Water: Nine Stories

WATER

NINE STORIES

Alyce Miller

Winner of the 2006
Mary McCarthy Prize in Short Fiction
Selected by Norman Rush

Sarabande Books

LOUISVILLE, KENTUCKY

Managing Editor
Sarabande Books, Inc.
2234 Dundee Road, Suite 200
Louisville, KY 40205

Library of Congress Cataloging-in-Publication Data

Miller, Alyce.
Water : nine stories / by Alyce Miller ; selected by Norman Rush. — 1st ed.
p. cm.
"Winner of the 2006 Mary McCarthy Prize in short fiction."
Includes bibliographical references and index.
ISBN 978-1-932511-56-7 (pbk. : alk. paper)
I. Title.

PS3563.I37424W38 2007
813'.54—dc22   2007010152

Cover image: *Nude in Pool II*. Black and white infrared sepia print. © 2004 by Kathleen Carr. Provided courtesy of the artist. (www.kathleencarr.com)

Cover and text design by Charles Casey Martin

Manufactured in Canada
This book is printed on acid-free paper.

Sarabande Books is a nonprofit literary organization.

THE KENTUCKY ARTS COUNCIL

The Kentucky Arts Council, a state agency in the Commerce Cabinet, provides operational support funding for Sarabande Books with state tax dollars and federal funding from the National Endowment for the Arts, which believes that a great nation deserves great art.

Contents

Acknowledgments

Glimmer Train: "Swimming"

Many Mountains Moving: "Hawaii"

Michigan Quarterly Review: "Ice"

New England Review: "Aftershock"; "My Summer of Love"

Northwest Review: "Dimitry Gurov's Dowdy Wife"

Prairie Schooner: "Getting to Know the World"

Sonora Review: "Cleaning House"

Witness: "Friends: An Elegy"

"Ice" received the Lawrence Prize and a Special Mention in the *Pushcart Prize* anthology; "My Summer of Love" and "Friends: An Elegy" also received Special Mention in *Pushcart Prize* anthologies. "Cleaning House" appeared in the anthology *High Infidelity*, edited by John McNally (William Morrow, 1997).

Foreword

Getting short stories right is a delicate business. Nathaniel Hawthorne characterized the genre as "short, quick stabbings at the axis of reality," which is about right, and which reminds us that, in the making of successful stories, the author's good aim is everything. And that the knifework, a.k.a. style, is also critical. And it reminds us that we want from the author's operations a thing of a certain distinct kind: we want to experience a representation of life that bears an unmistakable, if hard to define, emblematic force.

Alyce Miller has the eye and the skills for getting the short story right. I've chosen her collection *Water: Nine Stories* to receive the 2006 Mary McCarthy Prize in Short Fiction. (Against formidable competition from the other finalists, I should add. There were excellent stories in their collections, and striking realizations of off-center literary environments— the Madrid Metro, the world of diaspora Indian families, certain fantastical venues in modern America. I wish all these writers well, and thank them for the pleasure of their company.)

This author has published widely, and is no stranger to honors. Her novel *Stopping for Green Lights* was well received, and her collection of short stories, *The Nature of Longing* (1994), received the Flannery O'Connor Award for Short Fiction. Her work, fiction and nonfiction, has appeared in numerous anthologies.

Miller gives us solidly crafted neorealist studies in contemporary American unhappiness and dislocation. She writes vividly about people in various degrees of emotional extremis, and she avoids the temptation to invent resolutions for the dilemmas they're in. She deftly captures individual psychologies.

There are special strengths to mention. Her range is broad. She manages younger and older voices. She understands the nuances of repression. The stories built around black/white relationships are sensitively written. In evoking the lives of the "underprivileged"—hilarious term!—she avoids the paired dangers of condescension and romanticization. She writes at a consistent level, making sophisticated use of the free indirect style. And she adapts her language to the tone of the events she takes her characters through. So: this book contains a suite of strong, affecting stories, the best of which leave a sharp after-image in the reader's memory. May the added recognition this award brings encourage Alyce Miller onward in her calling, as she continues to deepen her art.

—Norman Rush

Water: Nine Stories

ICE

THEY HADN'T BEEN POOR WHEN SHE WAS GROWING UP, BUT her parents were Depression-era people, and they'd lived frugally all those years as if indigence were imminent. After years of renting odd, chopped duplexes, they bought a modest, but spacious, turn-of-the-century, Midwestern house, which over the years skyrocketed in value. Her parents furnished it slowly with other people's cast-offs and yard sale acquisitions, and now time had transformed many of those pieces into valuable antiques.

Ironically, though she made more money in a year than her father did every three, she was of the generation that could not have afforded to buy the house she spent her adolescence in.

Instead, she'd recently purchased a small bungalow in North Oakland, with a strip of lawn in front and a miniscule garden out back, which had cost ten times what her parents had originally paid for their house when she was a child. Every year when she flew home to visit, she brought photos of her house and her friends, because her parents didn't like to travel West, and the only way they knew about her job, her circle of friends, the men she dated, and the trips she took, was through snapshots, with dates and cryptic shorthands scrawled on the back: "March 3— White-water rafting in Northern California with Lloyd."

Her father still worked as the head research librarian at the university two towns over, and her mother who had devoted her life to raising children, now occasionally substituted in the public school, mostly to "keep myself out in the world," she said.

There had been four children (she was the youngest) and growing up, they had never really wanted for anything. At birthdays and holidays, presents had always been practical. The start of school each year spawned a one-day shopping trip in which one pair of new shoes for school and one pair of new shoes for Sunday school were the primary goal. She had gone through high school with four skirt-and-sweater sets, one jumper, and four blouses, regardless of the change in seasons and fashion.

But once she was free from her parents' spartan philosophy, she threw herself with a vengeance into a business major, won a scholarship to graduate school, moved to the San Francisco Bay Area, and treated herself to a lifestyle (as her mother called it) which permitted her to buy, travel, and dine out on whim. As a grown woman, she thought nothing of dropping a hundred bucks for dinner, wine not included, while she was occasionally nagged by the knowledge that her mother still dutifully clipped grocery coupons from the newspaper.

She was driven by a sensation most keenly described as a vague hunger, and tried to remember if they had ever gone without food. But they hadn't. The truth was she and her siblings had been more than well-fed, her mother had urged them to have seconds and thirds, and there was always copious dessert. Her mother had been an excellent cook with a wary eye on nutrition and economy. The children were all physically healthy and energetic. Yet why was it now, she could not cook for herself, and when she did, could not eat the food she cooked? Why couldn't she bring herself to plan an economical meal? Her refrigerator was an expensive side-by-side, with an extensive freezer for saving leftovers. But the few items in there went unused, and eventually became encased in thick white frost, rendered inedible. In the refrigerator itself a profusion of produce languished, hardening and overripe. Every few weeks she threw out in exasperation whatever had half-composted, and stuffed herself on a delivered pizza when she was too tired to go out. She ordered her groceries weekly by computer, which were then delivered routinely, whether she ate them or not. She had never mentioned these indulgences to her mother: not the manicures and pedicures (her mother did her own nails), not the exercise club that cost a fortune, not the fact that she'd spent five hundred dollars on the boots her mother had most recently admired.

It was a very cold Christmas this year, and she was glad she'd brought her new hound's-tooth coat, made of Italian wool and fully lined with dark blue silk. Her mother hung it carefully in the closet, smoothing the shoulder with a quick brush of her hand.

"Beautiful coat," remarked her mother admiringly, and she thought to herself, thank God she doesn't see how carelessly I toss it around. "You always have such lovely things."

Her father had carried her luggage upstairs into the room that had once been hers, but was now called "the guest room," or sometimes even "the spare room." She was struck by how little the space ever changed: there was still the same old inconvenient black dial telephone of her childhood perched on the table with its too-short cord. And the closet, a small, dark space, and too cramped to be serviceable, was used as storage for the discarded games and toys from childhood. She had once suggested to her mother that with a little remodeling, the closet could easily be expanded, to which her mother responded without missing a beat, "But that would cost money." Which was why when she had bought her house in North Oakland she had immediately hired a contractor to open the length of one wall and add a walk-in, cedar-lined closet, complete with a skylight and shelving system. She could stand upright, arms fully extended, and walk about. It pleased her to imagine that her clothes lived in a space larger than a multitude of houses in poverty-stricken countries.

Over the years, still single, she'd fallen into the habit of visiting her parents at Christmas. She was usually the first of her siblings to arrive. Her two sisters and brother were also traveling long distances, from New York, from Florida, and from Texas. One sister and her brother were each married, with children in tow. The other sister was engaged. Once they had all arrived, the house would swell to capacity, vibrating with their presence. It was why she liked to arrive early, when she could have her parents to herself, or sit in the living room on the old sagging sofa and read in silence, without interruption.

Now she opened up her suitcase and pulled out the presents she'd brought along for her parents. They'd been professionally gift-wrapped in silver, embossed paper while she ran errands on her lunch hour. She piled one on top of the other and carried them downstairs where her parents sat expectantly in the kitchen. It was a tradition she and her parents indulged themselves in: opening presents before the others arrived. A concession, she sometimes thought, to her singlehood, her childlessness. These circumstances would be perceived, but never voiced, by her mother.

"Oh, my goodness," her mother exclaimed as she laid the two

shimmering packages, one with red ribbon, the other with blue, on the table. "Oh, my, what on earth have you brought us? What gorgeous paper!"

"Open them," she said, feeling the anticipation of their surprise. "You'll see." And she sat back and watched, with confidence.

First her mother carefully pried open the envelope of the attached card and read it to herself. She looked up with a glimmer of tears. "Oh, that's so lovely," she said. "So lovely."

And while she and her father sat patiently, her mother slowly undid the paper (it would be folded and stored, along with years of other wrapping paper to be reused, in a box in the attic).

"Well, I can't imagine . . ." And she parted the white tissue paper to reveal the commissioned piece of stained glass—a sumptuous red rose in a blue vase. Her mother loved roses, had grown her own over the years in the small patch of yard known simply as "the rose garden." "Oh, my goodness!"

Her father leaned forward and peered over the top of his glasses. "Wow," he said. "That's exquisite." And he traced the leaded outlines appreciatively with his fingertips.

"It's for the front window," she explained. "Or wherever you want to put it, of course. This guy, the maker, lives in the Bay Area, and does fabulous work all over. He's world-renowned actually, and has done commissioned pieces for . . ." She stopped herself and added tentatively, "It's museum quality."

"Well, I've never seen anything so pretty," said her mother. "I just can't get over the detail." It was what she said every year, but each time it was sincere.

She lifted the glass cautiously up to the light with both hands. "Look at how it just glows. Oh, honey, you shouldn't have."

Her father said with childish eagerness, "Shall I open mine, too?"

"Of course." She was pleased to see them both so happy, and felt her body suffused with the warmth of generosity.

He, too, took time unfolding the wrapping paper, which her mother again admired and carefully folded. Inside the box lay a pair of hand-carved wooden bookends from England, an expensive replica of a set from the eighteenth century.

"Oh, look at those!" marveled her mother. "You always get us such beautiful things. Such generous gifts."

"I'm glad you like them," she said.

Her mother insisted that the stained glass be hung immediately, and there was some commotion about exactly how and where. Her father took on the job, and went to the basement for his toolbox. When the glass had been positioned "just so" in the front room window, the red panes of the rose appeared to have caught fire in the rays of setting sun behind it. Her mother announced dinner was ready, and the three of them sat down at the table.

"Since we're doing presents, would you like yours now?" her mother asked.

"Oh, let's eat first, we can do it later if you want." She felt the familiar knot of dread in her stomach. This was the moment she always feared. Presents from her parents had always been difficult. This difficulty had begun long ago. Meaning that long ago she learned not to hope.

Year after year, as she was growing up, had come the succession of uncomfortable birthdays and awkward Christmases. Her desires eternally spiraling into what her parents considered to be outlandish (even outrageous) requests, and they taming her lust for possessions with reasonable modifications coupled with implied disapproval. Like the doll that wasn't really a Barbie, but a cheaper imitation with a different face and painted-on hair. Her parents didn't know the difference, and couldn't understand why she had cried. Bitterly, but she did. There was the cheap vanity table which matched nothing else in her bedroom, when she'd begged and begged for a canopy bed and matching dresser. It had been on sale, and her father had been pleased as punch to have found it. She had learned, hadn't she, over the years not to expect? And of course there was the excruciating Christmas when she was ten. A turning point of sorts for her in which she was abruptly confronted with the absolute futility of her own desires.

It had all seemed so simple, so logical. A girl at school owned her own horse. A real horse with black mane. How she envied that girl! She had been invited to ride the girl's horse exactly twice, and in those moments sitting astride the saddle, she knew that at last she had found what she most yearned for. Never, ever would she ask for anything else. At night she would whisper over and over into her palms, "Dear God, if you get my parents to buy me a horse, this is the last thing I'll ever want." She spoke often of the horse, made mention of it morning and night, and as absurd as it seemed, she had been led to believe it might really happen when, in response to her pleas, her mother would smile and say, "We'll see, I'll talk to your father." And she'd come to believe that her parents would really buy a horse.

The smile, the tone, were all reassuring signs of complicity. Her mother at last understood. And so she had it all arranged in her mind and she explained to her mother about the exact horse she wanted. It lived on a boarding farm just on the outskirts of town where she had ridden half a dozen times on rental horses with the girl from school. The horse was a small, odd animal unsuitable for serious riding, but a perfect horse for a child, and it was, the girl at school informed her, being sold for a song. She imagined herself opening up her mouth and singing, and the horse arriving on the spot. She promised her mother she would baby-sit and clean and pull weeds to earn the monthly feed and keep for the horse. Her mother would laugh when she mentioned this, and respond offhandedly with what seemed like encouragement, "Yes, wouldn't that be fun? You'd take such good care of the horse, I'm sure." As long as her mother hadn't said no, the horse remained a possibility. When she fell asleep at night, the horse was the last thing on her mind. On weekends she would bicycle out by the horse farm, following the fence line until it came into view. She'd call to the horse and sometimes it would trot closer and she imagined the name she would give it, and what it would feel like to run the curry brush over its hindquarters.

"I'll do the laundry," she'd tell her mother. "I'll iron the shirts. I'll wash Dad's car. I'll vacuum the living room." She was obsessed with proving herself to be deserving. That's what it would take, and the horse would be hers.

And her mother would say things like, "Well, aren't you enterprising." And so she began to hope, against all hope, that her parents were plotting to surprise her with the small horse. Even now the memory of this childhood hurt wrenched her backward in time, to the year she thought she would rather die than go on living without the horse.

"Let's see what we have for you," her father said now with an air of expectation as he set on the floor before her a large box, the kind electronic equipment might be packed in. She knew from years of present-opening never to trust the size or label on a box. Her parents were given, out of practicality, to packing gifts in whatever was on hand: mittens came in toy boxes and socks were stuffed in old album covers. Once her brother had shrieked when he unwrapped his present because the box was labeled "AM/FM radio," but when he pried open the top he discovered a stock of new school supplies.

Her parents hadn't meant to be cruel. They were generous in their own right. She knew her mother meant only to make her happy, and could read her disappointment only as a failure of character. Now, as she pulled off the wrapping paper, she glanced up at their expectant faces. Deep inside me a disappointed child still lives, she thought sheepishly, and steeled herself to show appreciation for whatever was inside. Too many years had passed, she was an adult now.

But the memory of the sad little horse still came in waves. Needless to say, she hadn't gotten it. Instead, when her present arrived (and she, thinking it was a trick and that at the bottom would be an envelope with the keys to the stable in it, or a saddle), she opened it with slow, delicious excitement. She misjudged the happy look on her parents' faces, assuming they were collaborators in a big secret. This was their acknowledgment of how deserving she was. Only a horse could make them that happy. She had reached down inside the box. Something hard touched her hand. She fumbled with it, pushed back the packing paper, and wrapped her fingers around something round. For a moment she imagined it was a bridle. She pulled out by the head a plastic statue of a horse, a black and white horse with a little red saddle, rearing up on its hind legs. And when she paused to catch her breath, her mother said excitedly, "And there's another one on the bottom." They had splurged and bought two, thinking that would appease her. They had not trusted her, and had misunderstood entirely. They had presumed she would accept a substitution. Dully, she reached again into the box and pulled out a plastic bay mare. It had a sweet, pensive face. A horse for each hand. It was all she could do not to drop them to the ground and burst into tears. The gifts felt like a terrible trick. Somewhere in the back of her mind she could imagine her mother saying *You said you wanted a horse, so we got you two.*

She had excused herself and gone upstairs and flung herself face down on her bed, and wept, feeling sorry not just for herself, but for her parents too, whose good intentions had engendered such grief. She felt shame and

11

anger at the same time. She wondered what was wrong with her, and for the next month or so, she fell into a depressed state, tears springing to life much too easily over the first imagined slight.

Vestiges of those same pangs surfaced even now, though she tried laughing at herself. What a selfish, foolish child she had been! How preposterous had been her expectations! Inside the box before her was something bulky. Something large wrapped in white plastic. It was a comforter, the kind sold in department stores. So this was why her mother had asked so many questions about her new bed. What her mother didn't know is that she had bought the bed because her most recent lover was very tall, and he had complained that his feet hung over the end. They had gone together and picked out the wood and wicker frame, the box spring, and mattress, laughing about all the ways they would use it, and he had paid for half, saying he ought to contribute something. The entire bed had cost several thousand dollars.

The comforter her mother had chosen was standard department-store stock, chaste and sweet, little girlish, with pink rosebuds all over it. She knew better than to ask if it was filled with down. She tried to picture her lover wrapped in it, and the image struck her as absurd. But she managed a smile.

"I know it doesn't get as cold where you are as it does up here," said her mother sweetly, "but I still worry about you staying warm in the winter."

Her mother would have no way of knowing that she stayed quite warm during the rainy season, with two men actually: the new, tall one, and the more long-term, short one who was married. What on earth would she do with this comforter? She wouldn't have the heart to give it away, so it would join the striped towels, the polyester bed sheets, the flowery candy dishes, and all the other useless gifts collecting dust in the tiny attic of her house.

"Your mother picked it out," said her father. "We thought it looked like you."

She tried to make a joke. "I look like a rosebud?"

Her mother hastily added. "If it's not right, we can exchange it."

This was her chance. It was an opening, a moment she was being offered without reproach. She thought of the plastic horses, unridable and unlovable, that had stood as daily reminders on her dresser for the next eight years she lived at home. She had never played with them, and over time they found their way into the back of a closet.

"I think this is really nice, and so thoughtful, but I'm thinking I just might exchange it for a solid color. I'm actually working with a lighter palette in the room's color scheme." It was a stretch, a compromise. Her words sounded foreign in her mother's house. She waited for the awkward silence to engulf them all, but this did not happen.

"Well, of course!" her mother agreed, a little too eagerly. "They have other colors. I just remembered how much you and I always liked roses, too. We'll go together tomorrow to the mall. I'll drive you over myself."

She felt like a cad, a selfish, horrible cad, and she wanted to kick herself for her lack of graciousness. Wasn't it too late now for honesty? She could have exchanged the comforter without her mother ever knowing. She should have accepted the gift, without condition. But, wasn't it true, she still wanted to give them the chance to give her what she really wanted.

"Well," her father heaved a sigh and glanced over at her mother, "that's just fine. It really is. You should have what you want."

There was a tightness in his voice. Sarcasm? Disapproval? Why was it always so impossible, and always about little things, things that shouldn't matter?

Her life was so different from theirs. It always had been, only they refused to see it. She drove a brand-new car, she ate out at expensive restaurants, she bought expensive clothes at boutiques. She worked ninety-hour weeks and slept with men she was attracted to. She bought

13

season tickets to the symphony and theater, and she traveled in luxury to places her parents had only read about.

With the comforter folded back in its box and set to the side, they ate dinner, chatting informally about politics, the cold weather, her siblings, the neighbors, old friends. It was pleasant, and she found herself relaxing, enjoying the conversation, seeking common ground. She asked questions, took an interest. They wanted to see her snapshots. She showed them the new car, the walk-in closet, the tiny garden she'd had put in by a trusted landscaper, the jazz festival she'd attended, the group from work who'd gone wine-tasting in Napa Valley, and her business trip to Vancouver.

"You lead such an exciting life," her mother said with pride. "I can see why you are reluctant to marry and have children. As a single woman you're free to do so much."

After dinner she helped with the dishes (her mother had never invested in a dishwasher), and so they continued to chat while her mother scrubbed and she dried the dishes. Her father wandered through carrying wood up from the basement for the fireplace. Then he began to bring out boxes of decorations for the tree which stood bare in the living room. Her mother told the story how they'd driven out to the place they went year after year to "cut our own," and how they'd discovered an empty bird nest buried back in the branches, and decided to leave it there.

Standing there in the kitchen she felt her muscles stiffening from the plane ride, and knew she needed to get outside, in the dark, cold evening, and run.

"I thought maybe I'd get some exercise," she said to her mother, as the last dish was put away. "I'll be back in an hour, if I can stand it out there."

"Oh, goodness, you'll catch your death of cold."

"Probably." She laughed.

She disappeared upstairs and pulled out her tights, heavy socks, sweatshirt, windbreaker, gloves, and a scarf She overheard her mother, still downstairs, fretting to her father. "She's going out for a run. It's so cold and dark."

"Well, she's a grownup ..."

She came down the stairs, running shoes laced, gloves already on her hands. Her mother stood in the hallway watching her while she stretched her calves, then her quads, and reached her arms high overhead to loosen her shoulders.

"Do you want to borrow a hat?" she asked.

"No, I have a hood on this sweatshirt, I'll be fine."

"You might want to put a scarf over your mouth. You don't want to breathe in frozen air. It's so bad for your lungs."

"Really, I'll be fine."

But she was surprised by the bite of the cold air when she emerged onto the back porch. She'd forgotten this part of winter. The yard was white and slick with ice. It was too cold to actually snow, and the landscape had frozen into a wide drift of white.

She began slowly, feeling the tightness in her joints. She ran in short spurts, but her breathing was labored. She ran through the neighborhood. No one else was out, and most of the windows in the houses she passed were dark. A feeling of loneliness overtook her, the sense that she was always just on the edge of things, the way she had often felt as a child. Right now in Oakland it would be late afternoon, and still sunny and her garden would be blooming with purple bougainvillea, and her tall lover would be wishing she were there as he picked out a fine bottle of wine on his way home. He would be missing her, she was sure.

She took the gravel path behind the post office that led to the city reservoir. It was a half mile around, an oval of frozen water surrounded by the sweep of hillside to the left and a small hardwood forest at the

15

opposite end. She ran hard, sprinting around twice to make another mile. The gravel was full of ice, and slippery. Ahead, the silhouette of a small dark animal padded off quickly into the brush. In the still cold air she could hear the crunch, crunch of its body parting the stiff bracken.

At one time the reservoir had supplied the town with water. Now it existed as a place to fish or walk. Two boys in her elementary school class had drowned while swimming illegally in the reservoir. She and her mother had sometimes walked in the woods nearby in search of spring flowers, her mother warning, "Don't go too near the edge."

Now she stepped gingerly out onto the ice, testing it for thickness, the way she had sometimes as a child, an act as pleasurable as it was forbidden. She was close enough to the bank that she knew nothing was being risked, certainly not her life, at most her pride if she fell through. She jogged in place, testing the consistency of ice beneath her feet. It felt solid. A part of her dared the ice to break, but there had been several freezes already, and as far as her eye could see, the surface was mostly thick and white, with some places dark and glassy. She imagined the sharp, shrill sound of the blades of her childhood ice skates cutting across the manufactured ice at the skating rink on the other side of town. She had worn those skates long after they were too small, her mother insisting she had "one more season." And when she'd protested, her mother had asked sharply, "Why do you always want more than what's due you?"

The words conjured up here and now still stung, like the wind that had picked up and abraded her cheeks. Dusk turned to pitch-black darkness. She knew her parents would be expecting her soon. She pictured the concern on their faces, and the way the conversation would turn to wondering where she was. She could see her father putting on his overcoat and patched galoshes and coming out in search of her, the way he had on occasion when she was a child. Shivering on the ice she longed for the kitchen, still warm with her mother's labors. Tomorrow there would be Christmas Eve dinner, laid out in the best serving dishes on the antique dining room table, which her parents still loved to crow about having picked up for twenty-five dollars at an estate sale some years before.

Her brother would have arrived with his wife and teenage son, and her one sister with her husband and two children. Her other sister and the fiancé would fly in Christmas morning, and soon the house would be a clamor of voices.

Impulsively she began to jog straight across the ice to the center of the reservoir, where dark patches signaled thin ice and danger. She adjusted for the slip and slide of her shoes. Her breath smoked. She was being foolish, she knew it, and she imagined the sound of cracking ice, but it was only the wind knocking against the tree branches overhead. Any direction she now chose, she still had to cover the same distance back. She looked up. In the darkness the sky seemed just an arm's length away. Distances were deceptive. She kept jogging gently in place. As the wind cut through her, she hugged herself with her arms, breath steaming, legs stiff with cold. With each movement she expected to feel her feet go out from under her, or the ice to give way underneath. The temperature was dropping, and cold seeped through her clothing. She imagined the moment the ice broke, and how in seconds she would be plunging down through the dark cold water. There was no one around, and her cries, if she made any, would be absorbed by the dark, the snow, the silence. The edge appeared to be receding, and it seemed as if she were flanked by a world of ice. As her shoes thumped rhythmically in place against the frozen water, she imagined herself charging up her mother's back steps, shaking the snow from her shoes, and her mother asking brightly, "How was your run?" in that pleasant tone she had when she didn't know what she was really asking.

And she would match her mother's cheer with "Just wonderful"

17

forming on her frozen lips, because that's what her mother, after all these years, still wanted to hear.

She had no way now of knowing that she would do this, or that later when she'd gotten safely home, she would slowly unfold the comforter from its box, spread it out on the guest bed, and stare long and hard at the rosebuds, until the pattern became one long pink blur. Then she would wind the thick ends of the comforter around herself like a cocoon, and hold it against her body, waiting to draw out the chill of ice from her bones.

SWIMMING

WATER WAS A WAY OF FORGETTING. THE VERY BLUENESS CAST
its spell, drawing her away from remembering. Helen wasn't much of a
swimmer but it didn't matter because swimming wasn't the point. As soon
as she had stretched out into the irresistible length of pool, the water,
warmed by summer heat, took on the quality of skin. Sometimes she just
floated.

In the water it was easy to forgot she even had a body, the way the
space opened up between her neck and head and then her arms and
torso—soon she was the water itself From underwater, the world above
vanished. She squinted into the hazy depths, faintly tinted with yellow and
green scales like the belly of a fish, and considered how color was just a
trick of light. Below the surface thrummed the steady pulse of the pool's

own mechanical heartbeat, which assumed the rhythm of her own. She exhaled in slow bursts as if breathing life back into the water. Now she was joining herself to the sea, and sending her breath beyond until there was no breath left in her lungs. When she came up empty and gasping, urgent panic gave way to relief with the first inhale of air. Her vision was blurred by the sting of chlorine and the heavy water drops clinging to her lashes. Blinking, she saw just enough to know that the world above remained unchanged, and so she'd sink down again like an arrow, until she was stopped by the rough and slippery texture of the bottom against the smooth soles of her feet.

She used to live by the ocean, but she never swam in the whitecaps that pounded the shore, dark green and fierce. Instead, she walked the beach and stared out at water too cold for swimming. Locals who surfed wore wet suits most of the year.

Mostly it was tourists braving the glacial swells, except for those few days a year during Indian summer when the fog held itself back off the coast at night and the air warmed to an uncharacteristic desert heat. Then half of San Francisco, it seemed, congregated on the beaches near the Bridge.

But still, you had to be cautious. The ocean is capricious, and its unpredictability reminded her of a cat at play, soft paws concealing claws. The little waves lapping against the shore hid strong undertows and riptides. People who ignored the posted warnings had been swept off the cliffs and dashed on the rocks. If you hiked down to a seductive little cove along the shore you had to be certain you'd calculated high tide.

Now, more than two thousand miles east, across half a dozen states, in a place that had once been only part of the unending blur of what West Coasters contemptuously referred to as "the Midwest," she swam in an outdoor Olympic-size pool at the university where she taught art history. The azure water was the color of her first husband's eyes, though she didn't

think of him that way much because she had loved her first husband before
she really understood what love meant. She unfolded herself in the surreal
blue of pool, trying to deafen herself against the dull din of other swimmers,
and the constant chorus of splashes and spills echoing off the sides.

Sometimes she stayed in the water for several hours, even if it meant
floating almost lifelessly at the end of the pool, shoulders and neck gently
supported against the rim. It was summertime and she was through with
classes and students, through with an exhausting year that had taken its toll.
Sam, her husband (the second one), was at home working on the old brick
house they'd bought just on the edge of town. He was, among other things,
a skilled carpenter, and while the results of her efforts seemed to evaporate
into thin air at semester's end, his manifested themselves in new window
frames, kitchen cabinets, a new dining room floor, a cherry armoire for
their bedroom. There was something so substantive about what he did, and
something so ephemeral about what she did (*the artful dissemination of
ideas,* she jokingly told someone once at a dinner party who'd asked) that
she found it ironic when those well-meaning sorts pursued the perennial
question that plagued newcomers, "So what does your spouse do?" And she
fought the urge to snap back, "Much more than I."

With summer here, she'd often nap till noon, which was the hour the
pool opened. Still groggy, she'd pile a towel and lotion into her bag, along
with a book she kept meaning to read, and pull on her San Francisco
Giants cap to protect her face from the sun. Sometimes she'd bike in,
sometimes she'd drive, but either way before leaving she'd have to circle
the house to find Sam to say good-bye. He was always up high these
days—the roof, a ladder, a tree. He would wave down to her from above
in that hopeful way he had, and she would wave back, feigning casualness
and good spirits. After all, she was just saying good-bye for a few hours
before she went off to swim.

21

Unaccustomed as she was to the damp heat, the mugginess rendered her senseless. There were times over the course of these days, which had begun to bleed together like ink, that she lost track of simple things, like why she'd gone to the store or where she'd parked the car.

If she biked to the pool, she had to pedal uphill, so that by the time she arrived she was drenched in sweat. In any case, she timed her arrivals so that she wouldn't be the first one there. Once she climbed the stone steps so early she ended up facing a closed door, and stood there feeling desperate in the unbearable heat.

Inside the locker room, water puddled on the floors. The air there was soggy with the ripe smell of chlorine and wet suits. It reminded her of places she'd visited in the tropics where nothing ever dried. Women of all ages, young girls, teenagers, students, middle-aged women like herself, mothers, and elderly types ranged around in varying stages of undress. Flesh came packaged in many ways, she thought wryly.

She never used the locker room to change. Habit dictated that the moment she crawled out of bed, she reached for her suit drying on the rack by the tub and pulled it on. *There, dressed,* she'd think to herself. *Dressing made simple.* It was comforting to know that the first decision she made that day was so easy. It removed the burden of planning, and knowing where she was going next gave shape to the day. All she had to do was throw on cut-offs and a tee shirt, and after that, well, there were no more choices for a while.

The red suit was her favorite. She'd found it on sale in Los Angeles when she and Sam were down visiting her parents. She hadn't owned a suit for years, since if she and Sam went to the ocean at all, they headed to the Coast to one of the nude beaches. The suit was a fire-engine colored one-piece, made of shiny material, with a scoop neck in front and an open back. She secretly thought it was flattering.

22

When she walked out onto the wide pool deck, past the divers, past the children splashing to her right in four feet and less, she concentrated on the soft smack of her bare feet against the cement, and the gentle upward tug of the suit straps on her shoulders as if she were about to be released from the weight of sadness. The sun reflecting off the surface of the blue shimmering water was blinding. From up high in the trees, the relentless sizzling chorus of cicadas filled the breathless air until she felt dizzy with their sound.

After that, it was only moments before she slipped off the edge, and began gliding through water, the tight knots in her head coming undone, her long black braid streaming behind. Her arms and legs, naturally the color of walnuts, loosened like ropes. No longer able to tell where her body ended and the water began, she felt them merge, and all that was left was a red suit floating on blue water.

It went on like this day after day. At night she was unable to sleep because she couldn't breathe when she was lying down. While Sam snoozed peacefully on his side of the bed, without a care in the world, it seemed, she tossed and turned until finally giving up. Sometimes she would go stand by the bedroom window and look down into the backyard where, if the moon was out, the patio and plastic chairs and flower pots were illuminated as if by magic. Other times she stole quietly downstairs and roamed the house in the dark. Lights unnerved her, offering up the startling evidence of life around her: the rows of bookshelves, the sofa, the coffee table, the lamps, the chairs, the fireplace, a tool Sam had forgotten to put away. She preferred sitting for a while in darkness. Occasionally the headlights from a passing car spilled across the walls and briefly illuminated the corners of the room. Then she felt like a trespasser in someone else's house, familiar objects transformed beyond recognition into the strange possessions of another person. Their shapes pinwheeled through the quick splash of headlights, before disappearing back into shadow. She could remain like this for long periods of time, undefined in the darkness, recalling the way she'd felt years ago in Los Angeles during a long childhood illness when silence and solitude became the norm, and her mother's soft-footed comings and goings were the only intrusion. Once she awakened in the night to feel her mother's hand on her forehead. She lay very still trying to remember what they were both doing there.

Sam hadn't always wanted children. Initially, he was anxious about bringing someone into this world, considering the terrible state of things. And he worried that the world already was full of too many people and adding to the population was irresponsible, especially if, as he liked to say, you reproduced in a western , industrialized nation. *Six percent of the U.S. population consumes forty-five percent of the world's resources.* But Helen married him anyway because she loved him, or at least she thought she did most of the time, and it seemed like the natural outcome of the years they'd been together. Isn't it what people did? Sam liked children very much and was always chasing some neighbor kid around or hoisting one of his nieces or nephews up onto his shoulders. She figured it was just a matter of time before he tired of borrowing other people's kids, going off to zoos and parks and playing uncle. Soon he was whispering to her things like *Let's get us a kid, too,* and she felt a private joy, because she'd always wanted kids, and assumed that it would happen—naturally.

And she was glad she'd waited, wasn't she, because now they had more to offer a child. At least that's what their friends said too, particularly the ones who had also waited and were proving how such careful preparation and stability offset the downside of sitting up all night, at age forty, with a colicky baby. It was embarrassing, really. Helen had never thought about children in this way, as if they were something you could carefully arrange for, like a pet or a new sofa. *Nine months from now . . .* people would say with assurance, circling their calendars. She knew people, so confident in their abilities to reproduce, that they had "spaced" their children according to various calculations. A close friend informed her that a four-year-age difference between siblings was best, because by the time the infant came along, the older child was already firmly established in his own psyche. A psychically-established four-year-old? Helen had said to Sam.

Other friends touted the benefits of the stair-step approach, what Sam jokingly called *the bing, bang, bam* school of reproduction—the all-at-once-get-it-over-and-done-with strategy. Maybe best to have twins or even triplets! Suffer a few years, and then move on.

The mechanics of getting a child had never struck Helen as anything to give much thought to. In her own family, children had simply appeared. They were a fact of life. They arrived with seeming ease and regularity, expanding relatives' families into five, six, seven, eight, nine, ten people. This was before people began to talk about having only one or two children, as a lot of her friends now did. It was amazing how simple it had once seemed. *I'll take a boy and a girl, two years apart. I'd like the girl to be born first. No, on second thought, I'll take the boy first. It's nice for a girl to have an older brother. And let's throw in a little intelligence and good looks while we're at it.*

Over the years she observed various pregnant friends with a mixture of envy and repugnance: hands clasped smugly over burgeoning bellies, wearing the slightly vain expression of the expectant and the undeniable look of achievement. She watched these women turn inward (like birds nesting!), their complaints and joys focused through their bodies—the thrill of feeling the baby kick *(Here, you can feel it too)*, the weight of the fetus pressing on bladders, the soreness of expanding breasts *(My husband asked if we were just renting these or if we could keep them)*.

25

When Helen's turn came, she couldn't believe how easily she succumbed to the role. *Being pregnant makes you simple-minded,* she joked to Sam. This was back in San Francisco, and he would call her from work just to ask, *So how's the little mother today?* and she would laugh, *Oh, you big idiot, I'm just fine.*

Right on schedule, her own breasts swelled, and she often woke with morning sickness. She confessed to a wild, awful happiness, unlike any other she'd felt. It was terrifying and exhilarating at the same time because it was a happiness for which there is no substitute. It would ambush her unexpectedly, like the time she caught her own reflection in a store window on Union Street, and registered the words, *There goes a pregnant woman.* Throughout the day, she was often caught off guard by the powerful feeling surging through her. *I feel like a sentimental moron, a walking cliche,* she confessed, regretting that she hadn't been more generous over the years toward pregnant friends. Sam was happy too, and things were easy between them. He began to refer to the baby as "Sprout." He put his ear down to her stomach pretending to listen, and then repeating what Sprout had "said." This would make her laugh. They parodied their own expectations, and this would accelerate into silly enactments of parenthood and all the trials and tribulations that lay ahead. At night they'd huddle in bed and talk about the child. *Amazing that people actually choose to do this, isn't it?* Sam would say, and she'd laugh and remind him, *You have the easy job. Think how clever Nature is to trick women into believing we actually like this.*

They made irreverent jokes. It was fun and it was funny. But mostly she went about her business with a renewed sense of hope. There was a future, and the months would tick by, and then the baby would come. She could rearrange her work hours (she was teaching part-time at the Art Institute). Sam would keep the baby on weekends. They could take the baby places they liked to go. There was a satisfying balance to it all. *How old do you think the little bugger needs to be before we can drag him off hiking?* Sam wondered. They joked about stuffing the baby into the top pouch of a backpack and zipping it up inside. She yearned to press the palms of its baby hands against tree bark, to offer a minty eucalyptus nut up to its gleeful baby nose, to stand on a ridge overlooking a whole pine forest so that its baby eyes could take in a sweeping vista and see the possibilities available even in a difficult world. She liked imagining what the baby would look like, if it would favor her or Sam, or be a combination of them both. When she asked Sam what his single greatest fear of fatherhood was, he paused and said, *That the kid grows up to be a Republican.*

In the water, she was free of purpose and destination. Sometimes Sam asked her how many laps she'd finished, just to make conversation. She'd invent a number because she didn't have the heart to tell him that nothing much mattered any more. She didn't want to count. Count or count on. In the water, she simply was.

With the third pregnancy, she gained a fair amount of weight before it ended. Sam had become convinced she was swimming now to get in shape for a fourth try. At least that's what she told him, in a voice reminiscent of the parenting articles from women's magazines. She'd always been a little on the skinny side (growing up, she was known as *flaca* by her Spanish-speaking relatives on her mother's side), and both she and Sam had been surprised to discover what she looked like twenty pounds heavier. Her hips broadened and curved, and a mound of belly emerged. Even when it was all over, and she was home from the hospital, she would still awaken to a feeling of fullness; her body went on being pregnant. But that alone was not enough to bring the baby back.

27

It was embarrassing to talk about wanting to be pregnant in a professional setting, it seemed so unenlightened. (*With other options available to women, who on earth would choose...*) In her department at the university, childless women often viewed their procreating colleagues with thinly-veiled contempt. Helen had herself been guilty of reviling the oversized belly bloating itself beyond what seemed humanly possible, the awkward pregnant gait. And the way so many pregnant women dressed like dolls or little girls, as if pregnancy had reduced grown women to infants. There was one woman in her department who had recently given birth to a fourth child. She was cheerful and matter-of-fact, strolling the newest baby around in one of those high-tech carriages designed with sophisticated suspension that wouldn't jar the baby's neck or little brains. And the baby, seated regally in the comfortable stroller like a little pasha, took it all for granted, bestowing royal smiles on those who paid homage in the special voices adults reserve for infants. The woman's other children, all well-groomed and appropriately spaced in age, ran in a pack alongside.

One day when she was out for a run, Helen encountered them all on the edge of the city park. She stopped to talk, but her interest in the baby was disingenuous. In truth, it wasn't the woman's baby she wanted to talk about at all, she had the urge to talk about her own, all of them, the missing ones. Oblivious, the woman rattled on about motherhood, the "easy pregnancy," the "short labor," and the almost instant recovery (*When you've done this as many times as I have, there's nothing to it*). Then came the self-satisfied smile of one who can't imagine any other way. Of course she had no idea about Helen. And she had no way of knowing that her rain of words was not innocent, but full of malice and blame.

Helen had walked away fighting a tightness in her chest. The weight of her own grief pressed down on her and by the time she got home, she had just enough energy to crawl in bed for a nap.

Then came the recurring dream she mentioned only once in passing to Sam. The dream had started between the first two pregnancies. The events were simple and straightforward. Asleep, she found herself coming to on a steel table under blinding lights. A vague sea of faces floated before her. What came next was a kind of soft explosion from inside her body, a rush of water, and then the blur of faces began to take shape: Sam, a doctor, a nurse, all wearing face masks. She was having a baby! A moment later, in the dazzling light, she was handed something as slick as a baby seal. The weight and shape of what she held in her arms was so familiar she began to cry from relief—and happiness. Of course this version was the truth—the baby was here after all—not the awful absence and loss she could now consign to nightmare. How the mind could trick! And the baby, awash in light, turned its face up toward hers and smiled. Then came a deep conspiratorial chuckle eventually rising to shouts of joy. And it wasn't just the baby laughing, she was too, because together they shared a private joke. The dreams went on like this for a long time—Helen would waken in the night laughing so hard she ached, still feeling the baby's warm bulk so real it couldn't be any other way.

The baby remained with her throughout the day, and the joy she felt intermittently came back on her in waves—a terrible trick of the heart. Sometimes she couldn't be sure. Once she asked Sam, "Do you ever have dreams that are so real you can't believe they didn't happen?" And he nodded and said, "Sure" in such an offhanded way that she knew he didn't have a clue what she was asking.

What happens to a baby that isn't born? It was a child's question, but not far from the one Helen had often asked herself. The asker was Sam's little niece Constance who had come to say good-bye to them as they were moving away from San Francisco. This was after the second time. Clearly,

Constance had heard things from her parents (who stood mute, guilt written into their faces) and now she was waiting for Helen to explain. Constance was only seven. Before Helen answered, she reviewed in her mind all the things you can't tell a seven-year-old. You can't say, it starts with a wave of nausea and a sharp pain. Then comes the awful cramping telling you something is coming undone. You can't talk about the next stab and the next that makes you double over and sends you to your knees as if you're about to pray (Helen wasn't religious and so the kneeling part smacked of humiliation, not just humility). And of course Constance wouldn't want to know about the wash of blood that threatened to go on forever, that what was left of the baby was now soaking your clothes and the pavement as nervous passersby stepped around, afraid to ask. Or the gentle clink-clink of the delicate silver metal objects laid out antiseptically on the hospital tray just before you went out like a light. No, Sam's niece was asking something far simpler, far tidier. *I think*, said Helen, choosing her words carefully, *there is a special place near the water where the babies go to swim....*

One of Helen's friends, a staunch believer in reincarnation, suggested that some babies took several tries, that they chose their time. According to her curandera, Helen should just try again. *Try again.*

What could you say to such people? How many times do you try? In the Rainbow Grocery in Noe Valley, Helen met a woman once who'd miscarried thirteen times. On the fourteenth, she succeeded, and the result of that success was being strolled around the aisles, perched in the front seat of a shopping cart wearing OshKosh B'Gosh overalls and a little black, red, and green knit cap. The mother, about Helen's age, ruefully calculated she'd been pregnant long enough to produce exactly four and a half children. *Keep trying*, she told Helen, *it will happen for you too.* She said it so intently that for a moment Helen believed. Then she remembered she had just confided in a total stranger. She ended up leaving her groceries behind, and headed home where she tumbled into bed and took a long nap. When Sam came in that evening from work he found her that way in the dark. He sat down on the edge of the bed, and laid his hand against her stomach. That was when Helen sat up and asked, *So where do* you *think our babies went?*

When she swam, she forgot about time. She forgot about walls and other limits. When she swam, she was stretching into infinity, a world without end. She was a sea creature, and the more proficient swimmers streaming by in caps and goggles, earplugs wedged inside their ears, were chunks of driftwood or floating kelp. She was alone with the water. If she swam long enough, she ceased to exist.

Afterward, exhausted, she'd haul herself out of the water and sit dripping on the side of the pool, gazing out over the deck. It was as if she'd entered another country, a place full of sun-burned, bikini-clad girls, blonde and Midwestern, with pierced navels and triple-pierced ears, flirting with shirtless boys who trolled the periphery; a land of aging men in beach chairs, some paunchy and unattractive, who eyed the girls over the tops of books propped on their thighs. A refuge for university students sprawled like wingless insects on towels, summer schoolbooks shoved to the side, unread. And then there were the mothers, women wearing sensible suits and seeking shade, tending to the infants and toddlers with an endless procession of needs expressed and needs fulfilled: a popsicle, a wet diaper changed, a hug, a drying off. It was the children Helen watched, while pretending she wasn't, and in this way she realized she was no different from the older men lusting after young girls.

31

She came to recognize regulars. There was the little brown curly-headed girl with a body like a guppy who insisted in diving off the big-kids' while her proud mother watched, an infant on her hip. There was the towheaded toddler (so many towheads in the Midwest) who wore sunglasses and floated around in an inflatable plastic ring rimmed with action figures. There was the dark-skinned baby with enormous cheeks and round eyes whose mother bounced him gently on the surface of the water while he giggled and splashed.

How long she could find a reason to stare at other people's children without being arrested she could never determine. But one didn't simply walk away from miracles without an explanation, and she studied the mothers closely, wanting to understand.

On her way out, she'd choose the route directly past the kiddie pool. A sense of entitlement was building. She paused to stare unabashedly at the children playing below in the water. If some unsuspecting mother happened to glance her way, Helen would seize the moment to say something smart and knowledgeable, in that conspiratorial voice mothers use, like, "Isn't two a tough age?" or "Hard to get him out of the water, isn't it?" And in the moment the mother smiled back, Helen felt momentarily reassured. She too could belong.

A woman walked by holding the hand of a young girl with Down's syndrome. Helen smiled at the girl and then at the woman. But the woman was probably tired of smiles, and she didn't respond. The girl's attention was drawn to a bright candy wrapper that had been dropped on the deck, and was now ruffling ever so slightly in the breeze. She began to drag it along with her foot. The mother tugged gently, but firmly, at her hand. The girl resisted and made a grunting noise. She pulled toward the wrapper, and the mother pulled back. The girl freed her hand and let out a sound of pain. The mother looked discouraged. "Come on now, Amy," she coaxed in

32

a weary voice that signaled routine. Distracted, the girl gave up and reluctantly let herself be pulled along. The mother laid out two towels, and rubbed lotion on the girl's back. Then the mother got into the water, and called to the girl to join her, but the girl sat down on the deck and folded her arms hard against her chest. Helen looked away then. She wanted to say something to the mother, but suddenly the sunlight seemed too bright and the chirring of the cicadas made her dizzy. She set down her things and took a seat on the edge of the pool, dangling her feet in the cool water.

Children's voices echoed in her head. With the flat of her hand she shaded her eyes, then closed them. It had been three months since she lost the last pregnancy. A magazine article Sam clipped and left on the dining room table claimed that women who have miscarried once are ten times more likely than other women to be depressed. It urged counseling. Annoyed, Helen threw the article away. She was sick of numbers, statistics, of odds and chances and probability. She never mentioned the article to Sam and he had the good sense not to ask. She opened her eyes slowly. In front of her a young Asian girl in a black bikini cannon-balled off the high dive. Helen imagined what it would feel like to free fall. She pictured herself corkscrewing downwards, and the moment before slicing through water. She thought, this is the only thing that's going to save me.

Passing back through the locker room, she still couldn't shake the thickness from her head. It was the heat, that was all, it would pass. Still, her legs felt strange as if her weight belonged to someone else. Her breath had lodged so deeply in her throat it seemed unlikely to ever find a way out. There simply wasn't enough air in here. She had to get outside. Once there, she'd feel better. She'd get in the car, and head home where she could shower and take a long nap. When she woke up, she'd be lighter, more alert. She pulled her shirt and shorts on over the damp red suit. The clamminess of the suit felt like a second skin. She paused briefly in front of the locker room mirror to dry off her sopping braid. The sun had brought out freckles across her dark skin, the freckles she'd been teased about so mercilessly as a child. She washed her hands and rinsed the chlorine from her face. Then she walked out through the empty lobby and stepped into blinding sunlight.

On the cement steps facing the parking lot across the street, sat two children. As Helen started to pass, they looked up simultaneously, as if on cue. Both were so pale they appeared to be translucent. The little boy (at least Helen thought it was a boy) was wearing big, black-rimmed *spectacles*. No one would call these glasses.

"Hello there," said the girl. She looked about seven. The boy Helen guessed was maybe three or four.

"Hello," Helen answered. She was actually breathing again. One, two, three, four. In and out. The electric silence broken only by the occasional drone of a mower off in the distance. The shimmering heat. The cicadas. A brief flicker of breeze. The leaves on the trees barely rustling overhead. Then stifling air again. She measured her breaths as they came, more and more slowly now.

"What's your name?" asked the girl. She had on stained khaki shorts, and beat-up red and white Sketchers with no laces or socks. A pink plastic beaded bracelet, the kind girls make in summer camp, adorned one scrawny wrist.

"Helen," she said, stopped there on the step. "What's yours?"

"I'm Lizzie. This is my little brother." The girl thrust her thumb at the bespectacled boy. "He's *only* four."

"So you guys have been swimming?" Helen asked, even though the wet towels next to them and their damp, pale hair were dead giveaways.

"Yup," answered the boy. "We come here…"

34

The girl jumped in. "Me and him come to this pool every day in the summer. During the rest of the year, I have school, but he doesn't cause he's still too little."

"I see," said Helen, "and now you're waiting for someone to pick you up?"

It was a responsible question. In San Francisco, most parents wouldn't dream of leaving their children sitting unattended on the steps of a public pool. The parking lot across the street was full of cars, but not another soul was in sight.

The girl shrugged. "My mom's supposed to be here. But she's late again."

"Have you been waiting long?" Helen asked.

The girl shrugged again. "Ten minutes, twenty minutes," she said, with the arbitrariness of having simply picked a number out of the air.

"Well, maybe she got caught in traffic." Helen looked down the street to the intersection where a red light was blinking. "I bet she'll be along soon."

The little boy was staring at her, eyes owllike behind his thick lenses. His mouth was grotesquely purple from some awful candy he'd been sucking on, the remains of which bulged in his left cheek.

"Sometimes my mom comes, sometimes she doesn't," he said. "Sometimes we just walk."

Helen dropped down onto her heels to meet them at eye level.

"So you live nearby?"

Neither child answered. Instead, Lizzie fixed her gaze straight out at the horizon as if something of interest lay beyond. Then she swiveled around and riveted her pale eyes on Helen. "We live—sort of near here."

"Maybe you should go back inside and call home. Make sure there's not a mix-up. I can wait here with you."

"No point in calling, no one will be home," Lizzie said.

Helen straightened up and glanced back inside the open door to the lobby. A couple of university students, who worked the check-in counter, lounged behind the desk. "Maybe you should wait inside, you know, where there are people?"

"What for?" said Lizzie. "It stinks in there."

Helen smiled. This close to the children, she could easily memorize little details about them: the scratches on Lizzie's right leg (a pet cat maybe?), the tear in the little boy's tee shirt above the words *Grandma went to Las Vegas and all I got was this stupid tee shirt,* the battered styrofoam float toy at their feet—what was it, a duck? a giraffe? who knew?—and two raggedy, faded towels that Helen bet were known as "your swimming towels" in that sweet lingo of childhood. She could imagine the children's mother saying, "Don't forget your swimming towels!"

"Well, okay, then," Helen said. "You two be good." And she intended just to walk down the steps and across the street to the parking lot, but that was before she felt the unexpected pressure of a soft hand on her bare calf. When she looked down, the little owl boy had clasped her leg with both hands and was looking up at her.

"Can you give us a ride home?" he asked sweetly.

"Yeah," said Lizzie enthusiastically. "You could drive us."

"Of course not," Helen said hastily. "I can't do that."

"Sure you can. Isn't your car over there?" Lizzie pointed to the lot.

"No, actually, I can't," said Helen, shocked that children nowadays would trust so easily. "It would be—be illegal. If I gave you a ride, your mother would show up here and not find you, and think you'd been kidnapped."

"Kidnapped!" the little boy erupted into chuckles. "Kidnapped!" He seemed to get a special kick out of the word, which he repeated over and over.

"Our mother wouldn't think we were kidnapped," said Lizzie, with a slightly impatient edge to her tone. "We get rides home from the pool *all* the time."

"Sure, but not from strangers," Helen said.

"You're not a stranger," said Lizzie.

"But I am," said Helen, preparing to explain why.

"No you're not, we know you."

Helen was taken aback. "You know me?"

"You're Helen," said the girl.

"Yes, you're right, I am Helen. But what I mean is, you don't know me from *before*. And more importantly your *mother* doesn't know me."

"Which one's your car?" Lizzie asked.

"Over there." Helen gestured vaguely in the general direction.

"But which one?" Lizzie insisted. "What color is it?"

"Blue, but you can't really see it from here." Helen started to go. "I've got to get home now, kids. Nice talking to you."

"We live really close by," said Lizzie. "You could get us there in two minutes, and then everybody would be happy."

"You should only ride with people your mother has given you permission to ride with," said Helen, thinking how her voice had taken on a maternal quality.

Lizzie rolled her eyes as if to say, *And what planet did you drop off?*

"Our mother really wouldn't mind," said the little boy seductively. "Honest."

"Oh, yes she would!" Helen forced a laugh. "I know I would mind if I were your mother."

"But you're not," said Lizzie, "so can you please, please, please give us a ride home. Our mother would appreciate it, honest. She's so busy and sometimes she doesn't have time, and we will end up waiting here forever."

37

She stood up, gathering her towel.

"Look, Lizzie," said Helen, "and—what's your name?"

"Bruno," said the owl, blinking his transparent eyelashes rapidly behind the black spectacles.

"Look, Lizzie and Bruno, I'm a grownup and I can tell you with great certainty that your mother would mind a whole lot if I drove you home. No mother wants her children going off with strangers, no matter how nice they might seem. And I could get in trouble too."

"Where are *your* kids?" asked Bruno.

Helen paused. "I don't have any."

"Why not?" Bruno persisted. "Everyone has kids."

"And see," said Lizzie, "if you don't have kids, then you don't know what you'd let them do."

"Well..." said Helen, caught off guard. "Look, I really can't take you and that's that. And you shouldn't ask anyone else. Just promise me you'll wait right here till your mother shows up."

Lizzie chewed the side of her index finger for a moment and contemplated this.

"If our mother came and we were gone," said Lizzie, "she'd just go home and wait for us. She might be there right now waiting."

"I thought you said no one was at home."

"I said she *might* not be at home. Sometimes she goes out in the yard to plant flowers. Beautiful flowers. Big tall sunflowers that go all the way up to the sky. Sometimes we climb up there and touch the clouds."

"Yeah," said Bruno, "we go lots of places without our mother. Sometimes at night we take trips...."

Lizzie glanced over at him harshly. "Shut up, Bruno," she said.

"Look, I'm really sorry," said Helen. "End of discussion. Why don't you go wait inside the lobby?"

Lizzie shook her head. "If you don't take us, we'll just ask someone else."

"I told you that's not a good idea." She looked around. She hated leaving them like this, all alone in a public place, waiting for someone whose arrival seemed less and less certain.

Lizzie rolled her eyes again and made a disgusted sound like, "Tschhh!" through her teeth. She reminded Helen of a miniature woman.

"Okay, well, you kids take care," said Helen, starting back down the steps, but then something made her stop. She turned around. Both children were standing now.

"Look," said Lizzie, in a voice that suggested she was speaking to a small child, or a brain-damaged adult. "It's really okay for you to drive us. I'll give you twenty bucks if it's not okay. You'd be doing our mom a favor. And if she says anything, well, we'll just explain you're the lady we always talk to at the pool."

"Yeah, the pool lady," Bruno chimed in.

"Is that the kind of thing you normally tell your mother?"

"Sure," said Bruno cheerfully. "Our mother knows how things are."

Bruno bent down and grabbed his float. Lizzie handed him his towel. It seemed so natural, their eagerness a reassuring sign.

"Really," said Lizzie, "my mom is going to thank you for this."

And then as Helen began her descent down the steps, the children followed, Bruno hopping on one foot, then the other, with glee. At the curb she was cautioning them to look both ways (*Stop, look, and listen*). A car slowed down. The woman driver was looking over at the three of them. Helen's throat tightened. Of course, at last! She felt a mixture of relief and disappointment. She would introduce herself, say how delightful the woman's children were. But then the car sped up and went on past, and turned the corner. Helen insisted they all hold hands while they crossed the street. The small hands fit neatly into hers. When they'd gotten to the

39

other side, Lizzie broke free and began skipping ahead, but Bruno still clung to her tightly.

"Hey, careful, Lizzie!" Helen called out.

Lizzie came dancing back toward them.

"Careful! Careful!" she mocked.

Bruno accidentally dropped his towel in the gravel. Helen picked it up, shook it out, and folded it carefully over her arm. She unlocked the car. Lizzie ran around to the passenger side and claimed the front seat next to Helen. Bruno struggled briefly with the back door, then plunged in, flinging himself across the seat. Helen walked around and shut the door for him, and then gave a quick glance around the deserted parking lot. Where was everyone?

In the driver's seat, Helen inhaled the scent of chlorine and damp hair. It was the happy, familiar smell of children. She handed Bruno his wet towel which he spread out across the seat.

"To dry," he explained earnestly, smoothing the surfaces, as if he'd had practice.

"Here, take mine too," said Lizzie, tossing hers in back.

"Buckle up," Helen ordered, and listened for the click of safety belts locking the children into place. She turned around to Bruno in the back. "You okay, sweetheart?"

The owl eyes in the small pale face stared back. He was sitting upright, cinched in tight.

"Let's get ice cream," Lizzie said.

"What is this with you two?" Helen smiled. "First a ride, now ice cream?"

"We have our own money," Lizzie informed her, producing a battered little turquoise coin purse from the pocket of her shorts. "In fact, we'll buy you some, too. What kind do you want? Chocolate? With sprinkles? That's my favorite."

"That's not the point," said Helen. "We don't have time. We need to go directly to your house."

She turned the key in the ignition, and started the engine. "Wind down your windows, kids," she said. "It's hot in here."

"She said to wind down your window, Bruno," said Lizzie, twisting around in her seat. "Apparently she doesn't have central air."

"I can't do this by myself," said Bruno, so Helen turned around and demonstrated how the sticky handle worked.

Lizzie settled herself back into the seat, stretching her legs out in front of her. She glanced conspiratorially over at Helen. "Bruno can be *such* a baby sometimes."

"I am not," came the hot, exasperated voice from the back.

"Now, children . . ." said Helen gently and started the engine. "Let's be good to each other."

She followed Lizzie's directions. Turn left, turn right here. It seemed so easy. Surely no one would mind. And Lizzie was right. The quick detour for ice cream took only a few extra minutes—and it made them so happy. She refused their money, and laid out fresh crisp dollar bills at the window counter. They slurped their Dairy Queens (*No sticky fingers on the seats, please!*)—Bruno's ice cream was covered with Oreo-cookie pieces, and Lizzie's was piled high with toxic-looking sprinkles. Helen knew Bruno was making a mess in the back, but it was a happy, sloppy mess, the kind that kids make on a hot summer day after they've been swimming, and later she would get out the vacuum and clean the back, and think fondly of a small boy's pleasure.

Lizzie reached over and flipped on the radio. A song that Helen didn't recognize was playing, but Lizzie identified it excitedly, and began to sing in a small, off-key voice. That made Helen smile and Lizzie smiled back.

Helen began to feel more confident that she was doing the right thing. After all, this was life in the small-town Midwest. Wasn't this what they called "being neighborly"? In just a few minutes she would be delivering another woman's children to her door. The mother would be outside gardening, just as Lizzie said, and wearing a large-brimmed sun hat, and she would wave a thank-you to Helen as the children leaped out of the car. No questions asked. No harm done.

They passed the newest mall, then a long strip of fast-food restaurants, and a housing division called Lost Hills Estates that hadn't existed the week before. Helen looked over at Lizzie once or twice for reassurance. The little girl was happily taking in the scenery, and jiggling her legs. The plastic bracelet clicked softly against her small arm.

"Oh, turn right here," said Lizzie. "This is the best way. Kind of a shortcut."

"Okay," said Helen. She felt utterly relaxed, and her breath was deep and even. Hot sticky air wafted over them all, punctuated by little puffs of breeze. They passed a gas station mini-mart and Bruno called out the logo.

"You guys live a long way out here," said Helen. "I thought you said it was near the pool."

"That was our *old* house," Lizzie clarified.

"Well, you didn't tell me that part," said Helen.

"Yeah, we moved," said Lizzie. "We live in a *new* house now."

"What's the name of your street?" asked Helen.

Lizzie rubbed her nose hard with her fist. "I don't remember exactly," she said vaguely. "It's so new we don't have a street sign yet. But you'll see. We go past a school and then you turn at a mailbox. It has birds on it."

"I didn't know there were any schools out here," said Helen dubiously. She clicked off the radio. Lizzie didn't seem to mind. She was gazing out the window, licking melted ice cream from her fingers. Helen noticed how

42

the part in her hair had been made carelessly, as if with fingers or a brush instead of a comb. That was not the way a mother did hair, this was a child's effort. Lizzie dug down in the pocket of her shorts and pulled out a tube of lipstick. Then she pulled down the visor in search of a mirror. Not finding one, she began to apply bright pink lipstick in jagged motions around her mouth. When she caught Helen looking, she offered her some as well.

Helen shook her head. "I have to say I think it's a little odd that a smart girl like you doesn't know the name of her own street."

"I didn't say I didn't know it," said Lizzie, smacking her bright pink lips. A streak of melted lipstick stuck to her cheek. "Just relax, I'll show you."

Before long, houses gave way to pasture on either side of the road, and bales of hay rose up on green hillocks like over-sized cubes of golden fiberglass. In the middle of the farmland sat a life-size cardboard cutout of the front of a tract house, with columns and a banner across the roof announcing "Bay View Village. If you lived here, you'd be home by now."

"Is this it?" asked Helen, thinking that new houses were back off the road.

"No, silly, that's not a real house," Lizzie corrected. She pointed to a small road ahead and ordered Helen to make a right turn. More farmland. Lizzie was cheerfully pointing ahead at a field of cows. Behind them was an old barn with the logo *Chew Mailpouch* written on the side.

Bruno shrieked that he just saw a dragon.

"You didn't see a dragon," said Lizzie with great superiority. She turned to Helen. "He always makes things up. Why do little kids want to do that?"

"You both seem to be very imaginative," Helen said. "Kind of like you and the tall sunflowers and the clouds…"

"I don't know what you're talking about," said Lizzie.

Helen smiled. "It's important, you know, to have imaginations. It makes it more fun to pretend."

Alyce Miller

"Like what kind of pretend?"

"Well, you know, like pretending to be an animal or pretending you're rich or pretending you're somebody you're not."

Lizzie pondered this a moment.

"Like we're pretending now?" she asked. Her lipsticked mouth struck Helen as obscene and disconcerting. Helen began to slow the car.

"Do you really live out here? There's nothing out here except fields. If you don't live here, we're turning around." She pulled over to the side of the road and brought the car to an abrupt stop next to a drainage ditch.

"No, no!" Lizzie pleaded. "You can't stop now. Our house is so close. We're almost there. Please keep going."

"Yeah, keep going," echoed Bruno. "You're gonna see our house and our garden and all our pets and our bikes and swings and our mom and dad and aunts and uncles and everything."

"And if I don't?" Helen asked cautiously. She was beginning to doubt herself and her own sanity. She could picture terrible headlines and consequences, not to mention her shameful dismissal from the university, and the subsequent trial for kidnapping. The newspaper would feature photos of the weeping mother detailing the terror of losing her children. She imagined Sam's stunned expression and the disbelief of all her friends. *You did what?*

"You will," said Lizzie reassuringly. "You will." She put her small hand on top of Helen's wrist. The touch of her fingers brought instant calm. The soft child's skin, the tender pressure of her palm. Helen felt herself yielding. She gently eased her foot onto the gas, and turned the car back onto the road.

Lizzie smiled and stroked Helen's arm. "You see?" she said. And then she added, "You're brown, and I'm not."

"Yes," said Helen, "yes.'"

44

Lizzie's green eyes fixed themselves on Helen's and suddenly they were the only real thing of the moment, more real than the blue water in the pool. Helen continued to drive, the road unfolding obligingly into another two-lane paved road, the children's happy chatter ringing in her ears. Miles and county roads later, passing through a town she did not recognize, she was no longer asking the children where they lived, and they seemed to have forgotten themselves. Lizzie had scooted up close to Helen, her musty child smell rising familiarly in the warm car, one small bare knee crammed against Helen's bare thigh, head nodding on the edge of Helen's arm. She was telling a long, involved story about the time she dived into a river from a tall tree and how no one could find her and everyone thought she had drowned. "I was just living underwater, because if you really drown, you go to sleep forever," she explained

In the back seat, Bruno started singing "Found a Peanut." Helen glanced into the rearview mirror and saw he had snuggled up against the float toy, the wet towels spread beside him on the seat, his spectacles slightly cockeyed on the bridge of his nose. She took in the white eyelashes against his skin, the pale gray eyes, the strange frailty of his features. His mouth, open in song, looked moist and small. He was already on the stanza, "Got a stomachache, got a stomachache." Lizzie joined in, and then Helen. Not to be rushed, Lizzie began correcting them as they went along. It was a song without end, Helen remembered from her own childhood, that irritated adults and required stamina on the part of the singer. Now as they sang, the verses recycled themselves like waves cresting on the ocean, and invention kept them all moving effortlessly toward infinity.

GETTING TO KNOW THE WORLD

OKAY, SO YOU KNOW THE WAY OHIO LOOKS FAT AND badge-shaped, just like a buckeye? Well, starting at the top of the map where Lake Erie's carved out a crescent shape, if you trace a line southwest down through Bucyrus, then make a sharp right west before Marysville, and take the slow road past Byhalia—not far from Rushsylvania—you'll end up in the country where I was born, fanned by three generations of my people. Barely a pinprick on the map, smaller than the dot over the "i" in Ohio, that's it—West Mingo. Oh, and "Ohio"— it's an Iroquois word meaning "good river," though the only Indians around here now make up the logos on the high school's band uniforms.

You're not the only one whose eyebrows arc, wondering what I was doing growing up in a place like West Mingo. And you're right to figure ours was the only black family brave enough or crazy enough to still live within a twenty-mile radius of this sorry place. Unless, of course, you count our grandparents as separate, and then that would make two whole black families, right? (Just a joke.)

It seems to me how we probably got off a little easier, in part because over the years my parents became community fixtures and, in part because all six of us were girls (my mother had given birth to a son who died from a hole in his heart). Around those parts black *girls* weren't perceived as any particular threat, certainly not to white womanhood, or whatever worry it was that had these folks' knickers in a twist. Besides, none of my family was the type to bring notice to themselves. Just wasn't in their nature.

Still, lots of things happened. I'm sure I don't need to spell it out for you. Just think 1960s—backwater town. You saw *In the Heat of the Night*. You don't have to be a genius to figure out I was intimately acquainted with the words "coon," "nigger," and "Aunt Jemima." And it didn't help that I'm no sylph, being the only one of my sisters who developed low to the ground, round and solid like my mother, "built to last," she put it, "and not for speed."

From early on, my hair was yanked ("brillo pad," "sponge head," et cetera—how long did it take those fools to think this stuff up). I was kicked in the back, pushed, punched, pummeled, and even spat on, twice that I remember. Okay, so some of the kids were nice, as in maybe trying a little too hard, and some were just indifferent as if they didn't even see me, but others actively sought us out to blame for something they couldn't exactly put their fingers on. Played tricks, hid my books, stole my sack lunches, and even put sand in my sandwiches.

I tolerated it because these were just the facts of my growing up. Honestly? I knew nothing else. My best friend over the years, aside from my sisters, was a little moon-faced farm girl named Tammy, who got her ass kicked about once a month for sticking up for me. I used to tell her none of it was worth a fight, but she claimed it was the principle of the thing. "If you're a nigger," she'd say, "then I guess that makes me a nigger lover, because I do love you, Elaine." And proudly she'd wipe the blood from her nose, and count the bruises on her arms and legs, and her mother would make us homemade noodles from scratch and roast chicken, and tell us we had to stick together. I had no choice but to love Tammy back. What else was I going to do?

The irony is that of course my family had a lot more reason for resenting the white folks than they had for resenting us. For one, we'd been there longer than most of them. Half that county used to be the center of a farming community built by black ex- sharecroppers from the South. My ancestors had bought and worked that land ever since slavery ended. From the Emancipation Proclamation to the turn of the century and all the way up to World War II, black farmers planted their crops on their own land, and ran the general store and the town. Then things changed, and farming wasn't what it once was. People couldn't afford it any more, couldn't compete with the big companies. Everyone began selling off their acres, and heading to the cities to work in factories. They honestly believed a better life awaited them there. Typical black people. Whether it's going North or getting into heaven, we seem programmed to believe we're "gone find me a better place *up there*."

Not my grandfather, and certainly not my dad, both of them too hardheaded to think of doing things any other way. How they loved the rich, dark earth and the four distinct seasons in south-central Ohio. When they were both still alive, they'd get up before dawn, methodically going about their business in the darkened fields, just as we were waking up to dress for school. Two peas in a pod they were. My grandpa was Harold Senior and my dad was Harold Junior. My grandmother Isabel, who didn't like to waste words (but also had a sly sense of humor), nicknamed them One (my grandpa) and Two (my dad). And paying no attention to the fact that the county was getting whiter and whiter, and that Civil Rights was making the white folks meaner, One and Two dug in their plows and kept right on farming. Sometimes they even hired themselves some young white men to work, and that was always funny to me hearing them call my grandpa "sir," because those white boys were scared to death of him. Whatever they said behind his back never came to light face to face. And, boy, was he exact with a dollar, seeing to it they earned every cent.

About noon in the summertime when I was a kid, One and Two liked to break for lunch. They'd walk up the road to the general store (run by the mayor—and now a convenience store) just as they had for years, where they drank their root beers and talked farm equipment and government regulations with the white farmers, but never politics. Certainly not racial politics. Always respectful, always gentle-mannered, One and Two might have been mistaken in their overalls and straw hats for a couple of field hands. Or worse, I sometimes thought silently to myself, Uncle Toms. Consorting with the enemy and kowtowing to the white folks, while turning a blind eye to their ignorance and disdain. But they weren't Toms, despite what you might think. I can vouch for that. "We were here first" was their attitude, and they went about their business pulled up tall and straight-backed like they still owned West Mingo. If they were ever insulted and mistreated, they sloughed it off, the way you do when it's somebody else's mistake. White folks were just like the seasons to them—*there*.

By the time I was ten, One got too old to farm and took a job in town as the janitor of the three main buildings—the bank, the school, and the post office. He still tipped his hat to the ladies, and I think a lot of the white folks viewed him as a harmless, quaint old black man who made them feel nostalgic. Around this time, Two started slowly selling off some back acres to send my two oldest sisters Shirley and Brenda to college, and when he couldn't make ends meet with farming, he took a day job with a farm equipment company and began selling tractors to rednecks. He also tried boarding horses briefly, but none of us rode, and the horses took up a lot of time, so he sent the horses back home. My mother, who never criticized him for anything, remarked only once on a very hot summer day to no one in particular, "Your father's giving up too much."

I didn't know if she meant land or what, but her words spun there on the blades of the box fan, only to blow back out on the breeze of my own doubts. All I could think was that my dad, who never made mistakes, had done something wrong. What exactly did she think he was giving up?

I sure wondered that about myself every morning I put on my school clothes and got my hair braided to go to school with those hateful rednecks. Truth is, I belonged here more than they did. My family history grew out of this soil, my people had once owned the land they now rented. My grandmother could point out exactly where my grandpa proposed to her (the side churchyard, once a garden and now a paved parking lot), and recall exactly how her mother's vegetable garden used to look with its neat rows of beans and greens and lettuce and tomatoes, and where my great-grandfather laid the first stone for the foundation of their little house he built by hand.

I used to listen to my grandmother with just half an ear, as kids do, until I figured out that below the surface of her words lay something far more important. That she was actually telling me things I needed to know. And that's when I began to listen, and started spending time at the salon.

My mother did hair in the very back room of our sprawling house. My grandmother had always done hair, and years ago when my mother was a young woman she taught her the trade. "There's more to doing hair than

51

just doing hair," my grandmother used to say cryptically. I grew wild with curiosity. What was the "more to"?

My mother was a quick study and, though she'd been an orphan since she was only ten when my dad's folks took her in, she seemed to have inherited my grandmother's talent for attracting customers. It was as if she were the daughter my grandmother never had. Sometimes when I was little I'd forget, and think of my parents as brother and sister.

My mother managed a successful salon. I won't say she made a great deal of money. I will say she was good at what she did. A lot of my grandmother's clients passed themselves and then their daughters and then their granddaughters down to my mother as customers. "She's got the touch," they'd say. "Can't nobody do hair like Isabel, 'cept Isabel's daughter."

And it occurred to me that maybe someday, if I could learn hair, these granddaughters would trust their children to me.

These were women who drove in from other counties, as far as forty miles for a press and curl, to sit in one of the three red vinyl chairs in my mother's salon, and let her lavish the hours of attention that black women's hair requires. To tell the truth, I understood they came for more than hair. Amidst the smell of chemicals and hot combs and relaxers, I prowled waiting to catch scraps of talk. I pretended not to pay attention, my ear was tuned to every inflection, pause, and half-finished sentence. The funny thing is my mother wasn't much of a talker herself, being fiercely private and not one to waste words, but she was an excellent listener.

And though she could do all kinds of hair, white women tended to opt for an amiable hairdresser in town named Wilma who made them look like Jackie Kennedy. It wasn't my mother the women minded, I'm sure it was all those other women sitting around in their plastic sheets with goo on their heads talking their black women's talk. Moon-faced Tammy's mother used to make appointments from time to time, but try as she might, she seemed awkward in that room. When she was there, the talk was different. After her cut and style, she'd make a point of going into the bank or the general store and letting folks know how good my mother was at what she did. She meant to be helpful, but it didn't change the fact that white women preferred Wilma.

My sisters and I all took turns hanging out in my mother's salon. In varying degrees, we soaked up a catalogue of strangers' infirmities and infidelities, hospitalizations and bodily functions, men's sexual problems, marital skirmishes, and learning the way black people talk about themselves and white people, when white people aren't around to spy. These women didn't hold back, though I don't think anyone ever cursed, since most of them were Christian ladies. Soon I was learning to decode their oblique references, the unfinished sentences, the nods of the heads. Often they seemed to forget I was there until someone would clear her throat and then whoever was speaking would let her sentence trail off into that ambiguous horizon of "you know what I'm sayin" and the others would murmur "mmmm-hmmmm" and "uh-unh."

I'd hang tightly to the edge of those words until I was excused. Left to my own devices, I would wonder aloud. *What did they mean?*

My younger sister Beverly and I used to imitate them, pretending to be "grown women," until one day our mother overheard us and told us we needed to stop.

But she didn't forbid us from the salon, because we were able assistants. If she was working on someone's head, she might say, "Elaine, can you hand me that neutralizer?" and I'd run for whatever she needed, to the shelves of bottles, pomades and straighteners and relaxers, or the drawer of combs and pins and clips and rollers. I relished the warm dense smell of chemicals, the crowded knowing voices of the women, echoing like refrains against the hum of the fan in summer or the clicking of the space heater in the winter.

Later, if I asked my mother about something someone had said, she would remark matter-of-factly, "Whatever you understand on your own is fine, Elaine, but I'm not about to explain adult conversation to you."

"I want to learn hair," I begged her. She refused to believe me. She knew as well as I it wasn't really the hair I wanted, it was the knowing. Where else was I going to get such knowledge? My own naiveté frightened me, even when I was a child. I liked imagining all those women gathering in the back of my own house in the red chairs while I made them beautiful and happy. I wanted them to trust me with their lives and stories, just as they trusted my mother. I wanted to see my own life reflected back.

"Why can't I be a beautifitician?" I'd plead.

"For one thing, you can't even say the word right," she chided me gently. "For another, you're too smart not to take advantage of a good education. Life is hard enough without that burden too. The world's changing, Elaine. You have more choices than doing hair. Being a hairdresser won't get you far."

And by the way she landed on the word "far," I knew she meant a lot of things.

But as I got older I pestered over and over about following in her footsteps. I was envious of her operator's license, framed on the wall of her salon. Leona Mae Beaucaire, Licensed Operator. I imagined my own name framed the same way.

"Forget it," said my mother. "You're going to college, just like your sisters."

She and my father also believed that college was just a start, that the next step after would be graduate or professional school. "I've got two hundred acres I can sell," my father liked to brag. "That's twenty acres for everybody's college, with something left over for professional school. Doctor, lawyer, engineer, architect. Girls can do that work nowadays."

Formal education was not a family tradition by any means, but both my parents were avid readers, mostly magazines and best sellers, and every last one of my immediate family was smart as a whip. Between my two grandparents and my parents, there wasn't anything even approaching a college degree. My grandmother had come up from the South after a brief stint in segregated schools, but at some point she had perfected the most beautiful penmanship. I used to love it when she'd write my excuses for schools. "Elaine was taken ill with the flu and was kept at home with her mother yesterday to recover herself. Sincerely, Mrs Isabel Beaucaire." Each letter of every single word carried its own elegant shape, and every line slanted uniformly to the right in a graceful calligraphy.

My father graduated high school, and my mother went on one year beyond that to cosmetology school.

All six of us girls were good students, all hard workers, and every semester we all made the honor roll. I was preceded in school by my older sisters Shirley and Brenda, then Carol, and then Rhonda. Beverly, the baby, just two years younger than me, brought up our processional with straight A's and a particular affinity for mathematics. By the time I was old enough to pay close attention to the things that mattered, to sort them out from the tangle of useless information, Shirley was in graduate school, Brenda and Carol were already in college (Brenda at M.I.T. with a Nigerian boyfriend and Carol at Oberlin majoring in political science), and Rhonda was a junior in high school with an insistent eye on Harvard or Yale, and then med school. Personally, I think she just liked saying the words *Harvard, Yale,* and *med school.* She enjoyed maintaining a not so subtle superiority over the backward rednecks in her classes. She took pleasure in their confusion and annoyance at the thought of a scrawny egghead black girl off to the Ivy League and a life of privilege while they were destined to remain behind and pump gas in West Mingo or, if lucky, to attend the local community college.

All of my sisters took after my dad, tall and rail thin; Carol and Beverly were the two everyone said looked like models. They had his long skinny legs, and what my mother called "ironing board behinds." She'd say to me, "You and I—we're what you call healthy women, Elaine."

I took comfort in our sameness. Tried not to mind that my older sisters' hand-me-downs passed me by, and went straight on to Beverly, that my mother had to sew new clothes for me because nothing my sisters wore ever fit me.

To be honest, I wasn't just healthy, as my mother called it, I was chubby. I'd inherited my mother's girth with wide hips and behind, and I stayed short, to boot, while Beverly shot up past me in junior high. I had my father's thin ankles and wrists, and feet so small like my grandmother's I had to buy my shoes in the little girls' section of the department store way over in Urbana. When I was eleven, my mother had me fit for a grown woman's brassiere. I was embarrassed, but she kept telling me how pretty I was, and spent a little extra for the one with lace.

No one in my family ever commented on my being heavy. Not my skinny grandparents, not my skinny father or my sisters. That would have been considered downright rude. No one said, "No dessert, Elaine," or "No gravy for you, girl." And so I ate as I pleased, and grew up proud to look more like my beloved mother, with no one making judgments.

Now when I study photographs of me lined up with my sisters, it occurs to me I might have been inserted from someone else's family by mistake. Except that plainly I inherited my father's eyes, as well as his bad eyesight, and looked like a dead-ringer for my mother's half-sister Bernice who lived up in Cleveland.

My younger sister Beverly was the darkest and the most beautiful. Even the white kids at school treated her with reverence and regard. Every year, it seemed she was actually voted all those "most likely to's." I used to remark to Tammy, "Yeah, Beverly's most likely not to be black after they finish with her," and we'd laugh, but I'm not sure Tammy really got it.

True, Tammy caught on to a lot, and she was brave to be my friend. I mean that sincerely. The handful of wealthier kids, the ones whose parents owned businesses or whose fathers were doctors or lawyers, the ones who would go on to college or inherit the family business, looked down on her, and as we got older, there were white boys who refused to date her for reasons I could never determine. But there was one exception, an outcast like Tammy and me, named Ricky, who began hanging out with us. For a while we puzzled over his motive because being seen with us certainly did nothing to further his social status. He was small and frail for his age, as well as smart, a deadly combination. He lived a ways out of town with his mother in a rundown house. I never did find out what happened to his father, only knew he didn't seem to have one, and Tammy and I never asked. He started joining Tammy and me at lunch, unasked, and he would recite amusing facts to crack us up, and if we could tell that the snickers coming from other tables nearby were directed to us in some way, he'd remind us all the reasons we shouldn't care.

"Just think," he'd say, "when you're in your penthouse apartment in Los Angeles with Hollywood producers phoning up about your next movie, you won't even remember those lead-paint-eating morons. They'll still be here fishing for crayfish outta the polluted river."

Our shared laughter was temporary consolation. I really don't think my parents knew just how hard it was for me. For us, maybe. No, harder for me, I think, than for my sisters, because I was neither popular nor beautiful. Because I was fat, and because I'd worn glasses since I was six, and because I was square. I had to face the truth. The one thing I had going for me were my brains.

Sometimes I'd complain about the kids at school to my parents, who listened, but then reminded me I should feel sorry for those less fortunate. How could bullies be less fortunate, I wondered. Sometimes Beverly and I talked about the indignities we suffered, but when we compared notes it was obvious it was never as bad for her as it was for me, and I grew too ashamed to admit how much I actually put up with. You see, Beverly had real friends, even a couple to whose houses she went after school, and she sometimes went to dances with boys. She joined clubs, like Future Homemakers of America, and she was head of the drama club for a year, starring in *Cheaper by the Dozen,* the only dark face in the whole *Cheaper* family.

For a while I penciled on the inside of my closet door the number of times I heard the word "nigger" at school. Adding it all up was my secret way of knowing that I wasn't imagining anything.

At least I knew how to spell the word, I told Tammy, after someone scratched "niger" into the surface of my locker door. To the popeyed girl walking by who started to laugh at my consternation, I snapped, "Niger's a country, fool, and a river. What's so funny about that?"

Since most of the West Mingo kids weren't college bound, Beverly had a theory. Our teachers were the ones no one else wanted. They were "second-raters" hired out of mediocre colleges in Kentucky and West Virginia, full of barely disguised prejudice. "If they were any good, they wouldn't come *here,*" she told me. "Think about it."

I can say honestly, though, in all those years in West Mingo, I never had a teacher treat me with open hostility. It's a funny thing with bigots. A lot of them put on just fine in person, one-on-one, so to speak. It's not *you,* they like to say, because of course my sisters and I were models. We were going to uplift the race. It's those *others*. And I would argue that what went unspoken is what made things so much harder.

Learning started at home early in our lives. As soon as we could read we were given our own library cards at the real library, not just the Bookmobile that visited our school. Every couple weeks, like clockwork, my mother drove us over to Bellefontaine (pronounced "bell fountain" in those parts) to check out books. We would always each take out the maximum and then share. My father was specially proud of us all. "I have some very smart daughters," he'd say. "They're all going on to do great things."

As it was, Rhonda got early admission to Yale, and then announced to my parents she had joined up with a black nationalist group who were going to overthrow the System. At Christmas she returned with a suitcase stuffed with Cleaver, Garvey, and Fanon. Her conversation was peppered with provocative new phrases like *Power to the people*. She referred ardently now to *the brothers and sisters*, and a gulf widened between us. I was envious. Who was this new grownup Rhonda who had left home a little countrified girl and naive to boot, only to return with her globe-sized afro, army jacket, and big hoop earrings. About Rhonda my grandmother commented once to my mother, "I hope you talked to her, Leona. I hope you told her how to act—you know—with men."

With Rhonda's departure Beverly and I were the last at home. One evening at the table my mother remarked, "Seems to me we're going to be rattling around in this old house with just us." Without Rhonda, dinner time became a quiet time. My father would make a remark about something he needed to do or hadn't done, and there would be a pause, and then my mother would chime in to say she was thinking the same thing. And Beverly and I might tell stories about something that happened at school, and my father would ask if we had homework, and then Beverly

59

and I would get up and clear the dishes in preparation for washing, while my mother walked the unpaved block in the dusk down to my grandmother's house to take covered plates of food for her and One.

One and Two had built our house according to some random plan I could only guess at. It started with a few rooms built over a slab, and then each time a new baby arrived, they added a room, which meant that we grew up never having to share a bedroom, though for periods of time, Beverly and I would hole up together in one or the other's room. Out front, the house started with a wide screened-in porch with a linoleum floor that was cool to our bare feet in the heat of summer. My mother's salon had a separate entrance, and sat up half a flight of stairs. Thinking back now, it seems odd that we all shared one bathroom, but that was more common back then. If you were up in an airplane flying over our house, this is what you would have seen if you glanced down: a large, oddball flower, rooms spreading out like misshaped petals there in the middle of a field, tin roof gleaming in the sun. I remember once when a telephone repairman made a wrong turn out of one of the bedrooms and couldn't find his way back to the front door, he started calling, "Where am I? Where am I?" and my parents, soaking up all the implications of his fear, later laughed about this so hard I swear tears sprang to my father's eyes.

My parents were people who had seen a lot that they never spoke of. Their unflappable demeanors were a mystery to me. Maybe at a certain point they learned to be content within themselves while the world around them went crazy. Listening to Rhonda preach Revolution, my parents said very little. They didn't argue, they didn't agree. They just let her be. When you talk about "salt of the earth" and "backbone of society," you're talking about my parents. To this day, when my father comes to mind, I picture him in his faded blue coveralls, out in the back tinkering with some old tractor he'd picked up for what he liked to call "a song" at an auction. And if I wandered out to see what he was up to, he might remark something along the lines of "They don't make things like they used to, Elaine. The old stuff's the best."

While cities around the country burned, and riots broke out like chicken pox—bad riots—my parents kept right on. It wasn't that they didn't care. They cared deeply. Maybe too deeply. One of the only times I ever saw my mother cry in front of us all was when those little girls were killed in the fire-bombed church in Birmingham.

As a child in the South, before her parents died, my mother had witnessed the aftermath of a lynching. She of course did not tell me this herself. I heard my grandmother tell the story once to someone else, maybe another relative. It took me a long time to understand what my grandmother was saying, and it wasn't until later on in life that I grasped the full weight of what it would mean for a child on an errand, to stumble so unexpectedly upon the dead man. I never knew if he was actually still hanging from a tree when she passed, though that was the image I lived with. The story became something I knew about her that she didn't know I knew, and knowing this helped me understand more who she was. Unlike Rhonda, I didn't take her quiet ways as resignation. My mother was strong, stronger than any of the others knew, drawing inspiration from a source she never shared. Sometimes I'd see her praying, but my parents weren't regular churchgoers. After the AME church moved too far away, they tried a Methodist church closer by, then for reasons they never explained, stopped making any effort. My father confessed to me once that he'd never really believed all that much in God, especially since if there was God, He was probably white, but I shouldn't ever tell my mother he'd said that or she'd think he was going straight to hell.

In fact, the only times we did go to church were when relatives visited from out of town. And then we'd drive to the nearest Baptist church. My mother's half-sister Bernice and her husband Uncle Ray, as well as some of our cousins, used to visit twice a year, once or twice for the holidays and sometimes for the Fourth of July. The cousins were hip, city kids who attended a big urban school, and they called coming to visit us as "going to the country." They drove the three hours down from the East side of Cleveland in Uncle Ray's Pontiac, and arrived laden with suitcases. There were two boys and two girls, all close in age on one end or the other to Beverly and me. They'd line themselves up on the bed in my room and play the latest James Brown 45's on my little phonograph. They were appalled by us. "Y'all ain't even heard of the Chi-Lites?" or "How come you talk just like the white people on television?" They failed utterly in teaching Beverly and me to dance, though they tried with a feverish earnestness as if our lives were at stake. After a while their patience ran out. "You can't even keep a beat," one of the girl cousins teased. "Y'all need to come up to Cleveland and get some soul." They told us we danced like "hippie girls," and they'd imitate until we all were laughing.

If they came in the summer, we'd take the cousins "downtown," meaning we walked the quarter mile along the weedy roadside to the general store, next to the gas station and the City Hall, where we'd purchase popsicles and then sit out on the wide, wooden porch and wait for a cool breeze.

"It sure is slow down here," one of the cousins would comment, as we set our gazes out over the deserted street, while nearby empty fields sang lush with insect life. Occasionally a car would pass, engine droning, and someone would stare hard out of the car window, and each time I felt fear clutch my chest. Sometimes it was a kid from school who would look and wave. All I could do was pray that we'd hurry up and get back to the safety of my parents' house before something bad happened.

The time that Tammy showed up unexpectedly, I felt torn about inviting her in. I knew exactly what my cousins would say. And I knew how

Tammy, oblivious, would exhibit all the traits my cousins found inimical in white people, including dragging along her Three Dog Night records. I was ashamed of her, afraid I'd be judged right along with her. When she left, one of my cousins remarked, "That girl is *cun-tree,* you hear the way she talks, like somebody offa *The Beverly Hillbillies?*" And they had a good laugh about Tammy, while I, the coward that I was, never uttered a word to defend her. When I ran in to her a few days later, my cousins' voices ran like a tape in my head and, so uncertain of my own position in the world, it was awhile before I could allow myself to feel close to her again. Okay, so Tammy was a redneck—she'd be the first to admit it—but she had a good heart. And she was all that I had.

My cousins always were after Beverly and me to come visit (they even said, "Bring your little white friend!"), and we'd promise, but I knew exactly what their friends would think of us. "We're just the black white weirdos," Beverly used to say ruefully, and that about summed things up.

In seventh grade, Beverly let her hair grow really long into a big, carefully manicured fro. Every evening I'd watch her grease her scalp and plait her hair, and the next morning she looked perfect. So I followed suit. Our hair had never been straightened, much to our collective dismay over the years, but this turned out to be a blessing in disguise because our mother hadn't allowed us to ruin our hair like so many black women had. No hot comb or chemicals on any of us. Odd for the daughters of a beautician. But my mother had seen it all, women with hair so thin from "frying their heads," as she liked to call it. "When you're forty, you won't have to buy a wig," she told us. "You'll have thick beautiful hair to do anything you want with. You'll be the envy of all the other women."

In the magazines, natural hair was now *the* look. At night I carefully greased my scalp, and braided my thick hair into little, stubby plaits all over my head, and in the morning, I pulled the soft plaits open with my fingers, and picked out my hair with a cheese cutter. I looked better, I thought. I traded in the black frame specs for tinted granny glasses that Tammy talked me into. Tammy, who now identified herself as a "hippie" and a "freak," was ironing her hair stick straight, and sporting velveteen chokers and long silver earrings, and granny dresses. She assured me, one day, as we stood next to each other in the full-length mirror in her mother's house, that we both looked "very cool."

When I first showed up with an afro at school, the kids had a field day. "Hey, Jimi Hendrix." "Elaine's the psychedelic Negro." "What do you call that jungle hair?"

Ha. Ha. Ha. White people, I'd sigh, loudly enough for them to hear it. And they'd just laugh and turn away. You see, they saw me as that harmless and entertaining. They'd come up behind me and run their palms fast across my hair and snicker. One of the meanest, stupidest boys at school came up to me in the hallway, poked his face right into mine, and said for the benefit of a group of kids within hearing range, "If you weren't so black and ugly, I'd let you suck my dick."

Never had anyone talked to me this way before. The shock of his words temporarily blinded me. The school hallway disappeared, and all I could hear was a roar of laughter all around me. I had no idea why he said what he said. When I could clear my vision again, I fled to the restroom for one whole class period and let loose with tears. And even when one of my girl classmates tracked me down and tried to offer comfort, putting her arm around my shoulder, I couldn't stop crying. Though I couldn't have explained it to anyone else, I cried because even though I knew he was just an ignorant boy, when I caught my reflection in the bathroom mirror, I saw myself through his hateful eyes.

Lunchtime came around, and Tammy came and dragged me to our table with Ricky, while I sat poking at my sandwich, appetite gone. And then something unexpected happened in the middle of the cafeteria. A new kid, a tall boy from Dayton, named Kurt Kincaid, wearing a white painter's cap on his head, walked over and, in front of everyone, punched my nemesis in the face. Not once, but twice. "That's for Elaine," he announced loudly, and then he walked away. A hush fell over the room. The mean boy had picked himself up off the floor, his nose bloodied. He gave me the most hateful stare and walked out, raging that he was going to get his daddy to come down to school and get us all. I didn't know what to expect next, and took off to my home room to hide out. Word of the incident had spread all over school. Later, Kurt came right up to me, put his hand on my shoulder and said, "If you have any more trouble out of him, let me know, okay? I think you're a beautiful soul sister."

Beautiful soul sister? You could have knocked me over with a feather. Was this white boy crazy? Later, when I was feeling more like myself, Beverly and I had a good laugh over Kurt, and while I kept waiting for some repercussion from the whole punching incident, nothing happened. Now when Kurt passed me in the hallway, he'd wink. And sometimes he'd find me after school and walk me home, all the while telling me how much he had admired Dr. Martin Luther King, and how unfair he thought it was that blacks were treated differently than whites. He also told me—and I mean he said it straight up—that he was in love with black women, that they were more beautiful than white women. He explained this had all begun with a childhood crush on Diana Ross, and then his first girlfriend in Dayton was black. "You're just like me, we're no different, we're *human beings*," he'd say earnestly, as if to reassure us both, poor thing, and bless his heart. But of course he was missing the point, because I wasn't just like him. Not at all. I told him so. And I told him if that's what integration was trying to signify, then everyone had another thing coming. But I swear he didn't hear my words.

Still, you have to know that I was so lonely that I let him befriend me in a distant way, brown sugar fantasies and all. Occasionally he'd come over and we sat on our front porch and talked and listened to music. He listened only to soul—no Led Zeppelin, no Janis, not even Jimi for Kurt. He was all Marvin Gaye and Junior Walker and the All Stars. When he told me once I reminded him of Angela Davis, I burst out laughing. That's what I mean. He just wasn't looking. "But you do," he said earnestly. "The hair, the glasses . . ."

Oh, where to begin?

"For starters, Kurt," I said, "I'm about six shades darker than Angela, and about ten inches shorter and maybe fifty pounds heavier." I was being funny, at least I thought so, but he didn't get it. And it was wearing to try to explain. What do most white people know of grade and texture and shade and distinction. And, in my experience, this not knowing makes them anxious.

Kurt invited me to the movies in Bellefontaine to see *The Great-White Hope* with James Earl Jones. My mother agreed I could go, but I could see she was a little worried, and she wondered if maybe Beverly could go along, as well. But Beverly didn't want to go, so off Kurt and I went. It was kind of a date, but not a date at the same time. During the movie, Kurt kept squeezing my hand. Afterward, when we drove back home, Kurt pulled his truck over and tried to kiss me but I knew it was for all the wrong reasons, and told him so. He didn't push, just looked disappointed. He took me back to my parents' house and then insisted on coming inside to shake hands with my father. "You have a fine, upstanding daughter, sir," he said, pumping my father's hand, much to my father's surprise, who had never considered I'd be anything but.

Kurt couldn't see that his actions weren't improving matters for me. When I turned him down for a second date, he asked Beverly out, but she spurned him even more strongly. "He's really got a thing for black girls," she said, "and he doesn't seem to care who it is."

After that, he kept his distance, but when he passed me in the hallway he gave me the black power salute.

Poor Kurt. Poor us. I told Tammy I needed a boyfriend—and fast.

My plan was, to get my driver's license, and then start driving over to Bellefontaine on Friday nights, the closest venue for meeting a proper black boyfriend. How exactly this would happen I wasn't sure, but Beverly knew a hip black girl over there named Mimi Blair, who threw house parties, and this seemed like a good start for us both. It wasn't that I wouldn't date a white guy, I would and had, if you counted Kurt and Ricky. In fact, given the lack of options, all the boys I'd ever had secret crushes on had been white. Beverly sometimes dated white boys, but she'd never gotten that interested in any of them. She told me, "I'll fall in love when I go off to college." To me, it seemed like an awfully long time to wait.

I tried to believe my parents weren't wrong, that growing up in our bigoted, limited little town with one traffic light and one gas station and general store, where the preacher drove the school bus, and the gym teacher delivered the mail, was actually a character-building lesson that was going to prepare me for whatever else happened in life. As in the old adage, if it doesn't kill you, it makes you stronger. Like the divorce I'd eventually get in my twenties after college from the troubled husband I should never have married, but did. Like the two sons we had who were as much curse as they were blessing. Like the various jobs I held over the years, trying to make ends meet when my ex-husband was shirking his support payments. Like his distraught family who, embarrassed by his treatment of me, eventually shunned me. Like the fact that my oldest sister Brenda began hearing voices from the television and radio telling her to do violent things and was committed to an institution while still trying to finish her medical degree. Like the illness of my mother, who was diagnosed with dementia and began to deteriorate fast. She kept saying to me when I visited, "I'm not the way I was, Elaine, but where will the women go for a press and curl," insisting she could never leave the house my father built. Like Rhonda who, radical days ended, flew back to West Mingo from California after our parents had both passed away, claimed there was a will leaving her everything, and boarded up the house and ordered restraining orders on all of us so she could drive all their possessions back to the Bay Area in a U-Haul. Like Carol who taught political science at a university until she yielded to the life of a suburban housewife in Indianapolis, Indiana, and bought a station wagon to hold all her kids. Like Beverly who joined what can only be called a religious cult, and who faded farther and farther from me because I was "too worldly."

Everything that came to happen in my life could have been lifted straight out of those salon conversations I used to hear—the heartbreaks, the failed marriages (yes, there was a second one), the dreams gone awry, and the losses. It was no surprise that over the years the voices of my mother's clients ran in refrain through my head, as if narrating my life. Only then was I able to fill in the gaps they'd so cleverly stuffed with emphatic *mmmm's* and *yes, girl's,* and the exchanges of knowing looks, and the weighted silences. Was there ever a way to prevent the accidents of life? Was it because I was naive and hopeful that I rushed into the world thinking that once I was free of West Mingo nothing but happiness lay ahead?

When I hit my midteens, I was obsessed with fleeing West Mingo and landing myself in the real world, a place where I would live among people who looked like me, where I would finally feel I belonged. While Tammy was dreaming up a plan to go live in Santa Fe, New Mexico, on a desert commune (*Come with me, Elaine!*), I was busy imagining my new life without her.

Black is beautiful, the black-light poster on the wall of my room winked at me under the strobe light. I had just finished another dashiki dress stitched on my grandmother's sewing machine. Before her eyes went bad, my grandmother was an exquisite seamstress, and used to make all her clothes. Though I hadn't inherited the range of her skills, I could sew a straight line, and that's all you needed to make a dashiki.

Junior year of high school, I was accosted in the girls' restroom. "How come you wear muumuus, are you pregnant?" The speaker was one of three cheerleaders who stood next to me in the mirror above the sink where I was washing my hands. Another cheerleader sat on the radiator behind us and laughed into her hand deliberately so I'd notice. "Elaine'll have to go on welfare for the baby."

"I'm not pregnant," I snapped back. "I'm just chubby, and you know it."

They snickered. "Chubby—right."

"Is Ricky the father?" she went on. "Or maybe Kurt? You know, if you guys mixed your blood, you'd have a little mongoloid."

"A mongoloid is a retarded person," I corrected. "You must mean *mu-lat-to*," and I deliberately drew out the syllables.

"Whatever. My mother said that when races mix, the kids get all messed up, like they don't know what they are, and they look all funny like those little mongoloids, you know, retarded people." She furiously sprayed her hair and combed some more. The overly-sweet scent filled my nostrils. Her friend kept giggling.

Fed up, I asked the giggler, "What's so funny? Want to let me in on the joke?"

She doubled over and began gasping for breath in long, exaggerated inhalations. "Want to let me in on the joke?" she mimicked in a high voice, unlike mine.

I pressed her. "Can you please tell me why this is so funny to you? Does it make you feel good to try to hurt other people?"

She looked up, flushed bright red, and her face took on a stricken expression. "I don't know," she stammered. To her friend she barked, "Come on," and she got up and practically ran out.

I wanted to think she had realized something in that moment. That I had forced her into shameful recognition of her cruelty and ignorance. But the truth was she just didn't want to have to talk seriously to me or any other black person, and that when I refused to be comical to her, her only alternative was to run. The voice in my head said to the reflection in the mirror something along the lines of, *I'm tired of being the house Negro, good old Elaine who never gets mad about anything, even when we call her Tar Baby, Elaine who's always good for a laugh at her own expense, Elaine who's stoic politeness is mistaken for weakness.*

Face to face with myself once again, I had finally run out of excuses. I was ashamed of how alone I'd let myself become. If only I'd been one of my city girl cousins, I'd have hustled right over to Bellefontaine and rounded up six of the toughest girls I could find, and we'd have driven back to my town and kicked all those cheerleaders' asses into next week. I would have had them all so scared they'd have quaked in their little pink gym shoes each time I passed and gave them the evil eye.

But I had been raised by gentle people who found strength in calmness. Their silence was their fortress. Or was it? Could I blame them for this? Or was it my own fault? What was I missing? Then a terrible thought eased its way into my mind. Maybe, deep down inside, I really wanted to be lily-white and small and cute. Did I envy the pretty white cheerleaders wearing their boyfriends' letter sweaters and the way they cruised Main Street on the weekend nights, laughing and calling out to one another in bell-like voices? Was I secretly envious of their private society, the rituals I could never be part of? Thank God, I thought, there were no other black kids around to witness my shameful, Tomming self.

My father had always told me, "Words are just words, Elaine." What was he really saying? Go ahead and let people make fools of you?

I was smarter than all of them put together, wasn't I? I headed on to French class, burning with anger, because even knowing what I was up against didn't make me feel any better. *C'est la vie*.

My sweet, dear parents, you were saints, but how much was cover-up? How did you yourselves manage the humiliations all those years? What did you give up? And for what? Did I misunderstand something along the way?

What hadn't they told me? How often had my father been called "boy" in stores or forced off the road in his truck? What about the time I overheard him telling my mother the cops pulled him over and questioned him about the newly-purchased equipment he was hauling home from Bellefontaine? What about the time he was cheated out of a large sum of money by a couple of white men in town whom he had trusted and who later moved away? I don't know the particulars to this day, I only know my father swallowed that loss and never pressed charges. Why? Was this sanctity or pure folly?

What was true is that my parents had moved through their lives in their own way, parting the air gently like a curtain, letting others stand aside while they went about their hushed, purposeful ways. They had ignored, closed off their ears and their eyes, trusting in their own autonomy. They had perhaps thought they needed no one but themselves.

But I was different. So were my sisters. Our oldest sister Shirley was living in Columbus, Ohio, and working as an attorney. Brenda moved to Africa for a year abroad with the Nigerian boyfriend who claimed to be some kind of prince. (Ha! said my mother, and she was right, especially when Brenda discovered there was already a wife.) Carol and Rhonda flew home for Thanksgiving, Rhonda talking death to the honky pigs, and chastising my parents for staying in West Mingo. At the same time Carol was announcing she was pre-engaged to a rich white preppie guy from Connecticut whose father was in surgical supplies (this is not the man she married). She was also starting premed. She flashed around what I surmised to be some fake glass setting in a thin white gold band. And she spent a lot of time on the phone talking to "Bruce." "Bruce schmuce," I muttered to Beverly as I scraped out a pan in the sink. I could only imagine what Bruce's family would have to say about my beautiful sister. Truth be told, my sisters had all lost their minds.

My parents let them fuss and make fools of themselves. Marrying white, marrying black, it didn't matter to my parents. "Revolution?" said my father as Rhonda raged on. "There's not going to be any revolution. You young folks just don't know anything about anything. Wait till you're my age. You'll see things differently." My mother and my grandmother cooked huge meals, maybe in the hopes of stuffing us all into silence. My grandfather just shook his head and napped a lot. At one point he looked over at me and remarked, "The world's not the place I once knew." I watched how changed my sisters had become, and thought about why. They seemed strong and sophisticated and worldly. They had left West Mingo to become themselves. I considered my own pathetic existence, and after everyone had left, I took my mother aside. "Mama, I really need to go live someplace else, or I'm going to die here."

And to my surprise she took in my words and then said, "I'll talk with your father."

The rest of the school year crawled along at a painful pace. Tammy was still my friend, but her transformation from redneck to full-fledged hippie meant that in addition to the tie-dyed clothes and sandals, she was smoking lots of dope. We'd go out on Friday nights and get high from time to time. One night she fixed me up with a white hippie drummer in a local rock band who called himself Blaze. I'm not kidding. I don't even remember the name of the band. But I made a decision that night, and Blaze and I went all the way in the back of Tammy's truck. Just like that. It wasn't too bad, and Blaze bought me a burger and ice cream afterward. But more important, I felt as if I'd taken care of a terrible problem, that something was over that I'd been dreading. And when Blaze asked to see me again, I told him what we both knew, that it was better just to let things be what they were. That was how I got to the final week of my junior year, thankfully minus the burden of virginity, wondering what other sacrifices I'd have to make just to survive another year in this godforsaken place.

My mother hadn't forgotten my words to her after Christmas. Though she let time pass, as was typical of her, she hadn't ignored me. In fact, one evening she called Beverly and me into the empty salon, where she'd been cleaning up, and shut the door behind us. The scent of disinfectant from the floor mop hung heavy in the air. I imagined in vaporous form the women clients materializing like a Greek chorus in my head, chanting, "Get out, get out, Elaine. There's more to life."

The radio was playing country western, or what we always called "hillbilly music," because that's about all we could tune into on our dial. My mother clicked it off.

"Girls, your father and I've been thinking. And talking. We decided you two might be better off finishing up high school at a good school. Away from here," she said.

We were silent.

She went on. "I know what goes on around here, and what's passing for education. Times are changing. And you girls have put up with a lot over the years. Now I'm not saying you *have* to go away, but your father and I thought it was time to give you the option. What do you say, Elaine?"

73

She was looking straight at me. Here was my chance. My answer seemed to have been plucked from the air, and felt as natural as breathing.

"I'll go," I said. I hadn't even asked where.

"Beverly?"

"Where would we go?" inquired my more cautious sister.

"It's a private school up near Cleveland. You'll have Aunt Bernice and Uncle Ray close by, and they'll drive over on weekends to get you and take you to their house if you want. I think it's time you got to know your cousins better, had some different influences. If you don't like the school, you can come home any time."

Beverly said, "You mean we'd leave you and Daddy and Grandma and Grandpa?"

"You wouldn't be leaving us," my mother said gently. "This will always be your home."

"Isn't there a school that's closer?" I asked.

"This one is offering you and Beverly scholarships." She hesitated, then added, "They are trying to, well, recruit some Negro girls. I know what you're thinking, it means you'd be some of the first, but it's a good school, and with the scholarships we wouldn't have to dip into your college money, and you'd get to take interesting classes—college-prep classes."

I looked around at the empty salon, at the red chairs which suddenly looked worn to me, the battered stacks of back issues of *Ebony* and *Jet* laid out on the coffee table, and the freshly cleaned linoleum floor my mother waxed herself once a month on her hands and knees because, as she always said, this is the only way to do a floor right. My eyes lingered on my mother's operator's license hanging on the wall, framed carefully, her name centered within its borders. It represented how far she'd come from an orphaned child in the segregated South. She wanted more for us.

Now she was saying, "If it doesn't work out, Daddy and I'll come get

74

you right away, you know that. You can call us and tell us you want to come home. I just thought…"

And in that moment she paused, I detected tears in her voice.

"What I mean is," she said flatly, "I just don't think it's good for you girls to put up with what you do in the school here. Things are just getting worse."

"I think you're right," I agreed without missing a beat. "I think you're exactly right about that."

Beverly didn't say anything, but she wasn't objecting. We stood there, the three of us, for a moment or so, and then my mother opened the door of the salon, and we all walked out. I was going, no matter what.

Later, when Beverly and I talked it over, she said, "I don't know. We'd be living so far away, and we'd still be the only black girls at our school."

"But we'd be in Cleveland, and there are plenty of black folks there," I said.

"Yeah," said Beverly, letting out a deep exhale, "I'm tired of being a nigger to these people."

Just hearing that word come from her mouth shocked me. It was almost worse than hearing the white kids say it.

"They call you that too?" I asked.

Beverly looked at me as if I'd lost my mind. "What do you mean, Elaine?" And when I didn't respond right away, she said, "You think you're the only one?"

"Why didn't you ever tell me?" I asked.

She sighed. "It's so obvious, Elaine."

And so we gave our parents the go-ahead to make the arrangements. Beverly was just turning fifteen, and I was barely seventeen. As summer heated up and the humidity kicked in, I had a good feeling every time I walked past our old school that I wasn't ever going to have to set foot in again. Fourth of July Eve some drunk rednecks threw cherry bombs in our front yard and blew up some of Two's flowerbeds for no reason we could discern other than the obvious. My mother said because of this she didn't want Beverly and me going down to the Fourth of July fireworks celebration, we'd stay home and have our own party. So when Tammy stopped by in her pickup to take us out, she said absolutely not, it seemed too "risky," we were staying where she knew we were safe.

For the first time since I was really little, I felt like a prisoner in my own house, albeit a protected one. As if to compensate, my mother made sweet iced tea and we sat around in front of the fans and played whist with our parents. Off in the distance fireworks were exploding, each one of the pop-pops like a gunshot. None of us said a word about them. It was as if there were two Fourth of Julys that year—theirs and ours. I concentrated on the summer sounds of the crickets in the grass outside and breathed in the warm, sweet smell of rural West Mingo with its tropical summer air. This was my home, and in some ways always would be.

After that, I began to look outward instead of inward. I sewed myself new clothes with fabric my mother helped me choose from a department store, and worked on losing some weight. I would leave this place a new person. The old Elaine would be gone, and in September the new Elaine would be strutting down the hall of a new school looking sharp and powerful.

Toward the end of summer, shortly before Beverly and I were scheduled to leave, Tammy dropped around one evening in her brother's new pickup. I hadn't seen her for a while, but I think she and I both knew that our separation was inevitable. Still, she acted as if nothing were changing and wanted to know if Beverly and I could go "cruising" in Bellefontaine for old time's sake. We'd circle the square, see who was out, shoot the breeze, smoke a little dope. That's what white kids around here did to pass the time, and Beverly and I both agreed to go.

My mother came out on the front porch, slapping at the bugs and drying her hands on her apron. She looked hard at Tammy.

"Stay on the main road tonight, you hear me? No drinking and driving, right?"

Sometimes I wondered, how did my mother even know these things?

"Promise," said Tammy.

"My girls are going away soon. I want them to get there safely." Her tone had a strange edge to it. I think we were all feeling unsettled. She caught herself then and sounded exactly like my mother again. "Go on then, have a good time. Just get home before midnight so I don't worry."

Inside the pickup Tammy had secreted two six-packs, and a joint. Within half an hour, driving the back roads my mother had asked us to avoid, we were all "roo yapped," as Tammy would say. I didn't get high that often, and Beverly never had before, but it felt like the most natural thing to do on this particular hot summer night.

"I've got some acid," Tammy announced a couple miles outside of Bellfontaine city limits. "Want to drop a little?"

"I don't know. What does it do to you?" Beverly wanted to know.

"Makes you see things more clearly is all," said Tammy cheerfully. "Expands your mind." We were passing cornfields, and the sun was starting to lower, and everything was illuminated by the soft golden light. I tried imagining exactly where my mind would expand to. If I saw any more clearly, my brain would surely snap.

"It's not a big deal," said Tammy. "I've dropped with my brother before. You just laugh a lot. And this is good stuff."

To my surprise, Beverly agreed to try it. We entered town on the main street and circled the empty square. Tammy parked the pickup under an elm. "Nobody's here yet," she said, "we're early, so let's do it now."

We climbed out of the truck and took ourselves over to the band shell.

Beverly and I watched while Tammy laid out two tabs of acid on the bench and dissected one neatly into equal halves with a razor blade.

"Purple haze all in my brain—'scuse me while I kiss the sky," she sang happily. Beverly and I imitated the guitar line until we had Tammy cracking up.

"There's a cute guy," Tammy observed. "Someone for you, Elaine."

I looked up. A medium-sized, ordinary-looking black boy strolled by the other side of the square. I'd never seen him before.

"He'd be perfect for you, Elaine. Wouldn't he, Beverly?"

"Why me?" I snapped. "Because he's black?"

"Well, it's a start," said Tammy. "You keep saying you want a real boyfriend and you don't want to date rednecks."

"Well, I'm not chasing after the first black guy I see either," I said sharply, wondering if there would ever come a time in life when I wouldn't feel this annoyed. Still, I observed the boy, the roll of his shoulders, the dip in his stride. Cute, but not my type. I said so aloud. What Tammy had no way of knowing is that that boy would have never looked twice at me. Beverly, yes. Me, no.

"You're so picky, Elaine," Tammy said, as if the choice were purely mine. She handed me a crescent of acid tab. "Put it right here on your tongue. And then just let it dissolve slowly."

She offered Beverly her half on the palm of her hand. Beverly inspected it, as if she could tell anything more about it. It looked innocuous enough.

"I'm just giving you guys half since it's your first time. I'm going to do a whole, but don't worry, I can still drive, it just heightens my awareness."

It was a perfect summer evening. Not too muggy, for a change, and the remaining light in the sky had turned everything a warm, rich orange. The square started to fill with people, mostly teenagers, and mostly white. Some pickups and cars circled. In a parked Ford Tornado, a boy and girl play-fought in the front seat, and I heard the girl's voice high and excited, giggling. Beverly went to sit on the grass by herself. The last rays of setting sun sparkled in her fro.

"I'm gonna miss you, Elaine," Tammy said as she lay back on the bench in the band shell. She closed her eyes. Her long dress was hiked up over her knees, and her pale, mottled legs glowed like marble in the dusk. Then I lay down on the other end, looking up through the trees at the sky. We stayed there like that for a while, making small talk and laughing. And I waited for the acid to take hold.

The combination of the joint and beer had made me pleasantly mellow so I allowed myself to daydream. I was imagining my new school. I was thinking about the chance to start over. And then the colors of the evening began to brighten in the corners of my eyes. Little dots appeared along the periphery of my vision. They began to elongate into stalactites of color. The edges of the trees trembled, outlined as if by a child's awkward purple crayon. From the grass, Beverly murmured, "Everything's changing," and I said, "Yeah, the sky is moving," and Tammy chuckled. "You're both tripping."

I had a vision then. Of course it was only an acid vision, certainly nothing to be trusted. Fragments of color began turning like pieces of glass in a kaleidoscope. Then there were two Elaines, one I felt from the inside out and one I could see, separate from me. The one I could see was my old self running along to keep up. She kept calling out "Elaine!" and my new self would say, "Not now," as if she were in a hurry and had some place special to go.

The year was 1970. The colors and shapes of my narrow small life were undulating there in front of my eyes in the Bellefontaine, Ohio, band shell. Around me, the rural countryside was transforming itself, in slow-motion like the time-lapse film of a flower unfolding its petals. I pushed against the petals, and more petals emerged. They became doors, and doors opened other doors. I was being gently airlifted and traveling over cornfields and barns with *Chew Mailpouch Tobacco* stenciled on the sides. I passed an endless procession of small, sleepy towns, where people looked up and called out, "Look, there's Elaine!" Or maybe it was only Tammy and Beverly, wearing halos of light around their heads and laughing, "Look at Elaine! She is wasted."

Were they saints or devils? Beverly's mouth was opening wider and wider. Bits of gold sparkled in her teeth and hair. Then her peals of laughter became indistinguishable from my own. "Elaine," she kept saying. "Elaine, you and I, we're actually going away." Everything around me quickened. Riotous joy took over. Nothing bad could ever happen again. Then darkness fell really fast, and we all lost track of time.

Three weeks later, Two changed the oil in his car, and the six of us jammed ourselves inside—my mother, my grandfather, my grandmother, my father, Beverly, and me. And our luggage—brand-new luggage, I might add—green for me, red for Beverly—filled the spacious trunk. New clothes, shoes, toiletries, and Indian print bedspreads.

And then we were en route, toward the dip in the badge, passing Lake Erie, where generations before, my father's ancestors had fled over water from slavery to the Promised Land of Canada. And when they did return, they settled where they could work the land, to have something to pass on to the next generation, and the next. West Mingo, I thought, my heart knocking around in my chest, is surely behind me now. Heading north, I believed with every fiber of my new being that I was throwing off the shackles of the world.

AFTERSHOCK

October 17

Dearest D—

I am writing you from Somewhere Not in Northern California, Just above the Mason-Dixon line, but below Highway 70, on a fall day, in a place where there are four distinct seasons, but no large bodies of water, and where I have been for some time now ensconced in a different life, the life I refer to as "Life After D."

Hint: The leaves have been turning brilliant colors for a couple weeks now, and toward evening a chill creeps into the air, a reminder of what is to come.

In Life After D, time works differently, and through reflection and consideration of the world as I now know it, a world which is impossibly complex, and increasingly more difficult to negotiate, I am reminded daily that I am but a flicker of an eyelid, or maybe the final flutter of a butterfly wing. You always did say I mix my metaphors, but it is the movement of the eye and the wing I am analogizing, not the part with the whole.

Recently I learned, that every day small objects from outer space hit the earth, that we are constantly being bombarded by debris which could conceivably strike any one of us, and though it is highly improbable, it is not entirely unlikely. Some assert it would take a meteor the size of Australia to obliterate us, but others say this is an exaggeration. However the end happens, it appears we are doomed, and it's only a matter of when.

$$\text{Risk} = p(I)$$

P is for probability, I is for impact. Probability lies between 0 (not going to happen) and I (it's for sure). One in a million is notated this way: 1 x 10-6. One in a hundred like this 1 x 10-2.

Apropos, I am writing to express my concern about the game of seismic roulette you play every day that you drive across the portion of the East Bay Bridge which has not been properly retrofitted since the October 17, 1989, Loma Prieta quake we survived together exactly sixteen years ago. I have been researching this subject, and understand there is a sixty-two percent probability of a major quake in the Bay Area within the next thirty years. (See formula above.)

There appears to be evidence that some of the welders performed substandard work on the repaired portions, so that at any moment, it has been predicted, the whole section could collapse, killing hundreds, maybe more.

I am wondering if you are aware of this and if you consider it each time you drive back and forth into the City, which I assume you still do at least once a day, if not twice, and if you are at all filled with fear or apprehension.

I also wonder, D, if you ever imagine that moment when the earth cracks open like a walnut, and sends you and your beloved Audi shimmying off the edge into those gray, choppy waters below.

At this thought, do you accelerate as you cross the truss and cantilevered eastern span of the bridge that runs east from Yerba Buena Island to Oakland, which is the most vulnerable, as if speed will alter fate? It is only a matter of time, you know, until the next quake happens along either the San Andreas or Hayward faults, a fact you live with every day. How do you do it, as you sit idling in congested traffic shared by the those whose commutes add up to 140,000 round trips made daily? Does your adrenaline spike as you finally gather up speed to push through to the end, and do you draw a breath of relief at each end that you have managed to elude destiny as you find yourself again on terra firma on the other side?

At the end of your work day, do you stop for dinner (I'm assuming you still don't cook—and do you ever order the tamarind shrimp soup at the little Vietnamese place we liked so much?), do you worry about becoming a crime statistic, the murder rate having doubled so that it now well exceeds that of New York? Do you make a point of parking only in well-lit areas, checking and double-checking that the alarm is set, and do you pick up the pace as

Alyce Miller

you move from car to restaurant, glancing over your shoulder now and again when startled by a sound, drawing yourself up that extra inch in height? Do you really think you'll even hear the footsteps or the screech of brakes when they come for you, and have you felt the terrible silence in that moment when the cold metal barrel of a gun is pressed against your temple?

And, if you do make it home safely, do you at night, as you stretch your length across that California King mattress, do you, I ask, dream of the return of the Diablo winds, the same winds that stirred up fiery treachery in the Oakland hillside October of 1991? I wonder if you can still picture the way the tiniest flicker becomes a flame, and a flame becomes a ghastly wall of light against a hot blue sky, spreading through the Tunnel and up the canyon slopes of drought-dry vegetation, striated by groves of Monterey pines and eucalyptus, and upwards devouring wood frames and roof shingles, and bursting through insufficient single-pane windows? In three days it will be fourteen years since everyone evacuated with the speed of fleeing refugees, you at home that day, having taken the morning off, followed by a race against time, down those curving, stricken streets too narrow for fire trucks, believing you would never make it out alive. Knowing it could happen again, do you wonder how lucky you'd be a second time around?

Do you drive away from those same replenished and rebuilt hills each day, thinking not of the expansive and meditative views from your new capacious redwood deck, but wondering if you will return again to smoke and ash?

What, I ask, do you fear the most? The gun, the fire, or the water? What images plague your day: exploding gas mains, collapsing cantilevers, metal against flesh, the death-defying odds?

What do you remember, and what do you forget?

Dearest D, yes, I remember it all, every bit of it, from the beauty of our walks through fragile salt marshes and ferny trails through redwoods, to the roar of ocean surf on gray, windy days. And I remember sitting high in the hills watching the fog slowly devouring the city below, thinking of myself with you immune to the troubles of the world, as the lights below us vanished in that swirl of mist. Even so, I would settle into the sense of well-being and definition that made up the contours of my life.

There was a time when what I didn't know made me falsely happy. But now I can recall only the dangers in detail, the moments of near-misses and almost-there's. And after all these years, after all is said and done, I remember mostly the bridge and I remember the fire. I remember how fear and disbelief drew us together, and how we mistook it for something else.

And how we turned to each other those "morning afters" with something approaching wonder, believing in the connection of our own survival. It seems now that we are most faithful, you and I, in the absence of the other.

And so I wonder if and how you have come to imagine the end—shaken, damaged, or scorched—and if you still believe you are beating the odds.

Yours,

J.

HAWAII

THE DREAMS BEGAN WHEN HE WAS SEVEN. WHITE MEN WERE trying to kill him. He would awaken in their new apartment in Oakland, the lines blurred between sleep and consciousness, and wail into the shapeless dark, alarmed by the strangeness of his own voice and the strength of its need. Yet also reassured because it signaled he was not dead at all.

Soon the nightgowned shadow speaking in his mother Sharleen's voice glided from her bedroom.

Tajiri, what is it? her tone a mixture of worry and annoyance, like was he really scared or was he just messing with her again, trying to act out for attention—good gracious, Tajiri, (sigh) what am I supposed to do with you and these nightmares. More sighs and the rustles of her nightgown, the sweet scent of her body moving from the edge of darkness as she bent over to console him.

He could never tell her what "it" was. How could he? So he'd accuse her instead. "You aren't you! You aren't my mother!" and bury himself under his covers trying to escape. And when she'd try to uncover him for a kiss, he'd thrash around and moan until she yanked herself back and said sternly, "You better stop acting so silly."

Over time she got fed up and stopped taking him seriously. She said she saw it for what it was, playacting, an attention-getting ploy. In exasperation, she warned him, "You keep messing with me when I have company and I'm gone whup your little behind." When he pushed too far, she'd go for the belt, which was the only way she could get him to stop. Then she would feel terrible, her eye on the closed door of her bedroom where she prayed her company still slept soundly, and she would beg her son, "Be a good boy for Mother, please be a good boy," and they would hug then, and she would return to her own bed.

Lying there, his little ass still stinging from her quick strokes, Tajiri hardened his heart. From behind her closed door the humming sound he hated began, like the groans of the plumbing when the pipes filled with water. The floor vibrated, quick rhythmic thumps like breaths or heartbeats. They moved up through the walls, muted, but still audible. He lay very still and didn't breathe. Then there were the heavy footsteps filling Tajiri with dread, the clearing of a throat, the whispers, the slamming of the bathroom door. Shortly after, the toilet would flush.

In the dark, fists clenched into knots against his sides, Tajiri listened to his mother go about her shameless business with this or that man, her "boyfriend," she called this one, just as she'd call the next one and the next. They might as well have been the green, lizard-skinned creatures from other planets he read about in his comic books, who tyrannized cities. He hated the way the men made his mother laugh. It wasn't the same laugh she used with him, but one with a different, high-pitched and ripply sound.

What was it the white men said that put the rosy morning glow in her brown cheeks? Were they jokes? Secrets? "What y'all be sayin'?" Tajiri demanded of her over and over, even though she'd tell him to mind his own business. But he knew. They were the same words, like incantations, that threatened to erase him. In his bed at night, he was the slowly disappearing boy, being rubbed out like a mistake in a coloring book. In those long hours of darkness anything could happen. The cars passing down Telegraph Avenue whipped light through his curtained window. Shadows appeared on the ceiling just to mock him. He lay listening and watching until sleep finally overcame him, and just as quickly the early light of dawn woke him.

His mother, alone again, bed neatly made up with its too huge satin-covered decorator pillows, roamed the apartment. She wore the silk green-flowered robe a girlfriend brought her from Japan. There was the smell of oatmeal on the stove. She liked to sing as she ironed her work blouse. She let him have extra brown sugar for his cereal. "Don't be so slow," she'd tell him, "I can't be late to work." But there was a languor to her that took the sharp edge off her tone, and Tajiri knew on those particular mornings she was in what she called "a good mood."

She would drive him to school, looking fresh as a young girl in her starched and ironed blouse, and skirt and jacket, and smelling of the musky cologne that Tajiri couldn't get enough of. How he loved her, the shape of her long brown fingers on the steering wheel, the way she smiled unexpectedly when something amused her, revealing the flash of gold-filling in the back of her mouth that signaled happiness. He almost believed he had her back. Joy flooded through him. He would ask her to take him places, like the ocean, and she would smile noncommittally and murmur in her dreamy voice maybe she would, but she was floating away from him even then. Sometimes for a few days in a row she'd walk him over to the park and shoot basketballs with him, or let him play the pinball machine at the washhouse around the corner while she folded their weekly laundry into crisp stacks.

But then one of the white men would come again, often late at night just as Tajiri was heading off to bed, and there would be no bedtime story, just the admonishment to "Go on now." And the man would greet Tajiri as if everything was just fine, nervous and eager to please. And he would sit in the living room and laugh with Sharleen for a while and they would listen to music. Sometimes the men brought flowers or fresh bagels for breakfast. Some of them she met dancing, others at parties or barbecues. They were friends of friends, like distant relatives, people who showed up briefly, never to be seen again.

In the mornings Tajiri found residual evidence of them, the toilet seat left up, the steam from a recent shower still coating the bathroom mirror, the short bristles of shaved beard stuck to the white porcelain of the bathroom sink.

Ghosts who floated in and out. Then there were the spaces between them, the absences, during which Sharleen lived slightly grief-stricken adrift with her own discouragement and guilt. He would hear her for long hours on the telephone with her girlfriends analyzing, questioning, wondering how to make her life work. She'd do her stretches on the floor, her fingers wrapped around the cord, whispering in code, references that ignited discomfort in Tajiri, but remained mysterious and out of reach. She was so far away then, yearning for things he couldn't understand. He pined for her, mooning around until she'd notice and slap him away. "Stop being so nosy, boy," she'd snap, terrified he would hear the wrong thing.

90

When she was finally off the phone and heading toward the kitchen in her cut-offs and tank top, he would try to entertain her, show her drawings from school, offer to peel potatoes, sing her a song, but she'd sigh and say, "Shoot, I don't feel like cookin' tonight," and they might go out to get fried rice from the Chinese takeout down the street, or she'd scrub a couple of yams, poke holes in them with a fork tine, and lay them in the oven to bake for an hour. Sometimes she'd boil a little corn or fry up a cabbage with some onion. When there hadn't been a man around for a while, Tajiri's mother got headaches and forgot to set the table. She'd want to go lie in her dark room with the shades drawn, and she let him come in and rub her temples to ease the pain. He liked that because then she'd talk to him about her dreams and plans, and he saw there was indeed a future that included him.

On other evenings, they'd sit in front of the TV together and she'd make comments through forkfuls of cornbread and pot liquor like, "Mnmn, she shouldn't wear green, look what it does to her complexion." Tajiri loved it when she talked to him. "What does it do?" he'd asked. She'd cluck her tongue in mild irritation. "Look for yourself," she'd say. "She has too much yellow in her skin to wear green."

And he'd peer at the screen and marvel at his mother's knowledge. "Can I wear green?" he asked.

"Boy, you so good looking you can wear any color you want," and she was always finding deals on designer clothes for him, and making sure his baggies hung just so, and his polo shirts were freshly ironed, and his scalp was oiled and his fro shaped.

Sharleen worked for Pacific Gas and Electric in the billing department, Mondays through Fridays, doing customer relations. "I'm on the phone all day listening to people's excuses about why they can't pay their bills," she would tell Tajiri, "so you know I don't want to come home and have to listen to you whine about every little thing."

On the side, her hobby was collecting old things: clothes, furniture, shoes, plates, hats, silverware, knickknacks. She dreamed of opening up her own antique store some day. "Name it after me," Tajiri begged. "Call it Tajiri's."

"Boy, you so crazy," Sharleen would lean down and kiss him. "Now you know I can't call an antique store after you."

On most Saturday mornings she was up bright and early, man or no man, dragging Tajiri off to flea markets where she regularly bargained with two old black women in men's hats who sat on the tailgates of their trucks, guarding stacks of vintage clothing. Sharleen brought home armloads of silk bed jackets and pillbox hats with veils and cushions and old china, crowing over her deals.

"Mama, how come these people don't want their things any more?" Tajiri asked as she piled her bounty into their car.

She smiled and slapped the tap of his head affectionately. "Cause they're dead, honey."

"Dead people!" Tajiri felt his chest tighten, and panic rise in his throat. "We got dead people's stuff?"

They were surrounded by it. It filled the closets, the shelves, the cabinets in the garage behind their apartment. Even though his mother cleaned and washed and ironed and stacked the items away neatly, Tajiri could smell the faint musty odor of death on them. His mother, when she stepped out in the evenings, crisply ironed, every seam in place, looked like a million dollars—in twenty dollars' worth of dead folks' clothes.

She was inventive with style, and her girlfriends were always hooting when they saw her in some new outfit, praising her for her unique taste, complimentary and envious. She knew how to put things together—she could take an old scarf and put it with a pillbox hat, and match them both with the craziest old pointy-toed shoes Tajiri had ever seen. On nights she prepared to go out dancing with her girlfriends, the apartment came alive with laughter. They brought hair gels and accessories, and lipstick and eyeliner tubes were spread out on the vanity in the bathroom. The sprayed colognes blended in the air and created a scent that Tajiri came to associate with celebration. *We gone meet some men tonight.* And there would be gentle ribbing of Sharleen about finding her a black man, and Sharleen would roll her eyes and deny she needed anybody, she was doing just fine the way things were, and besides, white men were more likely to *help you out, not just take-take-take like brothers.*

And it was these moments Tajiri found his stomach knotting up, and the worry start. What did his mother mean?

"Good-night, Tajiri, you be good." They'd sashay out into the night, hair oiled, coats and jackets draped over their shoulders. As soon as the door shut, Tajiri flopped down on his stomach onto the living room floor to watch the television. His instructions were simple. If he needed anything, he'd go right across the hall to Jeannette's. Otherwise he wasn't to open the door, and he wasn't to answer the phone unless it rang twice, then stopped, then rang twice more, which was Sharleen's signal. At ten o'clock, Jeannette would walk over and check on him, and send him on to bed with a hug and a kiss, then go back home to take care of her own boy. And Tajiri would lie there on his mattress, with the action-figure bedspread stretched out over him, and feel himself overtaken by a growing paralysis in the silence. He'd hear the floor creak—footsteps! There would be music from the downstairs apartment, or voices in the hallway just outside their door. He'd get up every few minutes and peek into the living room to make sure no one had slipped in. Sometimes the noises seemed so close he thought his chest would burst wide open from

93

fear. What would happen if while his mother was gone one of her white boyfriends came looking for her? If only he could stay awake and alive until she got home...and in this way, stiffening his body into defensiveness, he would strain his mind so hard he finally succumbed to exhaustion and fell asleep. Only occasionally, when Sharleen returned at night did he ever awaken. And then it was just long enough to feel her bending over him, an angel from his dreams.

When Tajiri turned nine, his mother became engaged to Todd, a white man she'd been dating for a few months. Though Todd had initially brought Tajiri comic books and even took him once to the Exploratorium in San Francisco, Tajiri was wary of him. And it seemed that Todd was always around, to the point that Tajiri once asked Sharleen, "Doesn't Todd have a home?" and she slapped him. Just for saying that.

And when Tajiri turned to her with all the tears he could muster, she snapped, "Boy, don't you get smart with me. And don't you ever let Todd hear you say anything like that."

There was that catch of hesitation in her voice, signaling uncertainty that she had overreacted, but Tajiri knew, because he'd heard it a million times, that he was hardheaded, and it was tough for her, a single woman and all, keeping him in line, on top of everything else. He wished he could be different, but he couldn't. He didn't know what made him say the things he did, the way he talked back. It was as if the words jumped out before he could stop them.

Todd was around a lot in the daytime. Weekends he barbecued salmon on a grill he'd bought Sharleen right there in the backyard of the apartment complex, where all the neighbors could see him plain as day. Tajiri was too embarrassed to come out. Instead, he stayed upstairs and played with Jeannette's boy, hoping no one would link him to Todd.

Twice Todd took Tajiri to see the Oakland A's while Sharleen stayed home and cleaned house and made supper. He didn't say much to Tajiri, but let him have money for snacks, and on the way home the second time, he said, "I want you to start respecting your mother more—and me."

His words felt ominous to Tajiri, and so he didn't reply, just stared out the window of Todd's car and hoped that Todd would eventually disappear like the others.

Sharleen was obviously pleased Todd had taken an interest in her son. She would say things like, "You be a good boy for Todd, he's trying to look out for you," but Tajiri would feel only hardness in his chest.

Todd was nothing like Tajiri's real father. Samson was a dark-skinned, muscular, moon-faced black man who had taken off when Tajiri was three or four and headed to Hawaii to race motorcycles. Sharleen could never really explain his absence so that it made any sense. She gave vague and jumbled responses, said things like "Grownups can't always work things out. One day you'll understand," and left Tajiri with more questions than he started with.

"Where is Hawaii?" Tajiri wanted to know.

"Way across the ocean," said Sharleen sharply. But she didn't say which ocean, and Tajiri had to settle for knowing only that it was too far away to visit.

Sharleen once showed him wedding pictures when she was cleaning out an old closet. She was wearing a beautiful floor-length white lace wedding gown, with a crown of flowers in her hair. Samson was dressed in a tux, and stood with his arm around her and an ear to ear grin, the look of a man who expects happiness to follow. And there was little Tajiri, dressed in his christening gown and being held by some aunt he'd never seen again, a woman from Samson's side of the family his mother told him lived in New York. Tajiri was allowed to keep one photo of his father, and it sat in a small gold frame on his dresser. In the picture his father, a big man, with wide shoulders, was wearing leathers and straddling a motorcycle. What Tajiri liked about the picture was the broad, daredevil grin on his father's face.

"Your daddy loved to have a good time, and he wasn't afraid of nothin. He used to take me out on that bike and we'd ride Highway 1 up north to Stinson Beach and spend the day," Sharleen told him. And when Tajiri begged for more details, like did he get to go too, she gave a few, then grew tired of his questions, called it "pestering."

"Why did my father leave?" Tajiri asked, and Sharleen looked so stunned he felt as bad as if he'd hit her.

She spoke carefully then, measuring each word. "We used to fuss a lot," she said. "That's all."

Todd was, as she liked to tell her sisters and girlfriends, "stable," and they seemed, for the most part, to approve, knowing how lonely Sharleen had been and how hard it was to raise a child alone, and *Yes, girl, I know how these black men can be sometimes, so if you have to go white, I won't criticize you for it.*

On the day Todd proposed, he gave Sharleen "a rock," a large diamond she flashed around to all her friends with unquestionable pride. Sharleen had grown up poor in Mississippi, the daughter of a sharecropper, and the middle child of twelve. "Mother and Daddy loved us," she told Tajiri, "and we had each other, but we didn't have all that much by way of material things." She developed a love for pretty objects and clothes, and, according to her younger sister Olivia, she'd always had good taste. Everyone pronounced Todd's ring as beautiful, a perfect fit on Sharleen's slender brown hand. Sometimes she would hold up the ring and show Tajiri how it caught the light. Sometimes when she bathed, she set the ring on the edge of the bathroom sink and Tajiri would stare hard at it while he brushed his teeth. Behind him his mother's naked body lounged in the tub, concealed in warm, soapy water (Sharleen was very particular about never letting him see her unclothed). And before him the ring sparkled, catching its own reflection in the bathroom mirror so that it became two rings. Tajiri had to resist the urge to accidentally knock the ring down the drain. He imagined the sound of sloshing water carrying the ring away and out into the city sewers. He pretended the ring would ride on a current out to the ocean where a giant wave would pick it up and whisk it all the way to Hawaii where it would wash up on the shore in a place that Samson would be passing by. At that point Tajiri wasn't sure what would happen, whether Samson would stop and pick it up and realize whom it belonged to, and come to find him, but he let his mind wander until his mother's voice broke through his thoughts. "Boy, hurry up and brush your teeth. You are so slow tonight!"

Tajiri was careful not to look in her direction on his way out. He dragged his slippered feet going down the hallway floor—scrape, scrape, scuff, scuff—just to make a noisy, irritating sound. But she was too cheerful to take notice, was now humming to herself in the warm bath water, too caught up in imagining happiness with Todd.

Todd was considered good-looking (for a white man) by all of Sharleen's girlfriends. He had short dark brown hair and gray eyes, and he wasn't too pale. Todd was charming, or at least that's what everyone said. He wanted a wife, he wanted a family. "He's very traditional," Sharleen would say proudly. "He knows how to treat a woman." She loved that he bought her flowers, planned activities for her and Tajiri, took them on picnics at the ocean, hikes up Mt. Tamalpais, showed up with tickets to concerts, drove her up to Mendocino County for a weekend to stay at a bed-and-breakfast, and made her feel alive again. He was always promising things, like how he'd teach Tajiri karate and how to train the puppy he was planning to get for him. Sometimes he wrestled with Tajiri on the living room floor (this always delighted Sharleen, though Tajiri hated it when Todd would sit astride him and pin his arms down hard— too hard) and then took him out back to teach him the proper way to throw a baseball. He was the one who suggested Sharleen get Tajiri on the baseball team at school. "You don't want him getting all soft," Tajiri overheard him telling Sharleen. "You don't want him to grow up to be a sissy." The words that soothed Sharleen struck terror in Tajiri's heart. Todd had it all wrong. Tajiri was the man in his mother's life. He was all she needed. Until Samson came back, of course, which could happen someday. What would happen if his mother married Todd and Samson came roaring up on his motorcycle too late to claim his rightful place?

Things were going all wrong. Tajiri would hear Sharleen echoing Todd's words in conversations with her girlfriends. "Todd's going to make a man out of Tajiri," she'd say. "He needs that. Boys need a strong male influence. That boy is so stubborn and ornery I can't control him on my own. His head is harder than his daddy's."

After Todd began staying over every night and well into morning (even deciding how many cornflakes Tajiri could have for breakfast), he began to act as if Sharleen's apartment was his home. He would tell Sharleen how he wanted things in the apartment, chide her for leaving a damp towel on the back of a good wooden chair, put in a request for something he wanted her to fix for dinner. He moved furniture around, got rid of the old sofa and replaced it with a new black leather one he'd selected, got her proper curtains for the kitchen so passersby on the street couldn't look up and catch any glimpses, and made up the grocery list that he paper-clipped to a fifty-dollar bill. The more Todd was around, the more questions Tajiri asked Sharleen, in private, about Samson. *What kind of motorcycle does Samson have? How tall is he? Where exactly does he live? Why can't I see him? What kind of job does he have?*

The questions served only to agitate Sharleen. "Boy, you are really tripping," she'd say. "I have no idea where that man is. And I doubt he has a job. He never did anything for us. For me or for you. What you askin' me all this for? Your father's gone. I mean *gone* gone."

And if Todd overheard any of this, she would immediately apologize to him for Tajiri's rudeness, her eyes filled with a nervous light. "Don't think I don't know what you're up to," she'd say to Tajiri when she got him alone. "Don't push it, Tajiri. Don't ruin a good thing for us."

When Todd was around, Tajiri's friends were always asking, "That yo mama's husband? You gonna have a white daddy?" And they'd tease him and call him "white boy," just because of Todd, even though Tajiri had skin as dark as Samson's.

Tajiri was quick to correct them. "That man's not my daddy. My father's a black man who lives in Hawaii. He drives a motorcycle. He's big and strong and he could kick all yo's asses *and* yo daddies' asses too."

He'd threaten to beat up anyone who teased him about Todd. One day he took the picture of Samson from his dresser and stashed it deep inside his book bag so his mother wouldn't see. At school, he placed the photo on the shelf in his locker. "This is my real father," he informed everyone he could. He began to invent small lies, starting with how his father called him every week and escalating to the plane ticket his father was sending him for a trip to Hawaii.

"He's buying me a motorcycle, too, a big ole Suzuki 500," and embellished each lie with more lies. Pretty soon Samson had a big house with palm trees, Samson went surfing every day, Samson had a pineapple tree in his front yard, Samson owned his own motorcycle dealership. "Pineapples don't grow on trees," one boy said, and Tajiri knocked him in his head.

99

"It never gets cold in Hawaii," he went on desperately. "You don't need a coat. My daddy says in Hawaii you can walk around in your jams all day long and nothin else."

He told these stories so often he began to believe them himself. Once Todd, standing unseen above on the balcony of the apartment building, overheard Tajiri down in the driveway telling Jeannette's boy about Samson. When Tajiri came up the steps, Todd stood at the top, blocking his path. For a moment Tajiri thought he was going to push him backwards, and he stood still as stone. Instead, after a considered pause, Todd said, "Don't you ever let me hear you lie again, or I'll wash your mouth out with soap." And then he'd moved his hand along the edge of his belt as a warning. "I don't tolerate liars," he said. And just as he began to step aside to let Tajiri pass, he said something that Tajiri thought he hadn't heard correctly, which was, "Remember that, little nigger."

For the wedding Sharleen insisted Tajiri serve as the ring-bearer, and she rented him a mini-tux, with a red cummerbund, and black wing-tip shoes she polished to a mirror shine. She and Todd were to be married five hours away in Reno at a love chapel with an indoor gazebo. At first Tajiri refused even to try on the tuxedo and put up such a fuss about it that Sharleen, in frustration, took a belt to his bare legs. "Why you want to spoil my happiness?" she practically cried, as the belt hit *smack, smack*. "You are one selfish boy. (*Smack*) All these years I put a roof over your head and food on your plate, and now you got a daddy to do things for you, and you wanna deny me happiness?"

Several of his mother's girlfriends and her sister Aunt Olivia, and Todd's two brothers drove to Reno the night before and rented a hotel suite where they threw a champagne party, and everyone danced to Michael Jackson's *Thriller* album. Tajiri had never seen his mother smile so brightly. There were toasts and more toasts, and Todd told jokes and made everyone laugh. "Your mama's gonna be so happy," said Aunt Olivia, hugging Tajiri close to her. "Todd's the best thing that's happened. You be a good boy for your new daddy, you hear?"

The next day their pictures were taken in a session with a hired photographer. The woman arranged themselves in hats and gloves and filmy dresses. His mother stood red-lipped and smiling, her short hair oiled to a sheen and ringed with white baby's breath, the short antique-white dress with eyelets she'd found at the flea market and white stockings offsetting her ruddy dark skin. She was beaming.

Just after the preacher united them, Tajiri heard her tell Aunt Olivia, "Finally, God's given me a husband. And a father for Tajiri. Todd's good to us. I just got worn out trying to make it on my own."

And her face was radiant when she bent down to kiss Tajiri. "From now on, baby, I'll be the best mother you ever had."

Todd's older brother served as best man. He, like Tajiri, wore a white tuxedo. There was a photo taken of the three of them together, two tall white men and Tajiri sandwiched in between, dressed like a set of triplets. Tajiri tried closing his eyes each time the camera shutter snapped, until Todd put his fingers around Tajiri's collar and yanked. He said, "Keep your eyes open, Tajiri, don't spoil the picture," and on the next flash, Tajiri stiffened his body so he wouldn't blink.

On the back of the photo, which Tajiri's mother had framed for the top of his dresser, she scrawled "Tajiri, Todd, and Doug, Reno, Nevada, June 21, 1985." After that, the photo of Samson mysteriously disappeared. When Tajiri asked about it, his mother said it had fallen on the floor while she was dusting and the glass had broken. She said, "I'll get it repaired." Then she paused for a moment and fixed him with a hard stare. "Tajiri, Todd is in our life now. I don't want any funny business."

The photo of himself, Todd, and Doug made him angry. He would turn it face down, or sometimes even gently kick it around on the floor, hoping the glass would break, accidentally on purpose. Sometimes he even imagined opening up the back and taking scissors to his own face, leaving a blank space between the two men.

There was a mixed boy at school everyone called "whiteboy" and "ofay" and "honky" and worse, because if you didn't know better, you'd think he was. He walked and talked all proper and sat in the corner by himself doing his schoolwork. His hair was so thin and straight it was almost as if he didn't have any. After Sharleen married Todd, Tajiri sought out and beat up the boy every chance he had. Knocked his little pale faggot ass silly. Dragged him out on the playground in front of everyone and whaled on his butt. Every time Tajiri saw the boy he had the urge to hurt him again. But then the boy's mother reported the beatings, and the principal said if Tajiri touched the boy one more time, he'd be suspended, and she called Sharleen—at work, no less, to discuss the matter—and that night Todd gave Tajiri a stern lecture about fighting and put him on punishment for a week. No baseball, no friends, no phone calls, no television. During that week, Tajiri began to break things in secret. He started with the pencils his mother had bought him for school, then ripped an old storybook in half, then cut up some of his own clothes he didn't like, sneaking the pieces out to the dumpster behind the apartment. At school, he made missiles out of paper clips and rubber bands and paper and fired them at the heads of students. He tripped boys who'd looked at him wrong. He began to get in more trouble, for sassing the teacher, lying about his homework, stealing lunch money from other kids. One by one, in retaliation, Todd started taking away Tajiri's privileges. And Sharleen, beside herself with what she called "Tajiri's hardheadedness," expressed relief that now there was a man around to "set Tajiri right." "I just don't know what I'd do without Todd," she told her friends. "These days you can't hardly let a boy out of your sight."

Stupid white man, thought Tajiri, recoiling every time Todd drove him to school. He didn't want to be seen getting out of Todd's car. And if he was and the kids teased him, he lied and said Todd was a neighbor, or the man who mowed the lawn, the janitor, his mother's boss, anybody but who he really was. Once he said Todd was his old teacher from another school. "You sure he ain't your daddy?" the kids teased.

"Do I look like I have a white daddy?" Tajiri demanded, pointing to himself "Do you need glasses? Ain't you got eyes in your head?"

There were a couple of mixed girls at school, twins, but no one ever messed with them. They were nice and smart, and would help you with your homework if you wanted. Once Tajiri asked the girls if they knew where Hawaii was, and the three of them found it on the map that hung on their classroom wall. "My father lives there," he told them, and he stared long and hard at the small colorful dots that made up the chain of islands until the teacher asked him to take his seat again. There was a Hawaiian boy in his school, and there were other kinds of kids, too, besides the white ones, but you couldn't count the Asian and Indian and Mexican ones, neither white nor black, who stuck to themselves and talked funny. The ones Tajiri really didn't like were the Chinese ones who came from Vietnam on boats and ate all that garlic. At lunchtime those boys gathered in their tight little circle and played chess. Sissy boys. Tajiri couldn't stand them. "Chopstick-holding, noodle-eating m.f.'s," he liked to say when he passed them, just to see if he could get a reaction. He hitched up his pants and glared at them, trying to start something, and when they looked over at him, he stretched his eyelids back with the tips of his index fingers and chanted, "Chong chong, ching chang." He knew his mother would kill him if she found out. The odd thing was his best friend for years had come from Korea, but none of that mattered now. Someone had to take the blame.

In the meantime, Todd put a down payment on a modest bungalow in East Oakland, across the street from Aunt Olivia and her husband Uncle Pete. "To be close to family," Sharleen told Tajiri, ignoring the fact that Todd was the only white man for miles. Tajiri started midyear at a new school where Todd said he could "turn over a new leaf." But it didn't take long for the other kids in the neighborhood to see that Tajiri had a white father and to tease him about it. So Tajiri began to fight again. In turn, Todd grew stricter and harder, enforcing early bedtimes, and no music after seven, and only ten minutes a night on the telephone. If Tajiri wanted to call up a girl, he had to wait until Todd was out of the house, running an errand. And when Sharleen would fret and say, "Boy, you better get off that phone before Todd comes home," Tajiri would feel his insides tighten in rebellion, and he wouldn't obey—at least not until he heard Todd's feet pounding up the front steps in his cowboy boots. And even then sometimes he'd wait just until Todd came through the door to put the phone back in its place, like a challenge. And Todd would stare hard and say, "Were you just on the phone again?" and Sharleen would chew her fingernails and distract him with, "No, baby, that was me talking to Olivia, I've got some dinner for you."

Aunt Olivia, cutting up chicken in her kitchen across the street, chided Tajiri who had stopped over to borrow sugar for a triple-berry pie Sharleen was making for Todd. "Boy, you better start learning how to act. You keep acting so bad, you're gonna run that man off."

But it wasn't that easy. No matter how hard Tajiri tried, Todd was there to stay. And how Tajiri hated going places with his mother and Todd.

He would slouch way down in the back seat of Todd's car and pretend to be asleep. And when they would park and Todd and Sharleen would get out, he'd refuse to budge, and Todd would look at him and say, "You're asking for it, Tajiri, if you don't get out right now," and slam the door.

But the part Tajiri hated most was listening to the sounds his mother and Todd made at night when they were in their bedroom alone. Even though he would bury his face in his pillow, he could still hear his mother whimper and then cry out and then laugh, and Todd would groan, a long, lonely sound like a train whistle at night. Sometimes Sharleen called out for Jesus and then the floor would shake like the aftershocks of a quake. Tajiri tried plugging his ears with his fingers. He knew what they were doing. Kids at school called it "the nasty." It was unbearable to imagine his mother and Todd like this. As he fell asleep, he imagined Todd eventually devouring his mother in little pieces. He imagined waking up one morning to find his mother gone, swallowed up, and himself alone in that house with Todd.

Mornings after the noises, Tajiri could hardly stand to look at Sharleen's cheerful face, or the way she'd kiss Todd right on the mouth when she served him coffee, as if Tajiri weren't even in the room. It sickened him seeing his mother's beautiful full lips touch the thin pale line of Todd's mouth. More and more, he resisted being driven to school by Todd, who insisted on "man to man" talk while they were in the car.

"You better get good grades and not make your mother cry. I don't want a hoodlum stepson, you hear me? You stay away from the riffraff. You may be living in an all-black neighborhood and going to an all-black school, but it doesn't mean you have to act the way everyone else does. You don't have to be a nigger. And you know I'm using that word to cover white niggers too."

Tajiri stuffed the anger down inside, tried to swallow around it. Todd

105

had no right. No right at all. When Tajiri complained to his mother, she said, "Boy, you better never let me hear you lie about Todd again. All he's done for us, and you're gonna ruin everything."

When Tajiri at eleven got sent home for more serious fighting, Todd hit Tajiri with his hand for the first time, right across the face. And then he did it again, and again, up the backside of his head, on his ears, across his shoulders. He said he was going easy on him at first, just to make a point. Then one day, after Tajiri called him a name, he knocked Tajiri down. And Sharleen hovered nervously close by and pleaded, "Don't leave marks on him. Please don't leave marks on him."

Sharleen had never used her hand on Tajiri, because she didn't believe in that. Her daddy back in Mississippi had always used a belt or a switch, and it horrified her to see Todd's hand striking Tajiri's flesh. When she told Todd he should use a belt and not his hand, Todd just looked at her as if she were crazy. "In my family," he said, "my father always used his hand."

When it was over, Tajiri's mother was swollen-eyed and nervous, hugging Tajiri to her and begging him to be good. She checked his skin for signs of bruises and cuts. "I can't stand to see you hit," she said. "Please be good." And she would cry.

But in the same breath she would add, "Todd is trying to be a father to you. He works hard all day. He brings home his pay. He keeps a nice roof over our heads. Please behave, Tajiri. You're so hardheaded. Todd just wants what's best for you."

At a certain point, when the arguments continued, Sharleen told Tajiri she didn't want to have to make a choice. That was all she said, but Tajiri got the point. A choice between him and Todd. She seemed anxious and unhappy, and she was getting thinner. Todd told her she needed to start eating more, take better care of herself. Then Aunt Olivia started coming around on Sundays to get Sharleen to go to church with her. There were whispered conversations in the kitchen, followed by reproachful glances at Tajiri. One morning Sharleen announced she was praying for Tajiri's soul. "You need to come to church with me and get saved," she told him earnestly. "Turn your life over to Christ. He'll show you the way."

Todd didn't go to church, but he began to preach as if he did. This was usually at dinner, when the three of them were sitting face to face. "God made woman to be a companion to man," he said, "and a man's son is his pride. Make me proud of you, Tajiri."

But Tajiri couldn't. Hatred lurked deep in the pit of his stomach and when he wasn't hating Todd, he was outside with his friends thinking of ways to get away. He would never be Todd's son any more than the rain that ran off the roof of the house in the winter would turn to gold.

"Young man, I want to see these C's and D's turn into B's and these B's turn into A's," Todd instructed Tajiri, striking the report card with his index finger. He started paying ten dollars per A, except that Tajiri rarely got any A's. And when he brought home grades below a B, Todd said, "Now you'll pay me," and he meant it, collecting back any money Tajiri had made. Usually Tajiri ending up owing money to Todd, which meant then that Todd found ways for him to work it off, sometimes all day Saturday.

Then there was the list of daily chores for Tajiri, which included washing and waxing Todd's car, and cleaning the fenced-in kennel out back where Todd's newly purchased Doberman pinscher Buzz lived. Tajiri hated Buzz, and when Todd wasn't looking, he spit in the dog's food and made faces at the animal. The dog was mean, because Todd was training him to guard the house. There had been some burglaries in the neighborhood, and besides, Todd said, when he went out for runs, he didn't like the way some of the black men in the neighborhood looked at him. "I need some protection," he told Sharleen. "I'm not going to get my ass kicked by some of these hoodlum soul brothers out here."

Secretly Tajiri wished it would happen. He liked imagining Todd getting beat up. Who did he think he was anyway running around the neighborhood streets as if he belonged here?

"Some day I'm going to kill that dog," Tajiri told two friends one day, just to prove he was tougher than Todd. They were out back and he was lobbying small rocks over the chain-link fence around Buzz's kennel. If he hit Buzz, the dog would lunge and snarl, and the two boys would laugh.

"Yeah, motherfucker," Tajiri liked to taunt, "come on, now, you want a piece of me, come on," and he'd prance around and strut and pose, like Oleander Holyfield, and talk big with the fence between him and the dog. It made him feel good for a while. When Todd got home and went to take Buzz out, Tajiri relished the secret that the dog's animal muteness would never reveal.

When Tajiri turned thirteen, Todd told him, "You need to earn your keep around here. Your mother and I work hard all day for a living and you don't do a damn thing. Your mother takes good care of our house and keeps your clothes clean and pressed. You can show a little appreciation. And, by the way, I don't want you hanging out on the street any more. There's too much going on."

Now when the neighborhood boys were out just messing around, Tajiri was no longer allowed to join them. Pretty soon they stopped coming by for him, just stood around at the end of the street laughing and popping wheelies on their bikes and bragging about girls at school, while Tajiri sat up on his front porch, chin propped in his hands, staring dismally down the street. He knew what the other boys thought of him, and he knew it was all Todd's fault.

But what was even worse was what was happening to his mother. She was spending more and more time at church, attending Wednesday-night Bible study and Friday-night potlucks. She stopped reading her magazines and turned instead to the Bible. She said she had at last found courage in the Lord, that she had been saved, and she hoped Tajiri would find Jesus. She was always telling Aunt Olivia and her girlfriends that she was trying to wrestle the devil from herself, that if Todd hadn't come along, she might have wound up a tramp, never settling down with one man, and how would that have looked to Tajiri. "I had a son to raise," she said. "And he needed a real father, praise the Lord."

"Take a look at the list of chores on the fridge," Todd ordered Tajiri one morning. "I don't see any checkmarks next to them. There's no time for you to be lazy in this house. You better get to your responsibilities if you ever want to hang out with your hoodlum friends again."

"Dag!" Tajiri muttered under his breath. "You don't never let me do nothin."

He started to walk away, and had barely taken in a breath of air before he was yanked around and held in Todd's firm grip. They stood facing each other, Tajiri almost as tall now as Todd.

"What'd you say?" Todd wanted to know.

For the first time Tajiri thought he saw fear in Todd's eyes. Was it possible? He felt a small surge of power.

"I *said* . . ." Tajiri began, then relented. "I just said you don't let me do anything I wanna do."

Todd stared at him, but there was a relenting in the white man's expression. There was a giving in, or was it?

Tajiri looked away and prepared himself for a blow. But it never came.

"Suit yourself," said Todd. "You wanna do what you wanna do, then so be it," and he walked away. "Don't call me when you get sent to jail."

Dinnertime was often quiet. Todd liked to read the newspaper uninterrupted. Flick, flick, his eyes scanned the words, then he shook the paper and turned the page. Sharleen sat next to him and ate slowly, carefully, as if she thought she might make a mistake. She kept a concerned eye on Tajiri, and signaled to him silently if he ate too fast or forgot to keep his mouth closed while he chewed. If he reached for something, she would say, "Please ask for it."

It got so bad Tajiri stopped ever bringing school friends home, ashamed of the way things were. The other kids told stories of how Todd eyeballed them hard, and the way he yelled out in the street for Tajiri, and at school when Tajiri was within hearing range, they were always capping on his pale face and thin pinched lips, and the way he swaggered.

"Tajiri's got a mean old white stepfather," the boys would chant, and Tajiri would retort, "That man ain't nothin to me, he just married my mother."

Todd's older brother Doug married a pretty black woman named Laura who was already the mother of two mixed children, Bee and Leon. They were much younger than Tajiri, and when they came over to visit, Tajiri hated the way everyone expected him to entertain them. He'd sit in the living room watching them play Chutes and Ladders while he stared out the window to the street where his friends were. Sometimes Aunt Olivia and Uncle Pete came over, and the six adults sat at the dinner table long after the meal was over, talking and laughing.

Doug seemed nicer than Todd, but Tajiri was still wary. Doug was always trying to start conversations with him.

"So, you ready for a little brother or sister?" Doug asked out in the kitchen after one of the meals where Tajiri was rinsing off dishes. Tajiri didn't know what he was talking about. Doug went on. "I keep after those two for a niece or nephew."

Tajiri said, "I already have a brother in Hawaii."

"Really," said Doug.

"Yeah," said Tajiri, wondering where the invention had come from. "His name is Alfonzo."

Alfonzo was the name of the boy at school Tajiri admired the most. Doug changed the subject. "You still playing ball? Doing karate?"

Tajiri nodded.

"Here, man, let me help you with those dishes," Doug said.

"That's okay," said Tajiri, but he felt some of the stiffness leaving his body and realized how taut he'd been holding himself.

Doug's two children, Bee and Leon, burst into the kitchen and swarmed all over their father. He picked them both up, one in each arm, and hiked them into the air to make them squeal. Observing his tenderness with them, Tajiri felt a pang. "Daddy, Daddy, more up!" said Bee and kissed Doug on the cheek. Todd came into the kitchen then, carrying a stack of dirty plates. His eye fell immediately on Tajiri standing motionless by the sink.

"We need to get these rinsed," he said sternly. "You never let flatware sit like that."

"I know, I'm *rinsing*," said Tajiri.

"Watch your tone," said Todd.

Looking at Doug and his children, Tajiri realized in that moment just what a terrible mistake his mother had made in marrying the wrong brother. With Todd's eye right on him, he silently mouthed the word "motherfucker," and walked out of the kitchen. He was protected so long as Aunt Olivia and Uncle Pete sat at that table laughing with Sharleen. He was protected until everyone would later leave the house, and then he would take whatever punishment Todd dished out. He wasn't about to finish rinsing anyone's dirty dishes. Instead, without a word, he went outside and down the street.

Sharleen came running into the living room when she heard Tajiri fall. "What happened?" she screamed. "What have you done?" It was the sound of her wailing that Tajiri heard as he came to, and it was only then that he realized he'd been knocked out. For a moment he thought Todd had hurt his mother. But when he opened his eyes he saw she was weeping for him. "What did you do to him? What did you do?" She knelt down on the floor and began to rock him in her arms. The guests were all gone. The Chutes and Ladders board and pieces lay spread out next to him.

Todd stood to the side, wearing an expression of disgust. "He's just fine. Somebody's got to make a man out of him," he said. Then he used the toe of his boot to gently nudge Tajiri's arm. "Get up, boy, and quit worrying your mother," he said and then looked at Sharleen. "Go on, now," he said roughly. "Go back to what you were doing. This is between me and Tajiri."

But Sharleen couldn't stop sobbing. "Oh, baby, what did you do? Why did you provoke him? I see the way you are with him. Why? He never did anything to you."

Tajiri lay there, letting her fuss over him, while the fuzziness cleared from his head. His jaw ached, and he wondered vaguely if Todd had broken it. When he finally picked himself up off the floor, his mother got up also and stood to one side, teary-eyed, wringing her hands. "Tajiri, don't do anything back to him. Put it to rest. Please, let's stop all this. If you'd just come to church with me..."

Even Todd seemed to know he'd gone too far, and paced the living room until Tajiri was upright again. But then he came so close Tajiri could smell his breath. "Just know," he said, "I'll do whatever it takes to teach you to respect me."

Over the next few days Tajiri used the incident to bait Todd. "You gonna kill me right here?" he'd taunt. "Or you gonna murder me in my sleep, you ofay motherfucker?"

Something had changed. Todd wouldn't answer, just looked at Tajiri hard, as if to imply that either of those two things could happen. His silence, though, was unreadable.

A few weeks passed, and Tajiri did exactly as he chose. Todd paid him little attention. Sharleen tried to keep them separate, even planned it so Tajiri could eat dinner before Todd got home, and by the time Todd was pulling up his chair to the table, Tajiri was either in his room with the door shut and his headphones on, or over at a friend's. It was like a choreographed dance they'd worked out in the name of household peace. Sharleen tried to remain cheerful, and in the mornings when she got ready for work, she would call out, "Bye, Todd. Bye, Tajiri," as if everything were fine. Todd no longer drove Tajiri to school. Instead, Tajiri walked with three neighbor boys the mile to the high school. He felt fierce and determined. He was winning.

One afternoon when he came home, Sharleen called him into the bedroom where she was sitting on the edge of her bed. Her skin looked dull, her face drawn.

She spoke matter-of-factly, but the strain in her voice gave her way. "Todd wants me to put you out the house, Tajiri, but I won't let him. He says you're out of control, that you don't respect him. He wants to send you away to military school. Please be good. Please be good. I don't want to lose you and I don't want to lose Todd. He's a good man, you know, praise the Lord. He's given us a real home and a real life."

"Military school!" Tajiri scoffed. "I ain't about to go to anybody's military school."

He wrinkled up his face and turned away from his mother. He knew what he had to do. Out of earshot, he went into the room that served as Todd's office and phoned up Jeannette's son from the old neighborhood, and said, "Can I come stay with you?" He put his feet up on Todd's desk and fiddled with the keyboard of his computer. Todd had hung pictures of himself and Sharleen all over the walls—Sharleen in a swing laughing, Sharleen sitting on the grass for a picnic, Sharleen in a pale pink Easter dress, Sharleen and Todd posing for a professional portrait at Sears. At the other end of the phone Jeannette got on and said, "Does your mother know?"

And Tajiri lied and said yes. Jeannette agreed, but said that Tajiri had to promise he was going to work things out with his stepfather.

That wasn't how things happened.

"I ain't comin' home," he told his brokenhearted mother on the phone from Jeannette's a couple days later. "You choose. Either him or me, but I'm not living in that house with that man any more."

"Oh, Tajiri," she pleaded. "I can't leave my husband. Try to understand. I have a duty to him as a wife. If only you'd give yourself over to the Lord and not be so stubborn. It's your pride, boy. You've always wanted more than life could give you."

Tajiri didn't think that was true. There was only one thing he'd ever wanted, or so he told himself. Out loud he said to his mother, "I want to find Samson."

There was a long pause. "I can't help you."

"Somebody knows where he is," Tajiri persisted. "What about his family? I know I have a grandmother. And his brothers and sisters?"

Sharleen began to sob softly on the other end. "Why are you doing this, Tajiri? That man has never done a thing for you. You would only be disappointed, I guarantee you."

Tajiri hung up. He had hardened himself inside. He had lost his mother, so now he was going to find Samson. How much would a plane ticket to Hawaii cost? How easy it would be to find Samson. How many big strong black men racing motorcycles could there be in a place like Hawaii?

Sharleen agreed that he could stay with Jeannette and her boy for a week, until things cooled down. But after that he needed to come back home and work things out with Todd—like a man.

Even Jeannette was siding with his mother. "Tajiri, you need to make peace," she advised. "You're too old for this nonsense. That man is trying to do right by your mother. You're letting that hard head do all the thinking for you."

It hurt to hear her say that, but Tajiri nodded. A week was seven days, and a lot could happen in that time. Sitting on the steps outside Jeannette's apartment, he talked to her son about his plans to get to Hawaii. But he had no money of his own, so he was going to have to find some. Maybe he could ask Aunt Olivia, but she'd probably just pop him on his ears for asking. He could steal the money, take it from Todd's wallet when he wasn't looking. It would be easy. Todd didn't believe in credit so he always carried large amounts of cash. Jeannette's son wasn't so sure. "I don't know," he kept saying. "You could get in a lot of trouble."

After the week at their apartment ended, Jeannette drove Tajiri home. Todd was still at work, but Sharleen was there waiting for him on the porch. When he stepped out of the car, she wept and hugged him, and promised that she'd talked to Todd and things would be different, only Tajiri must try, he must try really hard and not get on Todd's nerves. She assured Jeannette it was just father and son nonsense, a misunderstanding to be resolved later. All the while Jeannette was nodding her head, Tajiri believed he saw the light of contradiction in her eye. He wanted to say,

You know, don't you? But he didn't. Instead he followed his mother into the house and let her make him dinner.

Tajiri would bide his time. The plan was this: When Todd got home from work and showered, he would leave his pants with the wallet in the pocket on the bedroom floor for Sharleen to pick up and tend to. Tajiri knew that wallet well: soft brown leather with a designer logo on the front. Soon the television would get turned on, there would be noise in the house, and Sharleen and Todd would eat dinner in front of the evening news, a habit they'd adopted in recent months. Tajiri would excuse himself, saying he had to study in his room. On the way he would slip into their bedroom and snatch the wallet from the pocket of Todd's pants. He couldn't take anything else except what he could carry in his jacket pockets. He would invent some excuse to his mother about needing to run down to the corner market, something about a ballpoint pen. Be back in five. The screen door slamming, his sneakered feet smacking down the outside steps for the last time, he wouldn't even look back. Catch the next bus. Be gone. Patience, Tajiri thought. Patience. In his room he pulled on headphones so he could listen to music for a while. His math book sat open on the bed next to him, but he flipped it shut, and gently fell asleep. He had a dream that he was already on the plane and that as they began the descent to the green island, surrounded by blue ocean, he caught sight of a moving dot on the landscape, until as they got closer, he saw it was Samson on his motorcycle. Then suddenly the headphones slipped off his ears, still attached to the cord around his neck, emitting a tinny blare of rap music that Todd so deeply disapproved of: *gangster crap*. This was why as he woke up, Tajiri hadn't heard Todd enter the room, and didn't realize, until the air moved around him, that Todd was standing over him.

"Get up, Tajiri. We need to get some things straight."

Tajiri didn't move. He had just been about to call out Samson's name in the dream. Samson had been so close it was certain he would have heard over the roaring engine of his motorcycle, and even above the sound of the waves slashing against the shore and maybe even the din of the endless traffic streaming through Honolulu.

"I'm talking to you, boy," said Todd.

Tajiri still didn't answer. He was imagining how he would call his mother from Hawaii, how she would admit it had all been a terrible mistake and leave Todd, and she would fly to Hawaii too. Samson would remember how beautiful she was, and whatever had kept them apart would all be resolved. They would get a house together. Every day after school Tajiri and Samson would play volleyball on a beach somewhere, wearing matching surfer's jams. They would climb on the motorcycle together, Tajiri's arms wrapped around his father's waist, and they would speed off with the tropical breeze blowing against their skin.

Todd grabbed Tajiri's arm. "I said I'm talking to you."

"I ain't got nothin to say to you, man," Tajiri said, shaking off Todd's hand, and rolling over. "Leave me alone."

"'Ain't got nothin,'" mimicked Todd. "How do you like that? You even talk like one of these street niggers. Turn off that music."

He reached down and yanked the headphones from around Tajiri's neck and threw them to the floor. There was silence.

Tajiri felt the pulse of his whole body pounding. It became the force of his eyes, mouth, nose, brain, skin, everything working together, like a perfectly oiled machine. He started to pull himself up off the bed.

Then came the clicking of animal toenails on the hardwood floor, and a moment later Buzz appeared in the room, muscles tense, clipped ears erect. He was rarely allowed in the house, and when he was, he carried himself with a nervous, dangerous air.

117

"You haven't done a lick of homework. So get up now and take the dog for a walk," said Todd, holding out the leash. Buzz whined and pawed the floor. "Now, Tajiri, get your lazy ass up!"

Tajiri drew back as the dog came closer and nudged him with his nose. He hated the musty smell of the dog, the sharp cruel face and pointed ears, standing erect. He hated the way the dog submitted to Todd, crawling on his belly across the floor if Todd so commanded him. But now Todd was silent, and the dog was pressing closer, his eyes intent on Tajiri's face. A low growl had begun in the dog's throat. What happened next Tajiri could not have predicted. But neither could he have prevented. He drew back his foot and slammed the toe of his sneaker full force into Buzz's face. The dog jerked back in surprise and yelped, going down on his haunches. Tajiri drew his foot back again. His leg was halfway through the air when he felt it land solidly in Todd's tight grip.

He didn't feel the sting of the leash right away, but when he did it was already whistling through the air a second time to land on his exposed arm. And then again with the swiftness of a razor, cutting a path across his cheek. He tried pulling away, but the leash caught him full in the face and in his panic he flipped over and landed on the floor. "Mama," he called. But there was only silence from the rest of the house.

Tajiri started to say something, but Todd's boot came down on his arm, and the leash snarled through the air once more and landed on his back. It cut through the material of his shirt, sliced on through his skin to what felt like bone.

There was no question, he thought, he was getting out of here. Book as fast as he could. Take Todd's money and never come back. Fuck all this. He struggled to ignore the pain flaring across his back and then his buttocks. He started to get up, but couldn't. Buzz had hold of his foot now, and the pressure of his teeth increased until he broke the skin, right through Tajiri's shoe. Blood had gathered on the dog's nose from where Tajiri had kicked him.

"I said, get up!" Todd's voice punctured the air next to his face. There was now pressure on every part of Tajiri's body, the weight of all the years he'd devoted to hating Todd, and the heaviness of Todd's boot pinning his side. It was like drowning, except there was no water. He inhaled, felt the catch in his chest, then the bulk of his own body collecting strength beneath him.

On a palm tree-lined road in Hawaii, a helmet-free, shirtless Samson was taking a curve at full speed. Bent over the handlebars, he braced himself against the stinging wind until he seemed to soar beyond it, Tajiri clinging to his shirtless torso from behind, the engine roaring in his head, along with the sea-salt of Samson's sweat and the unexpected tactile surprise of the man's warm, muscled flesh. In that moment Tajiri recalled the smell of that other man's body, not unlike his own, both familiar and strange as if he were both himself and someone else. Slowly getting to his feet in the tight airless bedroom in his mother's house, he breathed in tropical island sea, felt the warm pressure of wind on his skin and, recalling the arms of the man who had once held him, briefly, shook off the grip of the dog's savage mouth, and raised his fists.

DIMITRY GUROV'S DOWDY WIFE

YOU'RE PROBABLY FAMILIAR WITH THE DESCRIPTION OF ME in the widely anthologized Chekhov story. Depending on the translation, it goes something like this: "tall woman with dark eyebrows, erect, dignified, imposing, and, as she said of herself, a (quotes) 'thinker.'" Another version insists on this self-reference with the same quotes around it: "intellectual," perhaps again some frustrated translator's attempt to ironize in English what's already implied in the Russian. Which is to say, I am being exposed and ridiculed as something of a poseur, a bit full of myself. Everyone's having a little chuckle at my expense. Let me stand corrected. "Intellectual" and "thinker" are not my words. I have yearnings, yes, but I know also I am seen by the world as Dimitry's wife or wife of Dimitry.

In nineteenth-century Russia, a woman does not belong to herself As for the dropping of the hard signs after consonants when I write letters to my sister, and to my friend Nastya in St. Petersburg, it is not, as one translator's footnote tells you, "an emancipated affectation." It is what I learned at the university, a signal toward the future. I write letters and small essays, because writing is my only real link with a world beyond my own hermetic one. It is through letters that I often discover what I think of things, which is why I now write, alone in my room, with the light glinting off the snow.

Well, they are right that I am what is known as a dowdy woman. I am not ugly, but I am not lovely either. I was chosen as "a suitable wife," which signals attributes other than beauty. And they are also right about this: I am a reader, though their emphasis on "great reader" seems to embellish my small knowledge of German and French with which I have wrestled my way through Goethe's *Sorrows* and some of Flaubert and Maupassant. In English, if I am lucky enough to get my hands on a book, I prefer expressive poetry: John Keats and Robert Browning and Matthew Arnold. Dimitry never says much about my habits, but did show open disapproval when I praised Gogol's *Mertvye* dushi (*Dead Souls* in one translation, *Deceased Serfs* in another, *Moribund Servants* in the most atrocious of all), and he refused to accompany me to see The *Inspector General* when it played at the theater, calling it a pointless insult to our finer Russian institutions. Dimitry openly holds women in contempt, I know this, but what the translators don't know is that what Dimitry says and what he does are two different things. I would not have married a despicable man. A man with flaws, yes. But then are not flaws a condition of manhood?

It was while our three children were young that I began my constant reading, having long hours to pass inside our house with only the children and the servants while Dimitry traveled up to St. Petersburg on business or down to the Black Sea at Yalta where he finds the air easier to breathe.

—Moscow stifles, one day is very like the next, complains Dimitry, and it is apparent he yearns for the sea. He does not look at me when he speaks, but past me, then stretches out his legs, stands up, puts on his fur-lined coat and thick gloves, and saunters off down Petrovka Street. I happen to know he goes to the Medical Club to play cards with men he never calls friends. The nurse comes in and lights the lamp. She is pleasant enough, not too young, not too old, but we have nothing in common except my children, two sons and a daughter. I ask her if the children have finished their studies, and she confirms they have, and leaves, and that is our only communication. I am left alone with the wind howling in the chimney.

Some nights at my instigation Dimitry and I attend the theater together here in Moscow, taking the carriage through the snow, me wrapped in furs and feeling the chilled air brighten my cheeks. There is hope after all, I think, in the dark of the carriage, but in the radiant lights of the foyer I see that Dimitry forgets I am there and I find myself vanishing. It is the oddest thing how quickly I can fade in a public place. Is this my own complicity? How much must I blame myself for such absence?

My corporeal self often strikes me as a memory, like the boy I once loved when I was not much older than my own Sonia is now. I have kept his letters safe from dust and damp, sealed in a trunk in my room. They were beautiful letters, and he was a beautiful boy. His name was Anton. He died in the Army. I say died, because he never came back. Can there be death without a cause?

On our way home from the operetta, Dimitry grows more taciturn than usual, dismissing the performance with a wave of his gloved hand.

—The voices were weak, he says. —So thin I could hardly hear them.

Dimitry himself once sang, but his work in the bank keeps him too preoccupied for hobbies. Or so I believe. He does not speak his thoughts to me, and so I have now to wonder if boredom has driven him to

123

extremes in middle age. I don't begrudge him his vacations at the southern resorts, seeing as I do his face brighten at the prospect of a trip. Upon his returns, I count on him to introduce me vicariously to the gaiety which his sojourns elicit, to disrupt this silence between us.

Soon I will be forty years old. I have much to be thankful for: two sons and a daughter, a life in Moscow, and I have married well. This is what I tell myself as I wander through our house, dark in winter with the sun going down so early. I have been reading again by weak lamplight, and my eyes are strained and dry. I recently saw an announcement that the orchestra will be performing Tchaikovsky's new symphony in St. Petersburg, and I plan to ask Dimitry if we might go together, make a trip of it, see the city together. But I don't.

Christmas approaches. I write to my sister in Zhizdra. She writes back and complains about the provincial life there. Her husband is a low-level bureaucrat, a sweet-tempered man who loves her but will never leave his position, which means she too is there for life. She says I am lucky to live in Moscow (so much to do!), and she is right. I sigh to myself and think yes, I am lucky. We have our three children and two houses and sometimes we go to the theater. It is an odd thing, unhappiness. If I lose myself in other tasks, I forget about it. In this way I look forward to the holidays when there will be guests about, with whom I can find interesting conversation.

Lest you think I am only a complainer, let me explain that my children really are my greatest source of joy. Peter is the eldest, and he looks very much like Dimitry, has his quiet facility with young women, combined with a coldness that sometimes frightens me. Aleksei is the middle child, and he is most like me in temperament. We tease and tell each other jokes. He hides my things, a glove here, a pen there, makes me search for them before returning them like a magician's trick. We try to outwit each other, and whether we do or not, we collapse in laughter. My daughter Sonia is my jewel—just twelve now—on the brink of womanhood. Her skin glows with that knowledge. But she herself does not yet know, because she will still crawl onto my lap and put her arms around my neck to say good-night.

—Mama, she says this evening, staring up at me with big eyes, I so want a dog for Christmas. I have in mind the most darling puppy I saw near the square the other day. It is a little Pomeranian. Aleksei said I should ask you first and not Papa.

—Your papa dislikes dogs, is allergic to their fur, I remind her. Your papa would never let a dog live in this house. And small dogs make him nervous.

My jewel continues to sparkle. —Mama, please. I won't ever ask for anything again.

—I'll speak to your father, I tell her, with a sense of foreboding. —But don't get your hopes up.

She clings to me and plants kisses all over my cheeks.

When the children and I go out, people turn to look. They are a handsome lot, my children, and I am proud to think that my own plainness has been transformed into beauty. Sometimes their lives mean more to me than my own. At night I have cried copious tears over their imagined loss. In this way I test the breadth of my own feelings, remind myself I am capable of great love.

The holidays bring a sense of renewal and excitement. For some, the end of the year signals sadness. For me it is a culmination of all the happy moments from the preceding months. Alone in my room, I begin to organize gifts—I have not yet asked about Sonia's dog, have been waiting for a change in Dimitry's humor. It is his habit to go in and out of moods, sometimes for months at a time. He has been so removed of late that I hesitate to interrupt his thoughts. He appears unexpectedly in my doorway with a strange look on his face.

—I must go to St. Petersburg immediately on an urgent matter. It's regarding this young fellow I was telling you about, a rather awkward business to be sure. But it must be taken care of, or trouble will follow.

I refuse to counter with the obvious, that it is Christmas, that the children will be disappointed, that I will be alone again, that we will pass our holidays without him. He speaks distractedly. I listen with care. In between the words I hear other words, and the result is a jangle of contradictions in my head. He goes on, impatiently, and I begin to hear the echoes of other stories, other troubles, reasons for going away.

He says, —I tried putting it off, but it can't wait and must be attended to directly. If I had any choice in this, I would insist on delaying the trip. But a young man's future lies in my hands. Nothing to be done about it.

He waits, as if for an answer. In the firelight I see youthful exuberance in his face. He is a schoolboy narrating a delicious lie, knowing that beyond this moment exists a pleasure so worth the risk that consequences are immaterial. His eyes glow with the effort. What does he expect me to say? It has all been said, years ago when I thought such things mattered. When I used to weep at his departures, and cling to him like a child, saying, *Dimitry, don't go.* Because I wasn't sure what to do with myself when I was alone.

—Dimitry, I say now, Sonia is desperately in want of a little dog for Christmas. She saw a puppy in the square last week, and she has asked me if you would consider letting her have it. It is a very small dog, and she will take good care.

Relief clears his brow. I can only describe it as relief. He pauses, then his mouth jerks awkwardly, almost a smile.

—Of course, he says, she may have a small dog. I have begun to develop an affection for very small dogs actually. But she must promise to care for it properly, see that it's fed and not left to freeze to death outside.

I can hardly conceal my surprise. But a sense of foreboding accompanies my joy at this break in Dimitry's design. I don't mean to sound ungrateful, but his ready approval is most suspect. I know for sure that I have traded some dreadful truth for my child's dog. I rise up from the hearth where I have been laying out paper for wrapping.

—Is this bank business, Dimitry?

But he has turned in the doorway to leave and so my words fall in the wake of his retreating steps.

—I already told you, his voice travels back. A man's happiness is at stake.

Christmas passes, and my fortieth birthday goes without much notice in the spring. Dimitry has brought me a lovely gray dress and a new lorgnette from his most recent excursion. When I thank him, he smiles in that pitying way he has, as if I deserve little more than his sympathy. As if I have been wronged in some way that I am too ignorant to understand. I write my sister and tell her that we are happy, the birch trees are leafing, and Sonia's dog is the light of her life. We call him Strekoza, or "Dragonfly," because he is so needle quick. He is a beautiful little creature who prances through the house with long fur waving. Sonia is perennially beside herself to get home from school to romp with him. How my children and I dote on this canine darling whose active presence in our lives has proved a welcome disruption.

In the late mornings, while the children are hard at work on their lessons, I take Strekoza out. What I claim as duty is really a pleasure. Together we breathe in the cold spring air.

Soon I take to longer walks. They improve my figure and my stamina. The little red dog is good company, trotting along with determined curiosity. Sometimes people in the street pause to inquire about him.

—Does he bite? they ask, bending down, and I assure them he doesn't. —May I give him a bone?

These days I return home, feeling renewed, as if a door has opened in my life. I have some place to go, and it is never the same place. Walking

127

stimulates my thoughts. When I hang up my coat and move toward the fire with frozen hands extended, I feel the vigor of my own arms, and a new alertness in my mind. I read for hours without growing tired. At night before I sleep, I write in my little book. Even the nurse tells me I am looking younger these days.

This particular morning Dimitry takes Sonia to school, as has become his habit. I am pleased with his demonstrations of interest. Peter and Aleksei aren't the only ones in need of a father.

I have purposely never asked Dimitry about the matter of the young man in St. Petersburg, and have come not to think about it much, believing that whatever trouble there was is now resolved. Our lives have resumed a pleasant balance.

I go out with Strekoza, who has been barking at me to hurry up with my coat and gloves. On the street we are greeted by sunshine, and I raise my face to it, like a flower. Strekoza dances on his hind legs, then strains against the leash. "I'm coming, I'm coming!" I laugh with joy. We choose a new route that will eventually wind past Sonia's school, which is a good distance away, and then head for the little park. I'm ready for a challenge, the crisp air paints my cheeks, and Strekoza's enthusiasm urges me onward.

Now you readers already know details I have no way of knowing, regarding the lady they call Anna Sergeyevna, come down to Moscow, an interloper who somewhere in the back of my mind I have vaguely suspected. But what you don't know is that this particular day Strekoza and I walked by the Savyansky Bazaar Hotel, and I stopped directly across from it to adjust my right boot which had come unlaced. When I bent over, Strekoza leaped up on his hind legs and barked wildly, his miniature paws clawing the air. He yanked me several steps over the frozen ground so that in looking around to see what had upset him I slipped. Caught off balance, I struggled to keep myself upright and therefore missed what Strekoza saw and what you already know. The familiar heavy coat, the fingers in a fur-lined glove turning the doorknob. But fate intervened in the form of a loose boot string and a patch of ice on the walk, and so I never saw the figure of my husband pass inside the hotel to his most recent assignation. Perhaps it was her brand of unhappiness that drew him, her inseparable connection to another man, her own husband, and the impossibility of their love. Perhaps it was the fact that all the years I suffered, I held myself aloof and never demanded pity, or even tenderness.

At that moment in the street, I was still free of this knowledge. It wasn't until quite by accident I came across the story in a magazine, just a few weeks later, brought up short at the ending that gestures toward the anguished paradox in which I'm only implied. Putting two and two together was then as easy as knitting a row of stitches. I moved beyond the endless parade of spectres that had for years hovered in the back of my mind. Weighted down for so long by low-grade despair I did not myself know, I had forgotten my own longings and desires. But now plunged into the mundane specifics of my outwardly respectable husband's pathetic love affair, I almost laughed. For this I have been so melancholy? For this I have wept over nameless woes?

Chekhov's tale is lyrical enough, I grant him that, and he weaves an excellent yarn. But the story ends where it ends because it is guided by the poetry of language, another sort of truth to be sure, but a truth gained at my expense. Had I been allowed to speak, the story probably would have been reduced to an anecdote.

How boring to read this true and tedious little denouement: in fact, subsequently, Dimitry renounced his Anna and returned to me. Without any prompting on my part, he dropped to his knees one night about two months after and confessed the whole sordid affair in tears. I feigned first ignorance, then dismay, and finally uttered the words of forgiveness.

129

—I am a changed man, he told me weeping. —Do not forsake me, my darling wife.

And he flung his arms around my boots, a man fearing rejection twice, for surely his Anna must have come to her senses and he, no longer a youth, feared being left alone.

Now a leopard cannot change his spots and so I insisted on no further explanations, holding my small triumph in reserve.

—Don't trouble yourself so, Dimitry, I said, drawing on the bottomless well of benevolence at the disposal of all happy people.

Chekhov's fiction doesn't concern itself with the fact that neither the return nor departure of Dimitry could any longer rouse much sentiment in me. Over the years he has become like the weather, always present but impossible to measure, and his dalliances ceased to affect me years ago.

So what was it that time altered for me? It is this—whenever I so desire, I am the one to travel, and that includes places like Yalta. By myself I stroll the esplanade, chat up new acquaintances (and what lovely people I have found, gifted of manners and speech). I breathe in the sea air, and occasionally treat myself with abandon to confections at Vernet's. My children understand, even encourage me to go, claiming my skin has never looked so radiant, that upon my returns I am a girl again. Dimitry has taken to meeting me at the train station (his choice, not mine), and on the ride home he asks politely if I've enjoyed myself, and glances my way from time to time with—what shall I say—a quizzical look? I answer with suitable aplomb, my mind still lingering on the esplanade, the pounding surf and salty scent of the Black Sea infusing my senses. In the evenings if I'm not dining out he orders the cook to prepare my favorite dishes, and sends the children on up to their rooms. We take our seats at opposite ends of the long table, while I regale him, in candlelight, with various versions of my latest adventures. He listens with a mixture of amusement and pain. I talk of wanting to see London and Paris, and he doesn't blink an eye.

—But of course, darling, he says, you must see it all.

And kisses me on the cheek.

I am never named in Chekhov's fiction, not in the original, and not in the translations. It was written as another woman's story, and speaks, among many things, to the fragility and illusion of romantic love. But there is no such ambiguity for me as I sit here now, freshly home from the sea, my mind alert. Strekoza sleeps curled by the firelight while I scratch words and sentences on the page of my small book. There are no longer obstacles to my desires. If you should be in Yalta next spring on the esplanade, you may address me as Nadia, which of course means "hope." Know too that the little dog trotting at my side shares my passion for the water.

MY SUMMER OF LOVE

I WAS THE SON AND ONLY CHILD OF TWO FLOWER CHILDREN named Reed and Marie Braxton who met at Berkeley and were married when I was about three by a clown named Wavy Gravy who joined them "for as long as it feels good." My parents were staunch socialists who believed in sharing everything, including each other. My arrival was in strict contradiction to my father's philosophy about the overpopulation of the world. When I remained small for my age, my father blamed my mother, a resolute vegan, for refusing me meat.

Since my parents believed in openness about everything, I grew up with few secrets in a community of their friends near the Haight, knowing a little about a lot: various grades of marijuana, the salubrious effects of orgone boxes and meditation, options for birth control, and the relative

133

uncertainty of adult relationships which permutated like kaleidoscopes. My mother worked part-time as a receptionist at an avant-garde art gallery on Haight Street and volunteered in the evenings at the free clinic. My father had earned a teaching credential in college and occasionally taught at an alternative private high school where students didn't have to come to class if they didn't feel up to it that day, and where no one received grades.

The day my parents took me to the Amtrak station my mother wore a red-flowered skirt and a white blouse, set off the shoulders, and sandals. She and my father silently passed their morning joint back and forth as we drove down through the Panhandle. They had fought miserably the night before, something about a couple, Dana and Lightning from Los Angeles, who had been "crashing" with us since Easter. My father spent the whole night sitting outside on the front steps "getting his head together." Now my parents huddled in the front seat like two bad children, eying each other, as the acrid smell of marijuana enveloped us all in a forgiving haze.

At the station, my mother put on pink-rimmed granny glasses to hide her puffy eyes. She assured me over and over that my going to Aunt Evie was the best for now while she and my father worked through their "philosophical crisis."

"You know how much I adore Evie," she said several times as if to reassure herself. "I wouldn't trust anyone else with you." She asked me not to discuss their troubles with either Aunt Evie or Uncle Del. "Especially Uncle Del."

Then from her shoulder bag she pulled out my collapsible travel chess set and pressed it into my hands.

"You forgot this. Don't forget me," she whispered, her hot tears staining my cheek. I gratefully stuffed the chess set into my knapsack, along with a book on pawn structure and Nimzowitsch's *My System* and my wooden chess clock.

My father paced, his hands stuffed in the pockets of his cut-off sweats. He'd pulled his thick dark brown hair back into a ponytail, which meant he was most likely going to practice yoga in the Park later. He hugged me hard against him and I closed my eyes. Unlike the long-winded Polonius advising Laertes, my father kept his counsel short. "Stay cool," was the sum of his wisdom.

As I started to board the train, he called out, "Hey, if anyone on the train asks, you're sixteen years old." My mother burst into tears.

"Okay, Reed," I assured him.

My father had decided it was dishonest for me to call him "Dad" any more, since that implied inequality in our relationship (a slavish dependence on my part, and a perverse dominance on his) and so in keeping with our new parity, I repeated, "You stay cool, too, Reed," and slapped him five in the air.

I spent the entire train trip, all three days and two nights of it, among my miniature chess pieces, practicing memorized combinations for pinning, double attack, discovered check, smothered mate, and even a surprise checkmate by a pawn capturing en passant. The last was so poignant it brought tears to my eyes.

As requested, I phoned my parents each night from public phone booths, reversing the charges and assuring them the trip was going well. Other than that I gave my parents very little thought, relieved to be free of their conflict. Just like that, I stored them on a small shelf in my mind and closed the door. I ignored the other passengers and the countryside whizzing by, and concentrated on the endless possibilities of attack and defense on sixty-four squares.

In reaction to the endless variations on brown rice and soybean curd we ate at home, I downed copious amounts of Fanta root beer and dozens of Reese's peanut butter cups. A kind of gastronomical rebellion overcame me. At every opportunity I bought greasy burgers, still red in the middle, and topped with anemic tomatoes, stringy onions fried in fat, and tart, mouth-withering pickles.

Fortified by an endless supply of Oreos, I pored over variations of the King's Gambit accepted, and memorized a Spasski/Sakharov game from the 1960 USSR championship, as the train sang along the tracks. King-pawn openings were still my favorite and the controversy around the King's Gambit didn't diminish my appetite one bit for it. I was a romantic at heart and the chance for positional advantage through sacrifice only fanned my ardor. At thirteen, I hadn't yet discovered girls, and chess was my passion.

On our arrival in central Ohio, I emerged from the train with a violently upset stomach, into gray, muggy weather. It was early evening, and the air was thick with mosquitoes.

Aunt Evie and Uncle Del lived in one of those typical, spacious old Midwestern houses, with ample lawn, and a full attic and basement. This was in sharp contrast to our close quarters in San Francisco. I was given a room in the very back of the house which faced east, so that I got the early morning light. I shared a bathroom with my cousins Patsy and Edmund, whom I'd known intermittently over the years, and remembered only as "too old to play with."

Edmund was about to start his senior year in high school. He'd always been a dopey sweet boy who loved sports and hated reading. Years ago, during a family trip to Ohio, he nicknamed me Professor, which struck me as worse than corny. Now he had grown into a taller, more gangly version of his old self.

Patsy, one year behind him in school, had changed more dramatically. At sixteen, she was sarcastic and wild, and her childhood prettiness had ripened into a formidable adolescent savagery. She drew hard dark lines under her eyes that lengthened on either side to her ears; her hair was bound up with a rubber band and flowed from the top of her head like a waterfall. She painted her toenails purple and black, and wore two-inch tall green platform sandals. She dressed in halter tops made from bandanas and hip-hugger jeans that widened like open umbrellas at the ankles, making her legs appear pencil-thin.

She was teasing and sly with me, offering sticks of Wrigley's spearmint gum which she chewed in abundance, or sips of milkshakes that she stirred thoughtfully with a large red straw while staring dreamily out from the screen porch into the steamy grass below. She explained to me shortly after my arrival that acid was the only reality, and that her parents were merely two mindless puppets being manipulated by larger unseen forces. When I inquired more about details of the forces, she replied a bit impatiently, "the capitalist-industrial complex forces."

Patsy, I often thought ruefully, should have been my parents' child. It was as if we'd been switched at birth.

Aunt Evie looked exactly as I'd remembered her: the same ageless wide pale face and light gray hair parted on the side and held back from her forehead with a headband. For my first evening meal, she welcomed me with baked chicken, applesauce, and thick homemade noodles. The tomatoes and cucumbers were picked fresh straight out of her garden. It was the meal that settled my poor raging stomach.

Though she'd already eaten, Aunt Evie sat with me at the table, begging for details of my trip. When I went upstairs to bed, she followed me and fussed around my room, turning down the covers, and hanging up my jean jacket in the closet. As I brushed my teeth, she tucked me in almost apologetically.

"While you're here," she told me, "I was thinking maybe ten o'clock would be a reasonable bedtime for you. What time do you normally go to bed?"

I didn't admit I'd never had a bedtime before, having been allowed to fall asleep wherever and whenever I wanted. So I simply said that ten sounded perfect. Bedtime felt like a present she had just given me.

Since I was a small child, I had always adored my memories of Aunt Evie, and now those feelings spiraled out of control. I lay awake for sometime after she'd closed my door and left me to sleep, cushioned by a sense of well-being. In the weeks that followed, I seized every chance to sit on the kitchen stool while she baked or ironed or washed dishes. Sometimes she was silent, listening to the Saturday Metropolitan Opera broadcast on the radio, while I worked quietly on chess. In her more talkative moments she told me stories, interesting anecdotes about her childhood: how she'd baby-sat her two younger brothers for a whole week when she was ten because her mother went to the hospital for a gallbladder operation; how she'd fought with her father about going to college to become a teacher (she wanted to be a doctor); how she'd gone to Mexico for a month when she was twenty-one and lived with an Indian family in a mountain village where there was no plumbing or electricity. My curiosity aroused, I asked more and more questions and soon Aunt Evie was telling me all about the Depression and how later she worked in a factory during World War II, making machine parts. She ended up doing as her father wanted and became a teacher, though she had done little more than substitute over the last few years.

"I don't understand children these days, they're so wild," she confided sweetly in me. "I have nothing to teach them, and I can't stand yelling at them to behave."

Around the house, when she cooked and vacuumed, Aunt Evie wore a real apron. Even when she was sitting on the front porch in a chair, reading the newspaper, or stretched out on the sofa for a quick nap, her front side was covered by blue-and-white-checked cotton.

Quite to the contrary, my mother had never worn an apron, much less much of anything at all. Since I could remember, she wandered the house nude, her body slender and tanned, her breasts full and oblong-shaped like pears. She even courted disaster, cooking with hot oil, unprotected, believing, as did my father, that nudity was the key to spiritual freedom, and clothing represented hypocrisy and repression. Personally, I preferred wearing clothes at all times, though I was assured repeatedly by both my parents that it was fine not to, that the body was something to be proud of. There was a time when my preference for clothes caused them great concern, and my mother would gently point out how the other children my age at the nude beach were getting all-over tans, wouldn't that be nice to do. They feared I would grow up repressed and ashamed.

I came to associate Aunt Evie's apron with the aroma of chocolate-chip cookies steaming up the humid kitchen on summer afternoons. As the long sweltering hours after lunch piled up like days, and the yard sizzled and hissed in white-hot sunlight, I holed up with my chess set on the shady screen porch, waiting to be summoned to lick the raw dough from the beaters and, later, to test the first batch of cookies as they emerged from the oven. In that thick, tight air, the aroma of baking overpowered me like a drug, and sometimes I would sprawl on my back on the floor just delighting in the expectation.

If there was a thunderstorm, Aunt Evie would join me on the screen porch with a plate of cookies and glasses of iced tea, and together we would watch the lightning streak the dark sky, and count the seconds before the thunder rolled.

"That one was close!" she'd say. "Just right over there."

The heavy downpour that followed would dramatically lower the temperature, enough for me to run inside for a sweatshirt, and in the fine misty air, so delicious I wanted to drink it, Aunt Evie and I would play gin rummy or Scrabble, listening to the water drip off the green plants jammed against the screened walls.

"I see you're something of a chess player," Uncle Del commented one afternoon, as he appeared unexpectedly in the doorway looking out across the yard. He had caught me off guard by addressing me directly. His tone did not invite a response; his posture was rigid and exuded loathing. I kept my head bowed and my eyes on the board.

Uncle Del was something of a phantom in the house. He almost never spoke to any of us, including Aunt Evie. He reminded me of a white-flour-and-water paste my mother used to make for art projects when I was little. Aunt Evie never walked by my Uncle Del, but always *around* him, the way you might a piece of inconveniently placed furniture. He, on the other hand, looked straight through her, as if she were made of glass. Even when he addressed her, his eyes focused somewhere beyond. Or if he was reading, his eyes never lifted from the page.

And so it went. Uncle Del ignored me, Edmund tolerated me, Patsy confided in me, and Aunt Evie loved me.

One evening I overheard Aunt Evie tell my cousins, "You two be extra nice to poor little Oscar this summer, his mommy and daddy are going through a rough time."

Upon hearing that, I felt so sorry for myself that I went off and cried. Every time after that when I was feeling lonesome, I'd look at Edmund as mournfully as I could, hoping to pull at his heart strings.

But it didn't work, not really. Edmund was too preoccupied with his own life to be much concerned with mine. After all, we were five years apart, and his attention was on basketball that summer and when he wasn't at the neighborhood court, he was lounging on the front porch of a girl named Sabra who lived two blocks over. When I became a man in my thirties and again ran into Edmund at a family reunion I found him to be much like his father—unimaginative and uncommunicative. He had married a woman named Marjorie who looked almost exactly like Aunt Evie, but was far more severe, and they had three daughters, all of whom dressed like hookers and chewed gum.

That summer Patsy informed me repeatedly that Edmund was "just a dumb jock." A deep sigh would follow, out of some well of melancholy that stirred inside Patsy, expressed repetitively through her walls in the form of Jim Morrison's echoing monotone droning out, "Come on, baby, light my fire." Or the hard beat of Gracie Slick's untamed "Plastic Fantastic Lover." Over and over Patsy would listen as if in a trance for what seemed like hours, until the beat throbbed like a pulse in the house. I had glimpsed her, when her door was cracked, meditating on the spider she liked to draw on her hand in ink, her eyes lit up like candles.

"When I get out of high school," she told me many times, "I'm heading out to Frisco. It's the only place to be. Think Reed and Marie would let me crash with them?"

I shrugged. "Probably."

"God, Oscar, you're so lucky. Tell me again about stuff to do in the Haight."

Not sure what to say, I described people who hung out on the street and played music in the Park, embellishing my role here and there. I even told her how I went prowling through a manzanita thicket one afternoon and came across two wild-haired people in the throes of lovemaking there on the ground. I had actually run off like a startled deer, but suggested to Patsy that I had lingered, and served up several imagined details as truth.

"Is it true they sell dope right on the street corners?" Patsy wanted to know. "I mean, everyone just walks around buzzed in public, right?"

Unlike my parents, Aunt Evie and Uncle Del never seemed to argue, at least not that I ever heard. I couldn't begin to imagine Aunt Evie throwing pots and dishes the way my mother did when she was provoked. Household objects frequently zoomed by my father's head. He in turn would duck and laugh at her and call her a "crazy bitch," taunting her in her rage. Their fights left me with a sick, sinking feeling that neither could be trusted. Like so many of their friends at the time, my parents experimented with pills and dope, and things tended to get confused. Much of the time everyone was in a good mood, just lounging around, rapping and smoking, and cooking outlandish meals that took all day to prepare. Our house was always full of people, some of my father's high school students, old college friends, and neighbors who drifted by. But often, when my mother needled my father into a rage (and she seemed to do it purposely!), I fled to the basement and sat weeping between the cat box and the washing machine.

And yet there were times when the routine silence between Aunt Evie and Uncle Del took on a much darker edge than the open rancor between my parents, and I began to suspect a seed of evil germinating in the small callus of Uncle Del's heart.

Because of this I kept well out of his way. Uncle Del was inaccessible and unremarkable, with one exception: his impeccable table manners. Though he came from Pennsylvania mining stock, he prided himself in eating like continental aristocracy. He switched hands when using a knife and a fork, laying the utensils carefully to the side of the plate while he chewed. He took only mouse-sized bites into his mouth, pondering each one like a nugget of wisdom.

Before meals, he insisted on being given five minutes' notice, so that he could wash his hands and brush his teeth. And I knew for a fact that he counted slowly to one hundred while spreading the soap through his fingers, because I overheard him once doing it.

In the kitchen, where I kept Aunt Evie company, she would interrupt my chess study long enough to ask me, "Oscar, why don't you let your Uncle Del know it's five minutes to dinner." (She'd given up on Patsy and Edmund for this task.) I disguised my distaste for relaying her messages, because after all, it was Aunt Evie asking. At the sound of my voice, Uncle Del routinely appeared not to hear, engrossed in a book or magazine in the living room. Eventually his lips would move imperceptibly in an "Mmmm, hmmm" so that I could report back to Aunt Evie that I'd accomplished my task.

And within precisely five minutes he would arrive at the table like a dark cloud, seating himself with grave precision. He made a point of scooting the chair back and forth several times until he had settled himself against the cushion he insisted had to be placed on the chair just so.

"So, this is lovely," he would remark, as Aunt Evie set his plate before him. Patsy and Edmund always exchanged disgusted looks when he spoke, even made remarks under their breath. Hands folded in his lap, he let his eyes pass over the plate several times before pronouncing that it "looks excellent."

Aunt Evie always saw to it that meals were colorful so they would appeal to the eye as well as to the digestive system. She believed in good nutrition and the four food groups. And she always made sure everyone else was served first, while she busied herself at the stove or sink.

Before taking his first bite, Uncle Del would use his fork to gently prod what was on his plate.

"Now, let's see, how many tablespoons of flour were used in the gravy?" he might ask in a tidy little voice.

Aunt Evie's tone was as flat as the street they lived on. "Six," she might say, never breaking her momentum at the stove. "Now you all go ahead and get started before the food gets cold."

Sometimes, without looking at any of us, Uncle Del would issue into the air a verbal dissertation on the difference between certain types of green beans or potatoes, depending on what Aunt Evie served. He would hold forth on alternative ways to cook whatever it was that Aunt Evie had prepared, pausing only to wipe his mustache with his napkin.

Like Patsy and Edmund, I was relieved when he was away on business; the whole house seemed to loosen its joints and flex its muscles. But if truth be told, Aunt Evie was at her best when it was just the two of us.

The summer progressed, smooth and monotonous. One day flowed into the next, and I happily lost track of time. I was left alone in the afternoons to do as I pleased, but mostly I worked on chess. There were no neighbor children my age, and even if there had been, my poor social skills left me unequipped to pursue friendships easily. In the shade of Aunt Evie's backyard arbor I memorized the dragon and its countermoves. At night, on the front porch, my legs swabbed with mosquito repellent, I went over and over the King's Indian and its variations. I tried to teach Edmund, but he couldn't get the hang of it.

"God, it takes so long," he would say, shifting uneasily opposite me. While I studied the board he would throw imaginary basketballs into the air and send them through hoops with a "poof!" from his lips. Soon he would abandon me for better things, and I would be left alone until Aunt Evie would summon me for a walk in her garden.

"Did you know you can eat pansies?" she asked me one evening, offering several flowers as proof. I watched as she lifted the petals to her mouth. "They are beautiful in salads, you know. Go ahead, try this one."

She knew exactly how much to water each bed (she did it all by hand with a hose) and what needed weeding. Sometimes she put on gardening gloves and wheeled out what she called her "mulch cart," and spread black wood chips through the beds.

"Gardening is meditative for me. It gives me such a peaceful feeling, but then you probably understand the importance of that, with your chess and all." With her yard shears she might clip a rosebud or an azalea and thread it through a buttonhole on my shirt. I followed her around just for the pleasure of her company. She misunderstood and thought I was interested in flowers.

"I've given up trying to get Patsy and Edmund interested in gardening. They honestly couldn't care less." She said this without accusation. "Too bad I can't keep you all year, Oscar."

In the twilight we would sometimes convene on the stone bench at the back edge of her yard and stare together in silence out over her garden to the spread of a small park on the other side of the street. It really was just an empty lot with grass and several large trees, but she called it "the park."

"I'm so glad you could come be with us, Oscar," she told me one night. "My own children are at an age where I no longer understand them, when I have done my job as a mother, and now it is up to them to make sense of their lives. People eventually must grow up and become responsible for themselves, you know." She sighed. "Part of your job in life is to forgive them for the ways they disappoint you."

What was it, I often wondered when she and I sat like this, that stood between her and Uncle Del. Why the insidious silence that had begun to fill me with as much dread as the raging outbursts between my parents. Uncle Del lived so removed from the rest of us. He came and went each day without incident, like a casual guest. Sometimes when I looked at him closely, instead of feeling fear, I saw only a dull man whom I hated; at other times when he turned inwards, I saw a selfish little man preoccupied with some unnamed grief.

Once when I was walking by, I peeped through the open door of their bedroom and discovered they slept in twin beds, pristinely covered in neat

145

brown spreads, and separated by a nightstand with a lamp between them. I resisted the urge to go in and look further, afraid I'd get caught, and afraid of what I might find.

"I think, Oscar, you've put on a little weight here," Aunt Evie remarked one evening at dinner in front of everyone. I was having seconds of everything, as had become my custom. "Or maybe you've grown an inch or two." I didn't mind at all her saying things like this.

"He's been eating my desserts, that's why," remarked Patsy snidely. She was trying to stay slim. On hot days she wore skirts so short they seemed pointless, and her bare stomach was exposed, flat as an ironing board, as living proof that Patsy wasn't eating much. That summer Patsy worked on the outskirts of town at a drive-through called Dogs-N-Suds, where teenagers would go for whatever it was that teenagers did, and she claimed being around all that greasy food made her too sick to eat.

"Well, I think our Midwestern fare is agreeing with Oscar," Aunt Evie smiled and winked at me. "You're going to surprise your parents when they see you."

My mother had been writing me postcards and phoning twice a week. Her voice was often whiny and tinged with guilt. She made small talk about who was visiting or what someone in the house had said or how she'd seen a schoolmate of mine or what my dog Caesar had done. If he was around, Reed would get on the phone and tell me about the retreats and music festivals and demonstrations he was going to. I did not mention to them I had become a carnivore. I did not tell them that I didn't want to come back.

"So, how are they treating you back there in that vapid desert wasteland called middle America?" Reed asked with a chuckle. "Did you survive that great contradiction of patriotism and hypocrisy, the Fourth of July?"

146

"Sure, Reed," I said, but I didn't tell him how much I'd enjoyed the fireworks.

I didn't bother to mention I had just started going to a chess club held Tuesday and Friday nights two towns over in Tuscarawas County at the YMCA. I knew he hoped I was out meeting people my own age, like the boys who rode scooters and whistled at girls. So I let him think what he wanted, just said "yes" to his questions, and managed to add a knowing chuckle when he'd say something clever.

The truth was that I looked forward to the chess club. Usually Del, on his way to some meeting or other, drove me to these events in his air-conditioned white Cadillac. His overly-sweet cologne hung in the air, and I would try holding my breath as long as I could to avoid inhaling it. He didn't like me to wind down the window since it would compete with the air conditioning he was so proud of. We traveled mostly in silence, while Del fiddled with the radio dial until he found what Reed would call elevator music, the cheesy kind of sound that would get into your head and stay there. When he dropped me off in front of the YMCA, he always said, "Good-night," with such finality that I half-expected never to see him again.

Either Edmund, roaming town in his asthmatic Chevy, or Aunt Evie in her Rambler, would pick me up when I phoned to say I was ready, sometimes not until eleven or so at night. Aunt Evie never mentioned the conflict with bedtime, and didn't seem to mind if I slept in a little on the mornings after. Playing the Friday night tournaments, I was being matched with stronger opponents. I managed to get my rating up to 1650. There was an older player there named Bill who would go back over my games with me afterward analyzing my strengths and weaknesses. "You're a good player with good instincts," he told me, "but you're going to have to work harder. You're not seeing things you should. Look, you missed an opportunity here." He'd reset the board. "Now tell me what you'd do differently."

On a couple of the Friday nights that Aunt Evie picked me up I know for a fact that Uncle Del was not home when we arrived because his side of the garage was empty. Inside the house she fixed me iced tea and we sat on the screen porch together while I gave her a blow-by-blow account of my games. Though she didn't play chess herself, she told me that hearing about it was like listening to music, and she would close her eyes and absorb it the way you would a symphony.

One night, after Aunt Evie and I had iced tea, I couldn't sleep. It was either the caffeine or the unbearable August heat, but I was seized with panic, and leaped to my open window where I pressed my face against the screen, and began to suck in air. The night was particularly humid; thunder rolled distantly in the sky, and occasionally a streak of lightning crossed the sky, but there was no rain. Heat lightning, they call it back there, though once Aunt Evie explained it was really cloud reflections of lightning farther away.

Sweating in my pajamas, the silence thick around my head like a scarf, I set up my board and began going over a game I'd lost earlier. I'd blundered about six moves into the play and never fully recovered. I had a lousy position and played down a knight for most of the game. The correct move soon became obvious to me; I'd forgotten the traps for black in Ruy Lopez, and had fallen into one headfirst.

Vaguely, from the other side of the house I heard a small high-pitched sound that I couldn't readily identify: a cat yowling, I thought at first, no, a violin being tuned, no, a baby crying. The crickets under my open window kept up a staccato chatter, and the faint wail ran above it like a thin melody.

I climbed off my chair and went to the door. The sound came not from outside after all. I opened my door just a crack, and peered into the long black hallway. My eye was drawn to a thin string of light under Aunt Evie and Uncle Del's door at the opposite end. Though I had grown up hearing my mother cry, I found it disturbing that a man would. And yet I recognized it as such, a small anguished sound that started deep inside the chest. Murmurs, then sobs, followed by an outburst of bitterest tone. Then I heard Evie's voice, soft enough to soothe a burn: "That's enough now, Del, that's enough." I realized immediately I had been privy to something I should not have been, and shut my door. Despite the heat, I caught a chill and my teeth began to chatter. But not before a strange sensation passed over me, as if I'd seen a ghost.

The next morning I was relieved that Uncle Del was nowhere to be seen. I had not slept well, and sat at the breakfast table like a lump. Aunt Evie called for Edmund and Patsy to join us, saying he had something important to discuss.

"I've got to get to work," Patsy complained, swaying on one foot in the doorway. "What is it, Mother?"

Aunt Evie nailed her shut with a look. She spoke in a brisk, businesslike way. "Your father is going away to an insurance convention for several days and we're going to have a party, just the four of us, this weekend."

Edmund guffawed. "A party! Yeah, right."

Patsy rolled her eyes and started giggling.

"What kind of a party?" she wanted to know, in that sassy tone she reserved for making fun of her mother.

"A *party* party," said Aunt Evie. "You know, food, drinks, dancing. Just as I've always said I would, but haven't gotten around to, for one reason or another."

"Dancing?" blurted out Edmund. "We're going to dance—*here?*"

He spread his arms as if to encompass the hopelessness of such a concept in the crowded, forbidding living room that Aunt Evie had maintained in such an orderly fashion all these years. The same living room where Uncle Del read his paper each evening, waiting to be called five minutes before dinner.

Aunt Evie's face was flushed with excitement. She had made a list and produced it now, reading off the tasks she was assigning each of us to do.

"Edmund, I'd like you to scrub down the front walkway and mow the lawn, right out to the curb. Inside, I'll need you to vacuum every inch of the living room. Patsy, you'll help me shop. We'll have smoked turkey and potato salad for the main course, and then I want finger food and little sandwiches, you know the kind with just bits of this and that."

She turned to me. "Oscar, I'd like you to dust everything before Edmund vacuums."

"I don't believe this," Edmund muttered to me, shaking his head. "The old bat's off her rocker."

"And if any of you breathe a word of this to your father, I'll cut your throats! We're going to have a little fun around here."

I was so drawn to this turn of events that I abandoned my chess playing for the next few days and threw myself wholeheartedly into Aunt Evie's party preparations, helping her with little details, like getting chairs out of the attic, and folding napkins into triangles.

One afternoon Patsy and I worked on the invitations.

"Come on, little Oscar," she suggested, as we spread out note cards and envelopes on the kitchen table, "let's make them really freaky. We could put a little blotter acid on the invite and draw an arrow with the words 'Lick here one hour before you arrive.' Whoa, can you imagine?"

Aunt Evie appeared with a sample card. She called it a "mock-up." We were, she instructed, to write "SHSHSHSH" on the front of the invitation

150

and then on the inside announce her event as a surprise party. She didn't say for whom or why.

"How's Daddy not going to know about this?" mused Patsy as we labored over the invitations. "Everybody knows everything in this town."

I wanted to ask Patsy if she'd heard crying that night, but I was afraid. Uneasiness stirred inside me, but remained unnamed.

Patsy and I hand-delivered the invitations door-to-door on her bicycle in the twilight. I sat on the handlebars while she pedaled around town. She held the bike and I ran up and stuck the envelopes through the mail slots.

"You know this is going to be so square," Patsy moaned. "I'm going to have to get really stoned just to make it through the night."

The day of the party I was worried. What if Uncle Del came home unexpectedly? Or maybe the party was for him? What if no one showed up?

Aunt Evie's excitement was infectious. She strung paper Japanese lanterns on the screen porch and over the backyard patio. I trimmed candlewicks and filled two candelabras and several different candlesticks with peach and yellow and white candles. The local florist delivered a dozen red roses and two wildflower bouquets which Aunt Evie set on the mantel, the piano, and the dining room table. She combined these with flowers from her own garden. Patsy complained and polished silver for a couple of hours, and from the intensity of her concentration I could tell she hadn't smoked or dropped anything yet.

Aunt Evie's friend Lucy Campbell arrived early, dressed in black like a concert performer, to play popular songs from musicals on the piano. She started out with, "I'm Gonna Wash That Man Right Out of My Hair," and went on to tearjerkers like, "When You Walk Through a Storm," which had Patsy all teary as she lounged in her fringe vest and jeans on the living room floor.

And then Aunt Evie herself appeared on the stairs in a beautiful red

151

linen dress and matching red open-toed pumps. Her hair, which I'd never seen loose before, hung to her shoulders in soft gray waves. Edmund let out a low whistle.

"She's got lips!" he teased. Aunt Evie's red mouth smiled mysteriously. When she moved across the room, I was struck by the elegance of her walk.

Edmund served as the bartender, standing proudly behind the sideboard, with a wild paisley tie Patsy had found at a head shop wound loosely around his neck. His hair had gotten longer and shaggier.

My job was to welcome guests, and take sweaters and jackets, if there were any to take, and lay them on the little guest bed off the kitchen, though the evening was so warm it seemed doubtful.

Then, as if by magic, guests began to arrive, first one or two, then a whole herd at once. They were people Aunt Evie had known for years, teachers and doctors and neighbors she'd never gotten around to inviting for afternoon tea. The house was suddenly jammed with people and their chatter and the clink of glasses. The smoked turkey lay seductively in its platter of lettuce; there were potato and fruit salads, freshly-cut vegetables, and rounds of cheeses overflowing the dining room table like a cornucopia. The little sandwiches and finger food were gone in the wink of an eye.

Candles flickered and cast a cathedral light over the house.

I kept hearing Edmund clear his throat and ask in a funny formal voice, "Would you like something to drink?"

Patsy's best friend Anemone showed up, dressed in white hot pants and a red leather halter top, with two boys I'd vaguely seen Patsy hanging out with, Skip and Richard Somebody from down the street. They both had long hair (Patsy called them "heads") and Richard kept his tinted granny glasses on, though the light was so dim I wondered if he could really see anything.

Several guests stood around the piano where Lucy Campbell pounded out, "I'm Just a Girl Who Can't Say No." Everyone started singing along, including Aunt Evie whose voice soared over the rest—throaty and full of vibrato. Two older couples started dancing.

I took a seat on the window ledge where I could watch people drinking and laughing on the patio under the Japanese lanterns and couples in the living room dancing to Lucy Campbell's music. A chorus went up of, "Ducks and chicks and geese better scurry..." The party became a swirl of color, an abundance of happiness, spilling over the edges of our lives. It was the first surprise party I'd ever attended that didn't seem to be a surprise. At some point Edmund slipped me a vodka tonic that went straight to my head and soon the alcohol was rubbing at my cranium like sandpaper. So I ordered another, and felt better, at which point I agreed to dance with one of Aunt Evie's older women friends, Mrs. Simms. People were turning and pointing, and someone started laughing as I allowed myself to be twirled around like a baton.

Patsy and Anemone and their two boyfriends sat lined up on the sofa like criminals, laughing and hooting at the dancers, and passing a plate of cheese and crackers among themselves.

After Mrs. Simms curtsied and let me go, Patsy patted the empty spot beside her as an invitation for me to come sit. But I chose to go off by myself, overwhelmed as I was by an unexpected feeling of awe. It was probably the vodka tonics, but I found myself suddenly consumed by the knowledge that I would be leaving Aunt Evie soon. And I wondered what was going to happen to my parents and, ultimately, to me. Sadness gathered in the corners of my eyes, pulling the skin tight. But I couldn't summon tears.

What was in store for me, I wondered. For the first time I could imagine what it felt like to sit outside the principal's office at school, waiting to be reprimanded, though I hadn't done anything wrong. But it was the uncertainty of not knowing. And each time Aunt Evie floated by, her attention elsewhere, I was envious of her happiness. She was in her own world tonight.

After it was all over, the thing that most stuck in my mind from that night, when everything else had become a blur of tinkling glasses and the chords from Lucy's piano had taken over my head, was a particular image of Aunt Evie. About midnight she had walked back through the living room, only this time she wasn't alone. She was being led by a handsome man, maybe in his forties, with black curly hair and dark eyes. Patsy had found her way to me and now leaned her head on my shoulder. She reeked of marijuana smoke.

"Look at that," she murmured in my ear, "Mom's dancing with Mr. Chalk—he's a total queer, you know."

"I didn't know," I said.

"He's the freakin librarian at my stupid high school," she went on. "He and my mother lend each other *books*. Talk about *fruity*."

And then Mr. Chalk began to move, fluidly like water, and Aunt Evie became a swimmer in his arms. Her red dress took on a life of its own, the shiny material catching flecks of candlelight. Mr. Chalk guided her, lifted her gently to her toes, then spun her around. Everyone was watching, and someone started clapping, and Aunt Evie's face broke into a smile and she let herself be tipped backward.

Eventually Patsy tired of it all, and strolled out on the back patio with her friends to look at the night sky. And at a certain point, I realized guests had begun to leave, calling out their thanks and good-nights. But as long as Lucy played, Aunt Evie and Mr. Chalk continued to dance. At one point when Aunt Evie turned in my direction, her face a glowing moon, I thought I saw my mother, and then the tears came unexpectedly to my eyes. Why had Aunt Evie reminded me of my mother? Was it passion in her expression, as she twirled and twisted in Mr. Chalk's arms? Yet not the same frustrated passion my mother unloaded onto Reed when she felt he had wronged her? A longing for my mother welled up inside me. What if I had lost her forever? And then as I watched my Aunt Evie moving across the floor, I became convinced that it was her joy that caused my tears, and not my mother's sadness.

Mr. Chalk turned suddenly, spinning her backwards, and the heel of her shoe knocked against a small end table. An abandoned glass of red wine teetered on the edge of the table, and then fell predictably to the carpet. Mr. Chalk instinctively leaped forward to try to help, but she shook her head and smiled, signaling to him not to bother. Laughing together, they continued dancing together all around the pool of red wine that slowly spread around their feet.

When it was all over, Patsy and I sat together on the patio for a long time looking at the stars. Around her neck a ring of dark purple bruises ripened from where Skip or Richard had put his mouth. I fought off a deep urge to kiss her, now that my head was level with hers. But it wasn't really Patsy I wanted to kiss anyway; any pretty girl would have done. Patsy reminded me of the color yellow, with her hair frothing over the top of her head, and her face aglow in the dim moonlight. Later on, the women I would come to know and love, and eventually leave, became a collection of colors in my mind, like a rainbow.

"I can't believe it," Patsy was saying. "Tonight was a total trip."

"It was great," I said. "Your mother is cool, you know. I think *she* was the surprise guest."

Patsy chuckled. "My mother cool? That's a laugh." She paused. "By the way, I hear your parents are getting divorced, huh, Oscar? God, I wish my parents would."

This was news to me about my parents. I didn't know what to say.

"My parents can't stand each other," Patsy muttered. "And they're not honest about it like your parents. Mine try to fake it and it makes me sick. My mother has some weird idea about the nobleness of commitment. My father, well, you know he's a royal monster. Me—I'm never getting married, not in a million years."

I waited for her to go on. What did Patsy know? But then she shrugged her shoulders in resignation and changed the subject, which was her habit. "I've been thinking of changing my name to Sapphire. Is that too cool or what?"

An opportunity had come and gone, and I let Patsy's remarks drift off into the night. It was to be a long time before I had any explanation.

The following morning I slept in late. When I got up, the house was quiet. I wondered if Aunt Evie was in her garden or at the store. I crept partway down the steps and surveyed the living room from the landing on the stairway. Everything was back in its place, the evidence of the party swept and put away. The house looked exactly as it always did, Uncle Del's chair strategically positioned between the bookshelf and the television set.

But on closer inspection, as I came into the room, I could make out the deep red wine stain that had darkened overnight like blood. I wondered how Aunt Evie had missed that, so I went into the kitchen and got a rag and dipped it into soapy water. Back in the living room, I knelt down on the carpet, rag in hand, and began gently to scrub.

"Don't bother with that, Oscar." I wheeled around. Aunt Evie stood in the doorway. Her hair was pulled back in a ponytail and she was wearing a loose kaftan.

"Leave it," she said gently. "It's a good memory."

Then she called me into the kitchen where she made iced coffee and poured me a cup. We took our cups out on the front porch and drank our coffee together. Above us was a heavy gray sky, and humidity hung down over us like a thick curtain. Everything on the street, the shingle houses, the spacious lawns, seemed to leap out at us like a magician's levitation trick. In that heavy gray air, the foliage had gone bright green like a jungle.

"Tornado weather, but it's a little out of season," remarked Aunt Evie. "You get the stillness first and then ..." She searched the sky with her eyes. "You know what I think I'm going to do today? Go through some of Edmund's old things and see if we can't find some clothes to fit you properly." She leaned forward meaningfully. "I even think Edmund has an extra razor."

Suddenly self-conscious, I reached up and felt my chin. Later, when I checked in the mirror, sure enough there was a patch of dark stubble, as well as a thick dark line above my top lip. I passed my fingers over it disbelievingly, then went and sat in my window before I could get up the courage to try the razor. Aunt Evie had laid out two pairs of trousers, a shirt, and a sweater on the bed.

When I was married (eventually I did marry for a time) and in my forties I flew once, out of an unexpected sense of duty, down to Southern California, to visit a very old Uncle Del in a rest home where Edmund, now a lawyer for Lockheed, had arranged for him to be. I made the trip for Aunt Evie who was still alive in Ohio and occasionally sent me charming cards at Christmas and my birthday, which all oddly closed with, "Love, Aunt Evie and Uncle Del," though she had not seen him for years and never otherwise mentioned him in her letters. They never divorced, but Aunt Evie had been living on her own for years, it seemed, and I kept intending to make a trip East to see her, and then never did.

Uncle Del was a bent and crippled thing, pathetic to see. I doubted that he even recognized me.

"Hello, it's me, Oscar," I said.

"Yes, yes, Oscar," he murmured, his head settled into his neck. He was sitting in a wheelchair in the television room.

I reminded him about how I'd traveled to Ohio that summer to stay with him and Aunt Evie.

"Evie," he muttered. "Evie." His voice took on a thickness like milk. "She was my greatest sorrow, that woman was."

I assumed the years had not been kind to Uncle Del's memory, and tried to ignore his remark.

"Aunt Evie was wonderful to me," I said soothingly. "She was like a mother to me during a time I needed it."

His head shot up and his eyes, gone opaque with age and cataracts, skewered me without a blink.

"Evie was a whore. Just a common whore." The word "whore" fell from his mouth so unexpectedly it felt like a jolt.

"When I met Evie," he went on in a chiding tone, as if I were somehow to blame, "she was carrying another man's child, you know, that Dick Boston she'd met at her fancy college. Everyone knew about it." His voice was filled with contempt. "I married her as a favor, I did, because her father was so desperate to keep her name out of the mud, and Dick Boston didn't want anything to do with her once he'd had his way. I lived with her all those years knowing that I saved her, and there wasn't a day I looked at her and didn't see wickedness in her face."

I'd never heard this story before, not from my mother, and not from Patsy, and wondered first if Uncle Del was confusing Evie with someone else. And then, in the gap of silence that followed, I even wondered momentarily if Edmund was the son of another man.

But then Uncle Del continued.

"I was a naive young man from Pennsylvania, and she was beautiful and sophisticated. I thought I could make her happy. I worked hard, yes I did. And she wanted children so I gave her two, and you see how they turned out. We lived for years like brother and sister and I had to go to other women to console myself. Oh, you don't know what it means to a man to live with that kind of sorrow and humiliation."

I wasn't sure what sorrow and humiliation Uncle Del was referring to.

"I think you're confused, Uncle Del," I said, in the well-meaning tone we use with the elderly. "Aunt Evie had children with you."

Uncle Del's eyes narrowed like a hawk's. "She killed that child, you know. That's what she did, sure as I sit here. She went to a place up there in Cleveland. Dick Boston gave her the money. It was wrong, I tell you." He turned and stared at the ground, and I was certain he'd forgotten I was even there. "Even after what I did for her, she never did make her wrong a right. All those years..."

I excused myself shortly thereafter and never saw him again. He died about six months later, and Edmund sent me a note saying his father had been cremated and there was no memorial. Aunt Evie, though, is still alive and plans to go on living to a hundred. I have resisted the urge to ask either Edmund or Patsy about Dick Boston and the child, though the story has haunted me since.

I had heard Uncle Del cry that one hot summer night. And I remembered the tightness in his jaw when he would sit in the living room waiting for Aunt Evie to call him to dinner. So maybe he'd played the martyr all those years, judging Aunt Evie with every look and gesture, his face a constant reflection of some past indiscretion, either real or imagined.

I contrasted his sour expression with the wonderful brightness in Aunt Evie's eyes the night I saw her dance with Mr. Chalk. And now I understood the respectful way he touched her at her waist and held her hand. Aunt Evie was a woman who deserved that much. The two of them together made a wonderful flower that bloomed for years in my memory. And for this reason, I chose not to linger in the dingy undergrowth of Uncle Del's unhappy tale.

Getting back to that summer: the night before I left Ohio for San Francisco, Aunt Evie cooked me my favorite marinated flank steak, baked potatoes, green beans, stewed tomatoes, and apple crisp.

It was the last time we were all together. And as anyone of us might have predicted, Uncle Del had remarks about the food.

"Did you brown the meat first?" he asked.

"No need to," said Aunt Evie, an odd smile playing on her face. I am certain that it was me she looked at across the table before she said, "Actually, I used a neighbor cat, and simply parboiled it first, in case it had rabies."

And then she winked. I held my breath, in shock, but Edmund and Patsy both burst out laughing uncontrollably, kicking each other under the table for good measure. But Uncle Del didn't miss a stroke with his knife and fork.

"This is very good," he remarked, as if nothing unusual had been said, "very good indeed, though a tad more salt would have enhanced it."

For dessert there was applesauce cake and ice cream. And when I looked up at Aunt Evie as she was setting my plate before me, I realized she was wearing the same red dress she'd worn the night of the party. A small strand of pearls shone at her neck. No one commented. Edmund and I helped ourselves to seconds and thirds. After a while Patsy excused herself to go phone Anemone.

Later, as Aunt Evie and I walked in the garden, I asked her about the red dress. It was then that she confided to me that it was her fifty-third birthday. I was horrified I hadn't known and wanted instantly to go out to the mall to get her a present.

"No, Oscar, for heaven's sake, just walk with me. That's all I want."

We did walk, for some time, around and around, and eventually we strolled to "the park" across the street, where when I glanced back, I saw our house from a different point of view.

When we returned home, Aunt Evie and I stayed up late together and had more applesauce cake and ice cream on the screen porch, laughing over the fact that her birthday was our secret and no one else had remembered. There was no self-pity on Evie's part; she was enjoying herself immensely.

"I will miss you a lot, Oscar," she told me, slicing me the last piece of cake. "I am certain that you are going to be a very interesting young man."

So I took out my chessboard and showed her the giuoco piano opening, which she patiently practiced with my assistance.

"They call it 'the quiet game' but it's just the opposite. It leads to really wild, tactical play," I explained. Then, on a whim, I ran upstairs for my book on openings. "Here," I said, "It's your birthday. I want you to have this. You can practice from this, and we can play postal chess after I'm gone. We'll send each other moves in the mail."

"How thoughtful of you, Oscar," said Aunt Evie, taking the book into her hands. "This is a wonderful gift, though I doubt I'd be much of a match for you." She set the book on her lap. After we'd stopped playing the game, I noticed she'd kept one finger marking the page I had showed her, so she wouldn't forget.

Whatever it was my parents had to settle they settled, and I left Ohio shortly before September to return to my mother. The morning I left, Aunt Evie measured me and sure enough, I'd grown almost four inches.

I called my parents from a pay phone when the train stopped in Denver. Reed got on the phone long enough to explain to me he had split down to L.A. with Dana and Lightning, and was in San Francisco just long enough to pick up a few last things. "You'll have your own room when you come for visits. And I know you'll really get into the beach scene," he assured me, despite the fact that I couldn't swim a stroke.

The train ride home passed much too quickly. I was eager to see my mother, but along the way I met a girl from Nevada who promised she'd visit me in San Francisco. She was traveling with her mother who allowed her to come sit with me to play chess. Mostly we necked a lot in between looking at occasional combinations. Her name was Sylvia and she was the color red. When we parted hours later, we promised to love each other forever, and she gave me a friendship bracelet made of yarn.

At the train station in San Francisco, my mother screamed when she saw how tall I'd gotten.

"Oh, my God, Oscar, you're a man! What in God's name did Evie feed you back there?"

She made no reference to Reed's absence, just told me we were going to have a roommate, and that she was going to begin graduate school in the spring and become a social worker and realize her full potential.

That fall, when I returned to school, I continued chess, but also took up soccer. On Labor Day, I caught a PSA flight down to L.A. to visit Reed.

"We're having a thing at the pad tonight," he told me when he picked me up at the airport, "in your honor. Wow, did you grow or something?"

My head reached his shoulder.

The "thing," it turned out, was a party, with a bunch of Reed's new friends and some dogs and cats and various children in attendance.

Reed and Lightning worked in the kitchen frying up chicken for everyone. Hash brownies cooled in pans on the counter. Everyone was lounging around on mattresses and drinking beer and smoking marijuana. Gracie Slick's "White Rabbit" blared from Reed's strategically-positioned stereo speakers. An older, very tanned girl in tight paisley shorts and bare feet got up and started dancing next to me. I sat on the floor and stared up at her as she twirled and twisted, her eyes closed. I hadn't learned to coordinate my new long limbs yet, but watching the girl, whose rhythmic movements I took as a summons, I became convinced I belonged next to her. I put my chess set aside and rose as if in a fever. In a way she reminded me of Patsy; she had painted a flower on her cheek.

It was then in slow motion, that my mind replayed Aunt Evie, whirling in Mr. Chalk's arms, charmed by the movement itself, slipping like sand through a timer, slow and elegant. All those years, I thought, she'd suspected it of herself, and I had gotten to see it, what everyone else had missed: her yearning unwinding like a piece of string, and fluttering upward like the tail of a kite.

For years after, I would think often of how she and Del collaborated in silence to live together (they went on until their children were quite grown, and Patsy was already on her third child and second "relationship"). I was haunted by the image of Uncle Del, day after day in that large, empty house, sitting in his recliner, reading the paper, waiting for dinner, with the wine stain growing larger and larger between the two of them. As was his nature, he would never mention a word; it would simply be one more arrow through his cowardly heart for which he could blame Aunt Evie.

But for now, my mind was on the girl with the flower on her cheek. She invited me to walk on the beach, where against the backdrop of a chilly, pounding surf, I began to kiss her. Her mouth tasted like salt. She offered me a toke from the last of her joint. I accepted, inhaling as if it were the most natural thing in the world. Pressed against the girl, I imagined being swallowed up by the sea. A moment later, floating out of nowhere, came Aunt Evie's old blue-and-white-checked apron, looping and bucking against the wind along the shore.

CLEANING HOUSE

HER LOVER'S NAME IS WILLIAM AND HIS FINGERS WORK faster than a shuttle on a loom. He's volunteered to scour the bathroom while she tidies the bedroom. There is a feverish quality to their efforts, almost a celebratory spirit. The bathroom and the bedroom are the two rooms where she and William spend most of their time in leisurely showers and leisurely naps, oblivious to the hour on the clock. These are the rooms where, with shades drawn, they have whiled away their hermetic days. Ordered out for pizza, canceled appointments, unplugged the phone, gone in late to work or not at all, and gorged themselves on the luxury of two weeks, which have coiled around them to the point of near suffocation.

Sometimes she doesn't leave the bed even for a drink of water, but lies

165

parched, removed, staring at the ceiling from the tight, pungent circle of William's arms.

Sometimes they pretend they are two people stranded on a desert island, hopeless about ever being found, resigned to their fate: a slow undoing of life. Death hovers on the horizon, not in the form of sun or frost, but in the subtle draining of passion. They lie lifeless for what seems like hours. At those moments there's nothing left to say; each has been milked to unconsciousness. It is only when one moves that the other is aware of separateness.

"I'm using bleach in the bathtub," William announces, kneeling on the bathroom floor. A steamy vapor rises up from the porcelain.

"Paul will think I've hired someone to clean."

"In a way you have." William winks.

She's vacuumed the bedroom for so long she's sure the rugs have gone threadbare. She's like Lady Macbeth with her damned spot.

Tomorrow, Paul will return. This is as much as she has told William about Paul. You'd think little things would seep out through the pores of intimacy, when she and William lie in bed together. But they don't. She has drawn an uncrossable line in her mind. When she is with William, she refuses all references to Paul. She forgets, happily, about everything. Most importantly, with William, she stops holding her breath.

"Why did you ever marry Paul?" William asks on this, their last night together. He normally doesn't ask personal questions.

"I've forgotten," she says, and puts a stop to it.

Paul is so familiar she half-expects him to someday fade like the paint on the walls.

Perhaps if they'd had children. But children weren't possible, and this is something else she has never told William, who asked once, but only perfunctorily, if she had any. William has two children of his own who live in another state. He carries pictures as proof. She prefers to let him believe whatever he wants about her. Ironic, she used to think, that her own husband skillfully delivered into the world more than four thousand babies belonging to other women. It occurred to her she might have viewed those deliveries as a form of betrayal, but that would be too obvious. Besides, what does it matter now, she is past the point of wanting children. That desire belonged to a different time.

She won't talk about these matters concerning herself or Paul, with William or with anyone for that matter. She will not have them exposed, criticized, analyzed, or laughed at by the man she sleeps with. She keeps Paul's study door locked when William is there. Far more intimate to poke through a man's books and papers than to sleep with his wife, she figures. And, during William's stay, she does not, under any circumstances, allow either of them to borrow Paul's books, his pens, his telephone, or his writing tablets.

It is after midnight and she and William have exhausted themselves with cleaning and now lie side by side like two corpses. But they grow restless. The chill of late autumn gently on the ledge of the open window. It is not a hot night. Yet they pull apart as if it were, as if the very touch of the other is too much.

Lying there, she feels her heart pulse more rapidly, growing wilder in her chest, until she is convinced she hears the thump of Paul's step on the porch, the key in the front lock, and the scrape of shoe on the mat inside the door.

William pretends to be asleep. She can tell by his breathing that he isn't. She gets up for the third time and prowls gently through the house, without turning on lights. She knows exactly how many steps there are from the second to the first floor, how many steps it takes her to move through the dining room into the kitchen. There are shadows of tree leaves and lights from the street; there is the hiss of water in the pipes as she opens the faucet and pours a glass of water. She drinks slowly in the darkened kitchen, watching the shadowplay on the walls, finding her own quivering silhouette among the others.

In her mind she plans Paul's dinner tomorrow night when he returns. She reminds herself to check under the bed once again to be certain that William hasn't left behind a stray sock or kleenex.

And first thing, in the morning, when William and she have parted, and she has rechecked the closets and the drawers, and made sure one of his razor blades hasn't fallen under the tub, she will take their bed sheets, softened and soured by frenzied tussles, and drive them to the city dump, five miles away.

They can never be washed clean enough, she doesn't dare risk putting them in the trash cans out back, and she can't take the chance of being seen depositing them in a public trash can, like a crook.

There is anonymity at the city dump, as well as finality. Here it is that cast-off objects have collected in an anonymous pit tended by men in orange shirts and caps who shovel it all together. No danger of these objects ever reappearing. They lie beyond recognition in their open grave.

The man in the weighing booth, a heavyset, humorless fellow in a Harley cap, jots down the weight of the car as it enters, and then again as it exits. He never seems fazed that her car going out will weigh exactly what it weighed coming in.

"Ten dollars," he murmurs every time, quoting the minimum, without looking out at her from his glass cage.

Someday, she thinks, as the bill passes from her hand through the slot in the window, he may raise his eyes and actually look at her. He will separate her from all the other drivers of all the other cars moving through, and ask her, "What is it you dump here every couple of months, lady, air?"

She has anticipated that moment, when the man who guards the hellish pits of discarded junk, stubs out his cigar and considers her odd journey past the toxic-waste site and the recycled glass to where the white painted arrows lead, to dump something that weighs almost the same as nothing, something so light she might as well be passing through in an empty car. She has practiced numerous and humorous responses, none of which she will ever have the nerve to use. And, she realizes, he will never ask.

She sets down the empty water glass and stares around at the kitchen walls. Instead of going directly upstairs, she leans over on the countertop and lowers her head gently onto her curved arms. Her forehead finds comfort in the cool hardness of the tile. She can go no farther. Inside the dark circle of her arms, she inhales and exhales softly, twice. She pictures Paul's carefully locked study, tomorrow's bed made up with fresh sheets and quilt, all the care she has taken with him in his absence. In this way, she assures herself, she has been most faithful.

FRIENDS: AN ELEGY

THAT SUMMER THE THREE OF US GOT REALLY TIGHT FOR A while. Levonne and Dina had grown up together in Belvedere Arms, these projects on the East Side of the city. I first met Levonne through Blaine, and then when I started at the university that fall, she introduced me to Dina, and the three of us began hanging. Sometimes we'd roam campus and window-shop in the stores down High Street, or wander down to the Olentangy River with our ice creams. On hot summer days we'd start out from Belvedere Arms and saunter down Mt. Vernon Avenue in our jeans and platform sandals looking to see who was out. And sometimes we caught the bus out to the West Side to see Blaine and his cousins who lived just beyond city limits in a neighborhood called Bluefield. It was easy like that.

Once I got to know Levonne, she told me to call her by her nickname,

Lonnie. Her old man was Blaine's cousin, Victor. Otherwise known as Wild Man Victor by his sisters and girl cousins. Women went crazy for him. Where Blaine was on the quiet side, bordering on shy, Victor was outgoing, a classic charmer who could steal your eyeballs right out of their sockets while you were looking at him and make you feel good about going blind. He had a comical, disarming sexiness, drawing women like bees to honey. It was known that he had women stashed all over, brown girls, black girls, yellow girls, even a couple of white ones. Shameless in his conquests, he gave new meaning to the word *bold*.

"I just love women," he'd say, grinning and spreading his arms wide in feigned helplessness.

Lonnie wasn't pretty like some of Victor's other women (whom I'd seen him with but knew better than to speak of). Her skin had been pocked from teenage acne, and there was a small scar, like a stain, on her left cheek. One of her front teeth was snaggled, which may have explained why she rarely smiled. And she could be cold and evil-tempered, as well, but everyone said you couldn't blame her, considering the family she came from. Victor was always signifying on Lonnie, telling her that her head looked like a light bulb, teasing how her hair would never grow more than a couple inches, a fact she was sensitive about. He dogged her behind her back, said she looked like a man except for her big ass. But everyone knew she was his main lady. And in his own way and for reasons no one could really discern, I think Victor loved Lonnie as much as he was capable of loving anyone. Whatever brought them together remained a mystery to everyone who knew them. Yet occasionally when they were hand in hand, walking in front of Blaine and me, I saw something pass between them that I can describe only as understanding.

Sometimes when Victor drove Blaine up to campus to see me, he'd walk around with a baby propped on his hip (he had about five already) and a bag of Pampers in one hand, still rapping away to passing college girls: *Say, pretty mama, you got a minute?* Not unusual for him to walk away with the baby *and* half a dozen digits. Whether he really called them I don't know, I think he just enjoyed the conquest. As the saying goes, he went for them all: old, young, eight to eighty, blind, crippled, or crazy.

Needless to say, Lonnie was insanely jealous. You could feel it in the heat of her talk, see it coiled there like smoke in the gold iris of her hazel eyes. But she didn't let on to Dina and me that she was anything but naturally protective of her territory. She liked to claim she had Victor's nose wide open, how maybe when *she* was good and ready she and Victor would get married and settle down. All Dina and I could do was exchange knowing glances. We let her go on, because that's what friends are for, and besides, we both knew Lonnie wasn't nearly as hard as she seemed. What she did have, however, was something Victor loved more than he loved her, and that gave her a certain power. Their son, Little Victor, two years old, a pretty, pretty boy with the softest curly hair and big brown eyes, was Victor's only son and the love of his life. Sometimes he was called Victor Junior, sometimes just Li'l Vic or, more commonly, Mickey. And Lonnie was smart enough to know that Mickey was the glue that made Victor stick to her. It was the baby who kept Victor coming back for more. Without Mickey, Lonnie was just another woman, more trouble than she was worth, as easily discarded as the queen of spades. But with Mickey, she had a hold on Victor. And into Mickey she poured all her affection and patience.

Things were different with her six-year-old son, Alex, whose father was someone she periodically referred to as "that ole nasty red nigger." She hated the man and in turn she hated the boy, called him a "bad-assed kid." She hated Alex for the way he reminded her of his father, and over time she came to believe that it was Alex himself who stood between her and

Victor—and happiness. Without Alex around, she was convinced Victor would marry her and then she and Victor and Mickey could form a family. It was pitiful the way she took out her frustrations on Alex. Slapped and beat him over every little thing, ignored him for days at a time, called him stupid. Day in and day out she ground him down. Dina and I tried to stick up for him, but it only made Lonnie more hateful toward him.

On the other hand, Mickey could look her straight in the eye while peeing on the floor, and she'd just laugh and remark how cute his little thing was, cheerfully mopping up the mess with a paper towel, and telling him affectionately, "Go on, now boy, get some fresh drawers."

And, boy, was he spoiled. She gave him almost anything he asked for, let him bawl his eyes out in her arms over minor slights, and spent money she couldn't afford on a new outfit or shoes or hats for him. But with Alex it was always "get out of my face" and "quit clinging to me" when he'd sidle up against her. Rumor had it that things had gotten so bad with Alex that Social Services came and took him away because someone reported Lonnie hit him upside the head with a hammer. After he was returned home, he began lighting fires around the projects, in the dumpsters and on people's front stoops. He almost burned out a whole abandoned field. When the cops caught him, Lonnie beat his ass until he couldn't sit down. "He was born bad, just like his daddy," she liked to say, and then I learned that Alex's father was serving time in the state penitentiary. Dina and I tried to reason with Lonnie, but she couldn't see past her own rage. Over the many months I knew him, Alex developed a hardness in his eye, and an attachment for Dina and me that broke our hearts.

I frankly liked Alex better than spoiled little Mickey. We used to play games and read together, and I personally never saw any evidence of badness. He was always affectionate with me, and when I was out visiting in Belvedere Arms I'd take him to the corner market and buy him popsicles and gum. If I stayed overnight with Lonnie I'd bring along coloring books and crayons. My gifts made her jealous. "He likes you better than he likes me," she'd say in front of us both, and he'd get this look in his eye of being forced to choose. Sometimes when she had Mickey on her lap, I'd pull Alex onto mine, and she'd snap at him, "Boy, leave her hair alone," or "Get offa her, you're too big."

I told Lonnie she ought to treat him better, and she snapped at me for interfering in what she said was her business. "Take him if you like him so much," she said. "You can have him." She said this in front of him. I knew she was for real, and appalled, I told Dina. She said that maybe I should. She had considered taking Alex herself, but was leaving for college soon.

So I talked to Blaine about it. He agreed wholeheartedly that Lonnie treated Alex all wrong, and he'd noticed how fond I was of the boy. Blaine and I definitely wanted a kid some day, and we imagined for a while what it would be like to adopt Alex. But we were young—eighteen and nineteen—and I had three years more of college, and Blaine was starting classes in the fall, and neither of us had a nickel to our name. So in the end, Alex stayed with Lonnie, and when I was around I tried my best to undo the harm. I really thought I could make a difference.

Lonnie's family was no different. It was just her mother and two triflin' sisters who lived two circles over in Belvedere Arms. They all seemed intent on proving something was wrong with Alex, and bad-mouthed him regularly as a troublemaker. Dina didn't like Lonnie's family and thought they were downright mean. Behind Lonnie's back she criticized them as low-class, the way they'd go to the store with lint in their hair, wearing rundown house shoes and high-water pants, and how their ankles and elbows were always ashy. "They may be poor," said Dina, "but that's no excuse to be nasty." I used their bathroom once after the toilet had been stopped up for weeks. In the middle of the peeling linoleum floor sat a bucket full of rusty brown water with a rotting mop soaking in it so you could clean up after yourself When I told Dina about it, she looked incredulous. "You actually used their bathroom?" and shuddered.

Lonnie's mother was a light-skinned woman with a broad face. Her lower lip was often packed with snuff. When you walked in her house she wouldn't even say hello, she'd just look at you with the sweat rolling off her face and go back to poking her fingers in her plate of food. The whole place smelled like old cooking grease.

Dina told me once that Lonnie was treating Alex exactly the way her mother had treated her. And she was always murmuring how Lonnie's sisters were loose. I didn't have the nerve to tell her that before he met me Blaine caught the clap fooling around with Lonnie's younger sister, Mary, one night when he and Victor were out at Belvedere Arms. Blaine claimed she'd come over to Lonnie's, got drunk and climbed up on his lap just long enough for something to happen, a fact he regretted ever after. I chose to believe his version, to see the whole thing as a momentary mistake, something impersonal, a nonevent. He said he told me because he didn't want me hearing it from Mary who was apt to say the first thing that came to mind. She was always extra friendly to me and told me she was glad Blaine had such a pretty girlfriend (*Shut up*, said Lonnie, *you're just color struck!*). Still, every time I saw Mary I felt sort of sick inside, just picturing her and Blaine together like that. What had they said to each other? How could he have touched her? Impossible.

In theory, Lonnie didn't like white people and made no bones about it. When we met that first winter, it was clear she was going to tolerate me on a limited basis only, casting stares my way that matched the icy ground, and refusing to say hello when Blaine and I climbed into the back of Victor's car when we were off to Skate Land or a show. I didn't like her much at first either, knew no one in his family could stand her, and eventually came to ignore her, because Blaine assured me she just wasn't worth getting upset over. But over time she discovered we had the same birthday, only three years apart (she was older) and in a flash of that moment, she touched my arm and said, "We have something in common." After that, she grew warmer, started wanting to get together. She asked for my phone number. "I don't have a lot of girlfriends," she told me flatly, adding, "I don't really trust other women."

There it was, the crack in her invincibility. A soft spot had been exposed; she wanted a friend. And despite my better judgment I developed a real fondness for her, knowing I'd always have to watch my back. I suspected what she was up to, but couldn't really blame her. She wanted with Victor what I had with Blaine. He and I were pretty solid by that point, and she figured that by hanging with me, she'd see more of Victor.

In fact, she made no secret of this. When I was staying with her in Belvedere Arms, she would suggest I call Blaine and invite him over, figuring that Victor would come along, as well. And when the four of us were together like that, we had some very happy times. We'd cook up greens and fried chicken wings and bake some box cornbread in her tiny kitchen, and play tonk or dominoes on a beat-up card table late into the night. There was always music and laughter, and I could imagine us as one big family. And Alex would crawl up onto my lap and cuddle until he fell asleep, his musty little head nestled against my chest, and I'd close my eyes for a while and pretend he belonged to Blaine and me. It was like that.

If it was late and Victor didn't want to drive back to Bluefield, we'd all stay the night at Lonnie's. Blaine and I'd mash ourselves together on the single bed in the other bedroom where the kids normally slept. The children would sleep on the mattress on the floor by the door. "Don't do

177

anything until they're asleep," Lonnie would tell us with a stern expression. Through the wall emanated the unmistakable sounds of Lonnie and Victor screwing. Sometimes the whole floor would shake. Lonnie liked to call out, "Daddy! Daddy! Daddy!" and Victor would shout, "Oh, baby, oh, baby," and Blaine and I would crack up, burying our faces against each other. Behind their backs we took to calling Lonnie's place "the rocking house."

Once Lonnie asked me what it was like being with Blaine, "sexually, I mean," she said pointedly, and in a moment of frankness I confessed I didn't know, we hadn't gone all the way. She looked as if I'd slapped her. "Quit lying, you don't really expect me to believe that," she said. "I tell you everything." I tried to explain that I wasn't lying, that Blaine and I were waiting till—well—when we got married. Lonnie's face turned hard and angry. "You'll never keep a man with that attitude," she said. But I could see that it bothered her, and she was determined to find out what it was that kept Blaine and me together.

"You must be giving up something," she said to me. "Is it money?"

I shook my head. "Why do you always think people have to be getting something from someone?" It was her turn to be quiet, but I misunderstood her fury. She didn't speak to me for several days, but then she was often moody, and she might have just been mad at Victor.

Dina lived with her parents one circle over from Lonnie in a three-bedroom unit. They were hard-working people who had never approved of Lonnie or her family. Dina's father knew something unpleasant about Lonnie's father who had either died or gone away, but he wouldn't say what it was. Now that Dina was eighteen, they couldn't tell her who to hang around with, but they didn't mince words about Lonnie's bad influence. When Dina came down to Lonnie's, we'd sit outside on the stoop, just talking and drinking iced tea, or sometimes wander the projects for exercise, with Alex and Li'l Vic trailing in our wake. We'd call out hello to people sitting on their stoops, flirt with guys, or head to the corner market to buy slushies. It was Dina who got me started ordering ice cream in a cup instead of a cone, and eating it with a long iced-tea spoon. We both always ordered toasted almond. Lonnie was a mint-chocolate-chip addict. We took turns paying for each other, but none of us had much money.

Dina was easygoing and funny, and nothing seemed to fluster her. She was much cuter than Lonnie, but she had a tomboy spirit and refused to be seen in a dress. We were both tall and skinny, she with smooth dark brown skin and straightened hair, and me fair-skinned with curly hair. We were always borrowing each other's jeans and tops, a fact that seemed to annoy Lonnie to no end. Dina thought a lot of things were funny, even things that weren't, but when she fell out laughing, it was infectious, and I'd end up laughing too. Sometimes when Dina and I were both doubled over, Lonnie would just stop in her tracks and impatiently ask what the hell was wrong with us. I think she was jealous of the closeness we shared. "You act like two bulldaggers," she said. And that would only make Dina and me laugh more.

Dina didn't have a man, and claimed she was saving herself. She had finished her freshman year at Central State and was transferring down to Dillard in Louisiana. She wanted to concentrate on her education, not get caught up in all the complications of a man, she said. But sometimes she'd hang out with Blaine's brother Roddy who was super-fine, and they'd come along with us. When I wasn't in class or working, and Victor and Blaine had a break from roofing, the six of us would go places.

Victor was a regular master of ceremonies arranging our group adventures. He took us go-cart racing, horseback riding, swimming, bicycling, putt-putt golfing. His main goal in life, as he put it with that devilish smile of his, was to "have fun," and fun he had. Sometimes he'd arrive unexpectedly on campus by himself just to take me out on his motorcycle and thrill me to death doing ninety miles an hour into the wind. "You watch out for him," Blaine warned, "I wouldn't put it past him to hit on you," and I assured him he had nothing to worry about. I knew way too much about Victor and women. And I was just waiting for the day when Lonnie would figure it all out.

The West Side of the city where Victor and Blaine lived consisted of a series of white suburbs, in the center of which sat the small island of their neighborhood, Bluefield, a three-block radius of hand-built homes and unpaved streets, where everyone, it seemed, was distantly related through the tangled roots of a complicated family tree involving third and fourth cousins once and twice removed from the South. Initially, there had been a Bluefield one-room schoolhouse in what was now an empty field, with classes taught by a white Mennonite teacher, but by second grade, Blaine was walking over to the white school with his siblings and cousins, where most of the time they ended up being relegated to the special-ed classes. He and Victor would occasionally now laugh about that, bitterly, what Victor liked to talk about as his "mis-education." He had spent most of his school years in detention and suspension "just for being black," as he and Victor liked to say. "Yeah, they thought we were dummies, but we weren't so dumb we didn't take those white kids out back and kick their asses when no one was looking." "Naw, man, and remember that one teacher used to line all us little niggas up on the playground and make us stand there for the whole recess?" They had us all laughing, but it wasn't funny as they recounted their awful, early schooling. "Nothing's changed much there," Blaine told me. He worried about his younger siblings. And when I asked him why his mother didn't step in and do something, he looked at me nonplused and said, "You really think they care what she says?"

In the summer Blaine and Victor free-lanced all over the city as roofers for a guy named Bernie Steinberg (they called him "The Jew"), and they made good money that way, getting paid under the table. They also built up strong arm and back muscles, which Victor loved to show off by strutting around shirtless. The skin on both their backs and arms and faces burned to a smooth black olive color from the sun. "A brother can never be too dark," Victor liked to brag, flexing his biceps. He had recently added a tattoo of Lonnie's name to his left arm, carefully circumscribed by a heart-bearing Cupid. A competing tattoo on his right arm still proclaimed his love for a former girlfriend, a beautiful dark-skinned woman named "Cindi" I met once out in Bluefield when she came to visit Victor's mother. Cindi had become an actress and singer, and was living in New York. Lonnie always referred to her sullenly as the "boojee bitch," or "Miss Ann," and claimed that Cindi never really loved Victor at all.

When Blaine wasn't on campus with me, he stayed in Bluefield at his mother's little ramshackle house. It seemed she was always finding reasons to keep him with her, and even though she liked me well enough, I got the impression we were competing for his time and attention. He was the oldest of her children, and she depended a lot on him, whether it was help getting laundry to the washhouse or looking after his younger siblings when she had to go out. Her dependence on him had been part of his reluctance in starting college. She claimed she wanted him to go, but then she was always finding excuses for him to do something for her or the other children. "Blaine's a mama's boy," Lonnie warned me. "He ain't never leaving Bluefield, you know." She said it, in part, I think, because I often talked about leaving the cold, narrow-minded Midwest behind for warmer climes: Hawaii or California. I yearned for ocean and beach, in a place where it never snowed. I wanted to live where there were so many people that no one cared about what a particular person did. I was tired of being stopped by the cops every time Blaine and I drove across town at night (I'd taken to ducking under the dashboard just to save us the trouble), and I was frankly scared of the dead-ended life I pictured for myself if I married Blaine and we moved out to Bluefield.

Blaine claimed he wanted to leave, too, but it was always my plans we were discussing, not his. And to be honest, I hadn't calculated yet how Blaine figured into this future equation and he knew it. But we'd talk about warm places together anyway, and sometimes he'd lie on his back with his head in my lap, and I'd braid his hair and we'd imagine traveling after the summer ended.

The thing was, Blaine listened to me more than any other person ever had, including my family who lived four hours east. And Blaine took me seriously. Whatever I wanted to do, he told me, I had his full support. That summer he presented me with a pre-engagement ring, a little gold heart circled in diamond chips, and word spread quickly that we were going to get married. I called my parents and my father's only comment was a terse, "It's not likely." Blaine's mother said, "You're so young," but his sisters and girl cousins kept asking us when our wedding date was. The truth was, Blaine had said to me, "I love you," and so I loved him back. I needed him.

Lonnie and Dina liked any excuse to get out of Belvedere Arms, so they'd catch the city bus over to campus, and drop by my university apartment complex to pick me up. We'd go out then. Lonnie often left Alex and Mickey with her mother who just stuck them in front of the TV screen. I'd tell Lonnie she could bring the boys with her, but she rolled her eyes. "Wait till you have kids," she'd say. And I'd think to myself what good parents Blaine and I would be.

By July it was hot, hot, hot, and we'd roam those blazing sidewalks in bathing suits and shorts. Men driving by would go crazy. Some would slam on their brakes, some would pull their cars to the curb. Sometimes we'd lean in car windows and talk to guys, just messing around. We made up lies and names and phony numbers, and never gave ourselves away. It was still a big deal to see black and white girls together, and a lot of guys, both black and white, figured it meant we were easy.

Not so, that is, if Dina was telling the truth. I think she might have slipped up a time or two, but mostly she preferred guys as friends. Me, I'd done a little of this and a little of that, but Blaine was my first real love, and though we slept in the same bed several nights out of the week, I was afraid of getting pregnant, specially since Blaine told me he wouldn't want to use anything, but more than that I was picky about who would be my first, and I was mad I wasn't his first, though he said I really almost was. There had been a couple other girls besides Lonnie's sister, girls from Bluefield like Karen Freeman who had been his childhood sweetheart (forgivable!), but the thing with Mary really stuck in my craw. And once before me, he'd loved a girl, but not in the same way as me. Her name was Essie, and she was a little older, with a baby daughter she was trying to raise on her own. He had only wanted to help her out, he said, having seen what his own mother had gone through, and he'd offered to marry her, to give the baby the father he himself had never had. I forgave him for that, found it touching. And when I asked him if he was missing something from me, he claimed he understood and didn't want to rush me.

Lonnie rolled her eyes when Dina and I talked about being virgins. It was obvious she didn't believe us for a second. That's because she'd given it up to an old man at age eleven, and as she put it, "I never stopped." She gave birth to Alex just days after her fifteenth birthday.

And the truth was when she was low on money, she went on "dates" with "friends," which really meant, Dina said, she turned tricks and had been doing this since she was fifteen. Dina told me Victor suspected, but couldn't prove it. Lonnie's philosophy was, *Everybody fucks, so why not get paid?* She pointed out the hypocrisy of people who claimed sex was

183

sacred (she'd give me a hard eye and laugh). "Check out all those suburban housewives who married for money," she said. "Now there's some real prostitution."

Lonnie was much more worldly than Dina and I were, and sometimes her knowledge frightened me. She had her rules and her codes of honor, some of which were clearly spelled out and others which were unwritten. I had a feeling that there was an invisible line you could cross, after which Lonnie would write you off forever.

As far as the men were concerned, she didn't talk about that part of her life much to Dina and me, thinking we were squares. She was always telling me she didn't want to hurt my "little virgin ears," but explained once it didn't mean anything, she and the men were just helping each other out, a couple of them were married, and it was no big deal. And she did say she never kissed any of them on the mouth and in that way she saved herself for Victor. I asked her once why she didn't get a regular job, and she looked at me as if I'd lost my mind. "I have two children," she said. "I can't be gone all day."

I was working part-time, on the days I didn't have classes, as a cashier at a pizza place just south of campus. It paid poorly, but it was within walking distance, and I got one free combo medium each week and all the soda on tap I could drink. And occasionally I wouldn't ring up a pizza I sold, and could pocket a little extra. I decided this was okay because the man I worked for was a racist. He came right out and talked about how much he hated black people, and it seemed to me only fair that his ignorance should cost him a little. When I told Dina and Lonnie what I was doing, they cracked up and urged me to give away free pizza to everyone I knew. Occasionally, near closing time, they'd come by for free slices, and we'd pretend we didn't know each other. "Excuse me, Miss Lady," Lonnie would say in a loud, exaggerated voice, leaning across the counter. "Excuse me, but I would like a slice with pepperoni to go." And I'd cut her one and wrap it in wax paper and she'd pretend to hand me money, and I'd pretend it went into the cash register drawer. Every time my boss would say things like, "I sure hate to see colored people putting their dirty hands on my counter," I'd swipe more slices to take home for later. I asked Blaine if I should quit the job, and he said why, I'd just end up working for another racist, and at least this guy was up front. I saw his point. Besides, I needed money for books and clothes.

Dina's mother had taken her clothes shopping several times that summer for her transfer to Dillard, and once she invited me along and bought me a green cropped sweater on sale that Lonnie later grumbled about how I wore it too much. Dina's parents were proud of her, her good grades, her goal to be a medical doctor. Her summer job consisted of taking care of a neighbor's children three days a week. In fact, her pops trusted her so much sometimes he let her drive us around in his coveted old black ninety-eight. We loved that ride: wide comfy seats, push button windows, and air conditioning. Whenever Dina could get her father's car, we three went places—out to Hoover Dam, over to Chillicothe to flirt with men we laughed about later, or across to the West Side to Bluefield where Victor was always waiting for me. We used to laugh about that car. Lonnie called it The Boat.

It was convenient that Dina and Blaine's brother Roddy liked each other enough to pair up like a couple on the nights the six of us—me, Blaine, Victor, Lonnie, Dina, and Roddy—went out. I think the whole setup pleased Lonnie no end because it offered ballast to her life with Victor. And our group rambles guaranteed her a place in the passenger seat of his old souped-up red Chevy. When he wasn't roofing he was racing his motorcycle or ripping off cars for parts (he took them apart as fast as lightning in the alleys of Bluefield), or screwing any woman whose door he could charm his way into. How he managed to keep all his women separate, I'll never know. Or maybe they knew, but preferred not to see what was right in front of their eyes. His father, a deacon in their storefront church, used to warn Victor, sometimes in front of us all when we'd be sitting around the dining room table eating and playing cards. "You think the cheese on that pizza is hot, wait till you get to hell, Victor."

His father's rants only served as fuel for imitation, which Victor would do later, much to our amusement. He'd look at one of us and say, "You think the cheese on that pizza's hot..." and we'd all bust up.

That summer I had two new roommates in the suite I shared in a student apartment complex. They were two strangers, both white and both blonde, and both from the outer suburbs. Their names were Tina and Lee Ann. Tina was always polite, even if cautious, around my friends. But Lee Ann acted as if she'd never seen black people before or, if she had, as if she were scared. She'd finally made awkward peace with Blaine who was around a lot, but she was always scurrying around with her housecoat on over her clothes, as if she needed an extra layer of protection.

Behind her back, Lonnie and Dina had a field day with Lee Ann. And they also loved running into her when they visited me just so they could force her to speak. "How ya doin', Lee Ann?" they'd call out in loud, fake-friendly voices, crowding her in the kitchen or living room until she turned bright red and fled to her bedroom. "How's life treating you, Lee Ann?"

Later, when I was by myself she'd shoot me these whipped-dog looks, as if blaming me for something. Sometimes I thought she was just plain jealous, because she seemed to have no friends. But she told me once in a trembling voice that she was fearful of black people, that some girls who'd been bussed in to her high school used to corner her in the restroom and threaten her, as if I would understand.

In between classes and work, it was a mostly pleasant summer of high jinks. We picked up a mischievous pastime of "ripping." I'd done it before, but until that summer Dina never had. She was even squarer than I was. Lonnie was already a practiced thief, actually quite brilliant, and she taught us how to work a store as a team. We'd hit the big department and discount stores and while everyone kept their eyes trained on Dina and Lonnie, I could walk out twenty pounds heavier with all of our stolen clothes wrapped around my waist and chest. No one ever suspected me, they were too busy eyeballing my friends. In the dressing room we'd split up and then begin to chat loudly over the partitions. "Oooh, that'd go good with your yellow pants" or "I need something tighter in the legs," just to give the impression we were discerning shoppers. We'd spend a long time considering things, and sending things back out, and bringing things in, while keeping up a running conversation, until eventually the clerks were so confused we could have walked out with the cash register. Sometimes Lonnie and Dina walked in first and began trying on clothes. I would enter five minutes later, so no one would know we were together. Then Lonnie and Dina would leave the things they wanted stolen folded on the little chairs in their dressing rooms, and go out onto the floor to another department, and Security would begin trailing them around. I'd make my choices, slip them on, and simply collect whatever Dina and Lonnie had left for me. I was never followed.

The first time I stole anything I was only twelve. I swiped a purple skirt in a fevered panic just to show off for a friend back home. For the next six months the skirt hung unworn in my closet, a constant reminder of my wickedness. Guilt-ridden, I fantasized about returning it with a big apology and taking the consequences. I waited for my mother to ask me about the skirt, but she never did, likely believing it was just a trade with a friend. Finally, too distraught to enjoy it, I gave the skirt away to a poor girl, unloading any bad luck that might befall me.

187

Dina was also edgy like that at first, but Lonnie kept working on her. "Don't be stupid, girl, the stuff's there for the taking. It's not like stealing from people; it's corporations. The Man's got money, and rips us off right and left. What does he care if we get a little something for ourselves?"

"But I have a scholarship," said Dina. "What if I get caught?"

"You'll get over it," I added breezily, as if I knew anything. "After a while it feels good."

Eventually Dina saw reason and got hooked. The first time we went out together Lonnie and I let Dina do all the work while we distracted the store clerk. And she turned out to have a better instinct for it than either of us. It was scary. Dina, the goody-two-shoes, was not only cagey, but picky, and the combination was deadly.

Our best feat was the night we stole complete outfits for the War concert. And while Lonnie and Dina waited for me by the exit, I moseyed on over to the jewelry counter, with all our clothes wrapped around my waist, and managed to slip a silver ring off the hook and into my mouth. I even said to the clerk behind the counter, "Good-bye now" in my politest, most proper voice. That really got Lonnie and Dina who had observed the whole thing. "You're crazy, girl," Lonnie marveled, full of admiration.

The night of the War concert we didn't have the money for tickets either, so we hung out in front of the Agora Theater, parading around in our new outfits and shoes, and reveling in our cleverness. We were waiting on a guy Lonnie knew who'd promised to sneak us around to the side exit and let us in the back door. I called Blaine on the pay phone to tell him what we were up to and he just laughed and said, "Y'all are crazy. Don't get caught." He never worried about me, knew I always came out on top.

Lonnie's friend, a cute black homo showed up just as the first set was starting, and he motioned for us to follow him around back. We stepped out of the ticket line, with people glaring, and whisked off into the shadows down an alley. I thought, what if this is a trick, and the guy's got some buddies back here waiting to pull a train? But the guy was as good as his word. He opened the side door, and we shot in fast, but not before a ton of people turned around and saw us in the flash of streetlight. We scattered, blending quickly into the crowd. A few minutes later, groping among gyrating bodies in the heat of the theater and the blare of the sound system, we found one another again, and danced in the aisles with strangers.

Afterward, with music pounding in our ears, we emerged, drenched in sweat, and laughing. We were free, lighthearted, and clever. Life was good. I was so in love with Blaine it hurt. Lonnie and Dina teased me about him, talked about all the children we'd have, and their predictions made me love him even more. We took the bus down to White Castle and ordered a sack of greasy burgers, and then sat at a picnic table out back and gorged ourselves. Guys drove by and honked at us. It was mostly the black guys who'd pull up to the curb, and start conversations. White guys just slowed down and stared. I asked Lonnie and Dina if they'd ever go out with a white guy, and Dina shrugged and said she might if he was cute enough, and Lonnie said she just didn't find white men attractive, though if one paid her enough, she'd probably do what he wanted. Then they both turned to me and wanted to know if it was true. What? I said. They both started falling out. *You* know. But I couldn't tell them. I'd only been with Blaine, and then not really. What did I know?

Lonnie got up to find a pay phone while Dina and I polished off our Cokes. When she came back, Lonnie seemed uneasy.

"Where did Blaine tell you he and Victor would be tonight?" she asked me.

"Going to sleep early. They have a roofing job early in the morning.

Lonnie gave me a funny look. "You tell Blaine where *you* were tonight?"

I nodded. "You saw me call him from the show. Of course I told him."

189

"You tell that brother everything," she said accusatorily and slammed herself back down onto the bench. "I never tell any man, not even Victor, my business. Never."

Dina yawned. She was tired. "Come on, Lonnie, it's late, let's go home."

"We need to go out to Bluefield," she said, with a sense of urgency. "Victor's not where he said he'd be. I need to go find him."

Dina looked at me and rolled her eyes as if to say, so what else is new. Lonnie turned to me. "Are you coming?"

"Dag, Lonnie," Dina said, in a tone that signaled she thought Lonnie was out of control.

Lonnie looked at me. "What *you* gonna do?" she said, standing up, hand on her hip.

"Go home and sleep." I looked up at the night sky, dotted with stars. The burgers I'd just eaten were sinking heavily to the center of my stomach. I was feeling sleepy and content. The War concert had surpassed my expectations. Tomorrow morning at nine I had a French poetry exam on *Les Fleurs du Mal.* "Mon enfant, ma soeur, songe a la douceur d'aller la-bas vivre ensemble!" I imagined Blaine looking out the basement window of his mother's house at the same night sky. Even when we were apart, I never felt alone with him. That's what being in love meant.

"It's really late," said Dina. "Come on, Miss Levonne, let's go home. I don't have time to be chasing Victor all over town."

Lonnie turned back to me. "Do *you* know where Victor is? What did Blaine tell you?" There was a desperate edge to her voice. I tried not to sound impatient.

"If Victor's got to work early in the morning, he's probably sound asleep by now," I said, wearying of her.

She made a terrible sound in her throat to signal her disbelief. "And you're telling me you believe everything he tells you?"

"Yes," I said, "as a matter of fact I do."

"Then," said Lonnie, "you're stupider than I thought."

But I let it go. I could afford to be generous. Dina said, "Come on, Lonnie," and we went our separate ways.

It was about six o'clock the next evening when Lee Ann crawled out of her room long enough to answer the phone ringing off the hook in our suite. I was in the shower getting cleaned up and hadn't heard anything. Through the door Lee Ann was calling to me that it was Blaine on the phone. I came out then dripping wet, pulling the towel up over my breasts, thinking about what I was going to wear that night.

Blaine was explaining he had just gotten in from finishing a roof in Upper Arlington ("You shoulda seen this place—laid out: pool, tennis courts—you name it," he said), and he was so dog tired he needed to "cop some Z's" before he could make any plans. Besides, he was short on money for bus fare since his boss wouldn't have cash on hand until Monday, so would I mind if we got together later or even tomorrow instead when he could talk Victor or his friend Earl into driving him over. I was disappointed. After all it was Friday night, and I had been counting on our getting together. And I didn't care much for Earl, and hoped if Blaine came he'd come with Victor. But we ended up talking a while, and just hearing his voice and the patience with which he listened to me, I felt reassured and close to him again.

"So what you gonna do tonight?" Blaine asked. I told him I'd probably just stick around campus and get caught up on studying. He promised to call later on if he woke up and check in on me. When I got off the phone Lee Ann was in the kitchenette cooking up boxed macaroni and cheese in a pot on the stove. "Are you and Blaine going out?" she asked. And I realized for the first time that she herself had nowhere to go, and my comings and goings were of great interest to her. If I'd been a better person I'd have offered to do something with her, but I wasn't.

I dried my hair, did a little studying, and realized I was missing Blaine. It was late enough now that I was reluctant to call his house in case I awakened his mother. I was sitting there hoping he'd call me back, when the phone rang again. But it wasn't Blaine, it was Lonnie. "Is that you?" she said in a voice full of heat. "Get your clothes on. We're goin' over to the West Side to bust some ass."

I had no idea what she was talking about, and said so. I asked her if she knew what time it was.

"I don't give a damn. Some big shit's about to go down." Was she crying? I'd never heard her upset like this before.

"Lonnie, take it easy," I said, trying to console her, but she interrupted me.

"Victor's been fucking some little hillbilly Earl's got staying in his apartment, you know over there in the Hilldale complex across from the supermarket in Bluefield, and I've finally—(and she let out a deep exhale)—caught him in the act. I'm not going to tell you how I know, but I suggest you might want to see this for yourself, Miss Thang."

I didn't know what to say. Surely she knew Victor was all over town. It was late. I really didn't want to get involved.

"Are you comin' or not?" she said. "Me and Dina are catchin' the next bus; her pops won't let her take The Boat. We'll meet you downtown at the stop in front of Rexall's, but you better leave now, and I mean now. There's something you need to see."

"I just talked to Blaine earlier," I said. "He and Victor roofed all day and they're tired."

"Tired my ass," said Lonnie. "You sure are a gullible little bitch."

Me gullible, I thought. Good one, Lonnie.

"Get your ass on the bus, there's one in ten minutes," said Lonnie. There was a pause and then she added, "I need you."

That got me. Need always does. I agreed then to go along and see what wild imaginings we could put to rest. And maybe I could keep Victor from breaking her silly neck. Personally, I had never showed up in Bluefield without letting Blaine know first. It felt a little odd, ambushing him this late like this, but I consoled myself with the fact that I wasn't going out there to see him, I was helping out a friend. I pulled on a clean pair of shorts and a sleeveless tee shirt and my green platform sandals, and told Lee Ann who was hovering in her doorway that I would be back late, and made it to the corner in time to catch the downtown bus. Lonnie knew the bus schedules inside out, and was always punctual, and I knew I better be on time or she'd have my hide.

She and Dina were already there in front of Rexall's when my bus pulled up to the curb. Dina was strangely silent, chewing the side of her thumb and not looking me in the eye. Lonnie was pacing and snapping her gum and running her mouth all at the same time. She was steamed. The three of us ran for the West Side bus just as it was pulling away. The driver showed mercy and opened the front door with a hiss of hydraulics.

"You ladies just about didn't make it," he murmured, checking that we put the right amount of change in the fare box. When the bus lurched away again, Dina and I hung on to the same pole for support. She looked tired, or nervous, I couldn't decide which.

Lonnie had already taken a seat by herself toward the back, sitting ramrod straight, and looking out the window. She was acting like she didn't know anybody, including us. Once the bus was underway, Dina and I moved to the back, and squeezed into the seat right behind her. She still didn't acknowledge us. We stared at the back of Lonnie's head. Victor was right, it really was shaped like a light bulb, I thought, and then I started laughing to myself. Dina glanced over. She rolled her eyes, then got all tight-jawed. I stopped laughing. Something was up. You could have cut the tension with a knife.

At the Bluefield stop, Lonnie turned around in her seat and looked me dead in the eye. "If I weren't a real friend to you, I'd just let you find out on your own," she said.

We got off and stepped down into the heat. It was two short blocks of sidewalk until we made a left onto unpaved streets. Lonnie was walking so fast, Dina and I were practically running to keep up. We walked first past Victor's parents' house on Clifton Street, where the windows were all dark, and then past Blaine's mother's house on Draper. It felt a little like entering the lost colony of Roanoke. I pointed to the dark houses. "Everyone's asleep, Lonnie," I said.

"Hnnnhhh!" was all she said.

A moment later we spotted Blaine's dope fiend cousin Spider heading up the steps of his front porch.

"I can't stand that man," said Lonnie, which is what she always said when she saw Spider, but she called out to him anyway and asked if he'd seen Victor or Blaine. Spider stopped and studied us, then shook his head. "I think they went to Skate Land," he said.

"Lyin' Negro," muttered Lonnie. Then to Spider, she said, "Well, if you see them, tell them we're out here." She pointed to me. "She's trying to find Blaine."

"Lonnie," I said, "that's not true."

"It is now," she said.

I had no idea what Lonnie was up to, but from her determined expression and taking Dina's cue, I decided not to ask. So we walked in silence around Bluefield, and then headed across the vacant field toward the

A&P. The Hilldale apartment complex where Earl lived was just on the other side. I'd only been there once before with Blaine, just briefly when he went to buy some weed. Earl was older, but he claimed to have grown up with Victor and Blaine, even though it was not really true, and then he claimed to have gone away to California for a while to act in the movies before returning to Bluefield to wait for what he called "the next cattle call." Victor liked to say that Earl was crazy and had actually been institutionalized at Apple Creek. It was hard to know. Earl was always name-dropping and claiming connections that sounded mildly plausible, if you didn't listen too closely. Blaine and Victor were always making fun of him behind his back, and I thought they used him—for rides places and for free weed. Sometimes when Blaine needed a ride up to campus, Earl was the one to bring him, but he was a last resort since he was something of a pest and you could never get rid of him, and he'd mercilessly harass the black college girls in my apartment complex, lacking, as he did, the charm of Victor.

Earl's apartment was on the second floor. Lonnie stalked up the cement stairs first, her back stiff and straight. I whispered to Dina, *Exactly why are we going to Earl's,* but she just shrugged and looked away. Then Lonnie was knocking on the door, first just a normal rapping sound and then, when no one answered, she began to pound. Everything grew very quiet. She pounded again. This time the door slid open a little ways, but it wasn't Earl who answered, it was a small skinny white girl about my age. Must be the wrong apartment, I was thinking. But Lonnie pushed the door open hard, practically knocking the girl out of the way, and strode into the dimly lit living room as if she owned the place. Behind the girl who had answered I could make out two more girls sitting on mattresses below black-light posters on the wall. The Spinners were playing on the turntable. It was the song that had played the first time I ever slow danced with Blaine, and it had become "our song."

195

In profile, Lonnie looked like a mad little man. Her red plastic hair-pick stuck out partly from the back pocket of her jeans.

"Get your asses in here," she ordered Dina and me, and then pointed to the three girls. "These are the bitches I've been looking for."

So we inched our way in. The room smelled mildly of weed and sweat. Earl was nowhere to be seen. Two empty pizza boxes sat on a card table in the middle of the room. There were also some beer and soda bottles piled around, and in the corner a heap of what I presumed to be dirty clothes waiting to be carted off to the wash house. The place looked like a crash pad. It was starting to be clear. These must be the little runaways I remembered hearing Victor and Blaine laugh about weeks before, the ones they said Earl had "adopted." Earl was pitiful, wasn't he, so lonely he'd even bring home strangers.

"Which one of you little bitches is fucking Victor?" Lonnie demanded. Her voice was high and tight, as if she had something lodged in her throat.

One of the girls at the back rose up off a mattress and stepped over a small floor fan that was barely stirring the air and said, "I am." Just like that. Bolder than bold. She was wearing the shortest of shorts and a man's undershirt. Her legs were long and pale. She was staring Lonnie down, as if to say, "Who are you?" Bad move.

And then I felt Dina poke me in the side and she was pointing to something. And that's when I first noticed the writing on the wall. Words had been chalked in rainbow colors. Hearts with arrows had been scrawled by them. I thought of the tattoos on Victor's arm, one for Cindi and one for Lonnie. Only these hearts said *Lisa loves Victor, Lisa loves Victor*. I didn't want Lonnie to see that. I tried distracting her, but it was too late. She was already going for the girl's face with her open hand. And just as I heard the hard smack of flesh on flesh, I felt something hit like a rock between my eyes, because the next few words on the wall didn't make sense at first: *Betsy loves Blaine, Betsy loves Blaine* with big red hearts and yellow arrows drawn through them connecting the two names. Betsy? Betsy and Blaine?

Dina had backed herself against the dingy white wall, stood there long and skinny, like a shadow, and dropped her head.

What was going on? The words still weren't registering because each time they tried to put themselves in order they got scrambled up in my head. And there was Blaine's and my song spinning on the turntable, and there I was in Earl's apartment staring at three strange white girls I'd never seen before. I could have been floating above everyone, that's how it felt. When I was four years old, I was given my first ice cream. As I took a bite, the top scoop slid off the cone and landed on the sidewalk. It lay there, covered with bits of dust and grime, forever transformed into something detestable. Even though my father took me right back in to replace it, I couldn't stop crying. After that I knew the world was a different place, often untrustworthy. There are no replacements for loss. They only refer to the loss.

There was a roaring in my head, and my limbs went all weak.

"Who's Betsy?" someone in my toughest voice demanded. I was pointing to the wall. A little girl sitting on the mattress with a joint in her hand murmured, "I'm Betsy." I remember her only as a wraith, a figment of imagination that startles you for a moment until you come to your senses and know not to believe in it. But she was real. And it was late at night, probably after midnight by now, and I couldn't figure out how my life was intersecting with hers at this moment.

I turned to look at Lonnie. She had hold of the red plastic pick in her hand and was stabbing it into the air in front of the girl's face while she screamed at the top of her lungs, words weighty with violence. So I ask, whose pain was I feeling at the moment I pushed Lisa out of the way and went for Betsy? In a second I'd knocked her hard against the wall. I wanted it all to stop. I wanted the girls to disappear and for Dina to peel herself off the wall and come do something, to stop me, to stop us, and for everything to go back to normal.

Lonnie had lunged forward and grabbed hold of the girl named Lisa. I didn't feel sorry for the girl who looked terrified, I felt sorry for Lonnie who was pounding the girl, and crying and yelling at the same time, almost as if she was pleading with her. The girl was just kind of taking it, and then Betsy got up and came toward me and that's when I kicked her. I was shocked by the force of the blow. She was looking up at me like I was crazy, and telling me to get out of there. I had never hit or kicked anyone before in my life. But now that I had it seemed I couldn't stop. I bent down and slapped her hard across the face. She wasn't fighting back, she was curling up on herself like one of those little armadillo bugs. That made me madder. I reached for her again, not fully understanding what I was doing. Moments before there had been no Betsy, no writing on the wall. Moments before I had been happy and lucky in love. I had trusted in the knowledge that Blaine loved me more than I loved him, which was what my grandmother had always told me was the way it should be. And I had my pre-engagement ring to prove it.

The next thing I knew, all the air seemed to have been sucked out of the room. Through the open door came Victor, Blaine, Earl, Blaine's brother Roddy, and Spider, filling up all the space. We never even heard them coming. They were out of breath, as if they'd been running. Right away it registered that Spider had spread the word. He'd seen where we were headed, and he'd made a phone call. And when I saw that Victor and Blaine were carrying bags of White Castle burgers, I knew then the truth. They'd been on their way over here from the start, bringing food for the girls who were expecting a party.

Earl's big frame filled the room. He began to bellow. He was waving his arms and yelling. Behind him, like quicksilver, Victor had pulled Lonnie off Lisa who, emboldened by Victor's rescue, was now yelling back, "Who do you think you are, bitch, who do you think you are?" And Victor was warning her, saying, "Shut up, Lisa, just go in the back and stay out of the way."

And when I turned to say this must be some terrible mistake, all the figures blurred so that it was a moment before I found Blaine's face, and another moment to fully recognize him. He stood there wordless looking tall and gangly and helpless, dropping a bag of White Castles on a chair and trying to pull me toward him. Then there was Betsy saying, "Blaine, what's going on here?" but Blaine wasn't paying any attention to her, he was looking at me, and he was trying to talk.

The awful thing was that Lonnie couldn't stop screaming. Earl was now so close to me I could smell his slightly sour breath. He stuck one pudgy finger in my face and said, "You have no business breaking into my house. If you don't get out, I'm gonna kill you, bitch," just like that. He looked over at Dina. "You too, Dina man, I never thought you'd do me like this." Then he lumbered over to the two remaining girls and herded them protectively like sheep into the back room and closed the door on them. He turned and faced us all, telling us how we had no right to break in like this and injure "his guests." He threatened to call the cops and have us all arrested.

"Call the cops, motherfucker," Lonnie was screaming. "Call the cops, these little hillbillies aren't even legal! See what they do to you, just see what they do when they find out you're harboring little white girls."

I was trying to move toward the door, but someone had hold of my shoulders and wouldn't let go. "Wait," Blaine said. "Wait, please."

I pulled away, and got myself out on the cement balcony. There was no moon, everything was dark. For a moment, Lonnie was right behind me. From the corner of my eye I saw Victor grab her, right around her neck. Her

199

head flew backward. And before I took another step toward the staircase, he began to beat her, right there. All over her face and her neck. His fists were everywhere. Behind me, Dina started crying. Roddy put his arm around Dina and said gently, "Come on, girl, you need to get out of here."

And I felt my own sorrow tighten itself like a belt around my head.

After that, I remember only a few things: me begging someone to stop Victor, but no one did, because this was between Lonnie and Victor, as these things always were. Dina weeping. Softly. To herself. Me trying to get down the stairs, but being unable to move. And Lonnie down on the balcony floor, kicking her legs into the air and screaming. Blood streamed from her face. I had never seen anyone beaten before, and the person I should have been able to turn to—Blaine—was now a stranger.

Earl was yelling at everyone to get out now before he brought out his shotgun and blew us all away. "This is my house, my property, all y'all fools need to get out of here before I kill someone," he kept saying.

Not knowing what else to do, I ran down the cement steps. I was not alone, there were footsteps behind me, so I sped up, and when Blaine came too close I turned around and beat on his narrow chest with my fists. I had yelled myself into hoarseness so that my own voice was unrecognizable. I told him I never wanted to see him again, that I hated liars and cheats and he was both. I threw his words right back at him, the very words he had used over our months together to bring us closer. He kept stretching his hands out, trying to ward off my blows, begging me to listen so he could explain, but I knew then there was nothing he could say that would change what I'd just seen. *Black bastard. Asshole. I hate you. Get off me.* My voice grew more hoarse, as I lost it to a rough animal sound.

I'd been a fool. Stupid and in love. Lonnie was right all along. She had always known more than I ever would. And here I'd felt superior all along, laughing at her jealousies. No wonder Dina had kept so quiet when I bragged that Blaine was willing to patiently wait for me. What a joke it had been, me believing that sleeping next to Blaine at night had been enough, me taking pride in the fact that Blaine was different from Victor and all the rest. How long had they known? He'd been lying to me—how many times, I wondered, and for how long? Would he go to Earl's after he'd been with me? How soon after he'd touched that girl had he touched me? I felt so sick I could hardly stand up.

I got myself around fast behind the apartment and down the alley leading back to the parking lot. And there, ahead of me, were Victor and Lonnie on the other side by Victor's Chevy. They'd come down the other side. Lonnie was trying to pull herself up by holding onto the car door, and Victor kept smacking her back down, and he struck her again and again in the face. At one point her head snapped back, and she fell hard. For a moment I thought he'd killed her. She lay still and quiet, blouse torn, one breast exposed through her lace bra. I wanted to go cover her up. She looked, oddly, like a child at rest. Breathing hard, Victor kicked her for good measure, then began walking in circles, wringing his hands.

"Bitch, don't ever, don't ever, never, never, never," he gasped, "come dippin' in my shit again."

He saw me then, and his hand which he was tightening now back into a fist slowly relaxed and dropped helplessly against his side. "Shit!" he said and walked away, kicking the gravel in disgust. Dina was down on her knees next to Lonnie. She was shaking her gently and saying her name over and over.

Then Lonnie sat up and pushed Dina off her. "Fucking black sonofabitch!" she yelled at the top of her lungs. "I'll cut your fucking dick off." Her face was a mess. She looked ridiculous, and sad, with blood all over her face. Roddy and Spider were trying to block Victor and telling him he was all wrong, how you never beat on a woman like that.

Blaine was beside me again, trying to wrap his arms around me. "Sweetheart, please listen," he said, but I threw his hand off and told him to get away from me. In that moment I had never hated anyone more than I hated him.

"Come on," he pleaded. "We're not like this. Let's get out of here. We need to talk." I'd never seen him so intense, so focused. It was fear I smelled in the sweat breaking out on his face. And then he said, "I don't want to lose you."

And when I said, "You have," he dropped his head and stared at the ground.

"Get away from me. And don't touch me." He reached out for me and I tried to bite his hand.

"Please . . ." He pulled back. "This is bullshit."

Lonnie was pulling herself up from the gravel, holding her jaw. "You too, Blaine," she rasped. "Don't try to play innocent. You been in this shit all along."

"Stay out of this, Lonnie," warned Blaine. He tried again with me.

"Stay away, I'm not going anywhere with you." I started walking fast.

He caught up with me and grabbed at my arm. "Where are you going? You don't have anywhere to go."

That was when I began to scream. I threw back my head and made a whole lot of noise. Even when I wanted it to stop, the scream kept on. People began coming out of their apartments to see what all the fuss was about. A white girl screaming could only mean a couple of things.

Then came the police siren in the distance, snaking its way toward us through the thick air. Victor jumped in the Chevy and started the engine.

"Get in!" he ordered Lonnie through the open window. "Get your big ass in here before I leave you."

We all knew he had outstanding warrants, and he had to go.

Without a word, Lonnie dragged herself the couple of feet to the car and, with Blaine's help, dropped herself into the passenger seat, blocking the side of her swelling face with her hand. Even now she still obeyed Victor. He had broken her jaw. The whole side of her face hung loose. Her right eye was closed shut.

Dina said to me, "Get in the car, girl. Get in now!" and I crawled in back because I didn't know what else to do. Dina and Roddy jumped in beside me. Crammed together, Dina and I stayed silent. It was Roddy who, visibly shaken, kept saying, "Damndamndamndamndamndamn" under his breath. I don't know where Spider went, but he seemed to have disappeared. In the dark, Dina turned and gave me a look that I want to describe as sympathetic, but it might also have been one of disappointment. With me? Or with all of us? Then she turned her head and looked out the window at the lights from the A&P parking lot.

As the car lurched forward, the door closest to me flew open and Blaine flung himself in, slamming the door hard behind him. "Let's go," he said in a voice I didn't recognize.

Victor gunned the motor, and we were off, the six of us.

Except, everything had changed.

"Drop us off on campus, bro," Blaine ordered Victor, after we'd gotten onto Sullivan Avenue, heading away. His voice was deep and ragged. Lonnie sat in the front seat weeping softly, while Victor drove, cursing under his breath, hands clenching the wheel. He wouldn't even look at Lonnie, who had slouched down in the front seat, so all I could make out was the top of her head.

"Just me, not him," I said to Victor. "You can drop me off, but keep him."

Victor gunned the engine and merged onto the freeway, taking us the fastest way. I think he wanted us all gone. He got into the passing lane and sped all the way to campus.

As I pushed my way out of the car, Dina squeezed my hand. I didn't say anything, just slammed the door behind me.

But then I could hear Blaine right behind me as I hurried into the lobby without so much as a backward glance. He knew better than to try to follow me past the lobby. He gave me that much. Instead he stood back a few feet while I waited for the elevator, but he didn't get on with me. I took the elevator up to the fifth floor and got out in the silent hallway. I stopped there for a moment as the elevator doors closed behind me and tried to breathe. It's over, I said in disbelief to the garish turquoise carpet. It's all over.

I don't know where all Victor went with Lonnie that night, but somehow she found her own way to the hospital. They were broken up for a few weeks afterward, Lonnie so ticked off that Victor was scared to go around her. She'd threatened to kill him and then claimed she had a contract out on his ass, which she might well have, and then she claimed she'd call the police on him too. She had to have her jaw wired, and the doctor prescribed pain pills. I saw her maybe a week later when she was still swollen and bruised, and hopping mad. She refused all pity, she was at war with Victor, and she was mad at me as well. And yet she knew she held the winning card. She still had his son. About Blaine, she asked me in a surly voice, "So what are *you* going to do, take him back?" as if she thought I were the stupidest person in the world. I told her no, of course not, and she said she hoped I knew how much I needed this dose of reality, that I lived in a dream world. "Men are all the same," she said. "I don't care what they put on your finger."

I didn't know whether to hate her or thank her.

What I never told Lonnie was how that same night Blaine waited in the downstairs lobby until six in the morning, sleeping on the vinyl sofa below the television blaring from a shelf on the wall until the security guard came over and nudged him awake. That finally when the sun rose he got the nerve to come upstairs and knock on my door. That Lee Ann, not knowing any better, let him in. When I asked him to leave, he started to cry. I had already cried all night long, falling in and out of sluggish sleep, and was finished with tears. The sunlight pouring into the living room turned everything flat. I went back to my bed, conjuring up dry sobs again against my pillow. And then without asking, Blaine crawled in next to me and very slowly put one arm around me and when I didn't resist, then the other. He held me like that, carefully, for a long time without a word.

He left around eight to go roof a house on the West Side, because it was supposed to rain on Monday. When I got up I made myself a cup of instant soup, and sat nursing my hurt and anger. I didn't work Sundays, and so went back to bed for a while. When I got up again, I was all alone and I knew what I had to do. Because I saw no way around it, I anonymously phoned the cops and turned in Earl for "harboring white runaways." I liked the sound of the phrase. I said my name was Mrs. Arnetta Smith and I spoke in my most proper white voice, emphasizing the trigger words like "little, white, and underage," and borrowed Lonnie's word "harboring," and ended with the phrase "hiding out in the apartment of a black man." It was mean and wrong, but I had no other place to put my anguish. If Earl wanted to play rough, I could too.

Blaine knew I did it. I didn't even need to tell him. He knew me that well. He told me later on I'd done them all a favor. "Those little girls didn't mean nothin' to me. The whole thing was nothing. Just stupid stuff. I'm glad you called the cops. Got them sent home. It's over. I want you."

It was a dangerous thing I'd done for all kinds of reasons and I knew it. Monday morning Earl was arrested, and the girls supposedly vanished, at least for now. I heard this much from Lonnie, and then Blaine's mother. "Someone called the cops," said Lonnie, fishing. I said I wasn't surprised. "It was someone *white*," said Lonnie pointedly. "A *woman*. Earl knows and everyone thinks it's you and he says you're going to pay for this."

I lied and feigned ignorance. It was likely one of Earl's neighbors had called. I reminded Lonnie about all those people who swarmed from the apartment building that night to see what all the fuss was about, how there had been lots of witnesses, any one of whom could have made the phone call. I never actually admitted to anyone what I'd done, not even to Blaine.

We took a walk down along the Olentangy one day and looked into the brown water, and he reminded me how the summer before we'd rented a boat and drifted along imagining it was the Seine. I said I still yearned for travel, that I had to get out of the Midwest, and see the world. I wanted him to say he felt the same way, but he didn't.

He held my hand in the tentative way a careful stranger might, and when I went to sit on the grass, he insisted on taking off his denim shirt and spreading it out for me so I wouldn't get my jeans damp. But I moved five feet over and wouldn't talk, so we sat like that for a while, and he just waited patiently, chewing on a stem of grass until I was ready to go.

Later that evening, he was lounging in the reclining chair in the living room when I came in from work. Lee Ann had let him in again. He was still in his roofing clothes, and he smelled like tar. He'd been waiting for me to come home and forgive him. But I didn't. I took one look at him and walked back out. I had no place to go, though, and when I came back a couple hours later after walking the main drag past all the shops, he was still waiting.

"I hope you know I'm not ever leaving you," he said. I said nothing and took a bath. When I came back out he was watching the evening news in the living room with Lee Ann. They were talking, so I went into my room and closed the door. He stayed out there watching late-night shows until I'd fallen asleep. I woke up once in the night to feel him there holding me tight.

Things got more complicated after that. Two days later, after he'd been released on bail, Earl stormed up to campus, shotgun in hand, to threaten me.

"It had to be you who called the cops," he insisted, holding the gun stiffly at his side. "I talked to Dina and I talked to Lonnie, and they ain't did it. I know it was a woman, and I know the call came from campus." He glared at me. For a moment he had me scared until I realized he had no way of knowing that. "I'm lookin' at potential jail time," he said, "and I've had to hire a lawyer. It's costing me. It's costing me plenty."

With the shotgun now turned toward me, I wasn't about to argue with him. I recalled the stories about the mental institution and I played it cool, even invited him to sit down, and poured him a glass of water. I pretended not to notice the gun exactly, which he eventually set down on the floor at his feet as he relaxed. I told him that I'd be honest with him if he'd just listen. Sure, I said, I'd admit there was no love lost between us and that I was glad somebody turned him in, but I wasn't stupid enough to do it myself.

He leaned forward then and said, "Those little girls were mine. They were my friends. Blaine never messed with those girls, you know," but I knew we were both lying. "Those little girls liked *me*."

I didn't say anything.

"They'll be back," he insisted, "when all this blows over. I told them they're welcome at my house any time."

After a while, he admitted sort of sheepishly that probably one of his neighbors had called the cops, one of the prejudiced white folks who hated seeing black and white together, and I agreed that's likely what happened. But I could see he was still wary of me. He told me then that I should get back together with Blaine, that we belonged together. I said I didn't know about that, and then he brought up acting school and said his dream was to return to California and make it big in Hollywood. "I have talent," he said. "With this voice, I'm going to make it big, you watch." I let him prattle on. It was the price I paid for what I'd done. But on his way out he turned and said, "You know, if I ever find out you did it, bitch, you're dead."

He didn't mean it. He was mad because the little girls were gone and he was all alone again. He was mad because Dina and Lonnie and I'd shamed him, and because he knew no one believed his dreams and lies. Helplessness makes cowards out of us all.

And so Earl fussed and fumed around for a few days around Bluefield, telling his story to anyone who'd listen, and threatening to "kill the bitch" that turned him in. He had his day in court, and the charges eventually were dropped, mostly because the girls had evaporated—for the time being. Two of them, and maybe all three, went back to some little coal-mining town in West Virginia, or so rumor had it.

But the truth is I kept seeing them, or girls like them, quick glimpses on my way into Bluefield, getting in and out of cars, disappearing over backyard fences, but by the time I got close enough they were gone. Like phantoms. Traces of vapor on the air. Young white girls floating into my peripheral vision. I'd seen their footprints in Blaine's mother's dirt yard, the rings left on her kitchen table from their water glasses, smelled the scent of their hair on Blaine's shirt. I knew, deep in my soul, that they never actually left.

Blaine started staying with me almost every night. Several times my phone on campus would ring and a girl's voice would ask for Blaine and then hang up. I asked Blaine about it, and he disavowed any knowledge, assuring me he wouldn't give my number out to anyone. I checked his pockets, searched his wallet, even came right out and asked his mother. I might as well have been trying to pry open a sealed tomb. She told me, "I don't know nothin' about those girls that Earl had over at his place, you'll have to ask Blaine and Roddy."

Sometimes I believed him—that nothing had ever happened, that a lonely girl made it all up, that I'd misread the writing on the wall. Maybe it hadn't been Blaine's name at all. But Lonnie and Dina had seen it too, though I never asked them about it.

Lonnie, her jaw healing and bruises fading, kept at me. We now had something in common—heartbreak. "What you think you gonna do, get back with Blaine?" I said I didn't know. She knew he was staying with me, and didn't believe me when I said I wouldn't so much as kiss him. Dina told me I should forget about the "stupid little white broads," what did they matter, that men were just like that. "You got you a good brother who loves you for real," she told me over and over. "All men mess up sometimes. You should let it go."

I did and I didn't. Months later, Blaine and I were still together, and on the surface things returned to normal, but underneath everything was drastically altered. For one, I was no longer the same person who memorized French poetry and swiped pizza slices from my racist boss. I was straining at the limits of my world, and yearning to be somewhere else. We sublet an apartment together for a few months, because I felt safer when he was there than when he wasn't. At night we'd study and then make dinner. Sometimes we'd watch documentaries on television. Sometimes we'd take long walks and talk as if we were a real couple.

In the same week that Victor was hauled into county jail for outstanding tickets, Lonnie and Mickey were riding in a car with two of Blaine's girl cousins and their children when a drunk white man hit them and killed all four children on board. In the emergency room one of the doctors told him what he'd done, and he sneered, "It was just a bunch of niggers." The family overheard it. Mickey was thrown thirty feet and died of a broken neck. The funeral was one of the saddest things I'd ever seen, and somehow I connected all these events in my mind, and they became woven into the same fabric.

Lonnie never got over Mickey's death. Now it was just her and her little firebug Alex. Shortly after Mickey's death, Victor threw Lonnie over for his next favorite girlfriend Deborah who had just given birth to Victor's second son. She named the baby Victor II. But as I say, replacements are only stand-ins for the thing you once loved more.

I didn't see Lonnie much after she and Victor split up. She started hanging out in a bar on Mt. Vernon Avenue. Dina, home from college for a vacation, said Lonnie had started messing around with coke in a serious way.

Sometimes Victor would stop by and visit us, but I didn't know what to say to him any more. I knew I would never be able to forget his brutality toward Lonnie. Even when he came by once to fix a broken window, handling the parts so gently and explaining to me how to make the repair myself, I couldn't forget the violence of those hands. And I noticed for the first time not just his tattoos, but all the scars on his forearms from working and fighting. I think he kept wanting to apologize to me, but every time he got close to doing so, one of us changed the subject. Finally he got up and stood there for a moment looking almost helpless. And then he said, "I miss my son," and burst into tears. I should have taken him in my arms and hugged him. I should have told him I was so sorry and it would be all right. Instead I just stood there, hands at my side, and said, "Things will get better, Victor," because it seemed the wise thing to say, and he said, "Yeah, it's a real bitch," and then he went out the door.

Dina came home from Dillard mid-semester because it turned out she'd gotten pregnant by a football player. She didn't tell me this, I heard it from Blaine, who heard it from Victor, who heard it from Lonnie when she called him one night, drunk out of her mind. I could imagine Lonnie almost gloating over the news. Dina got her own apartment in Belvedere Arms and wore a fake wedding ring and told everyone she was married and her husband was overseas in the military in Germany. I would have called her, but it turned out she didn't have a phone, and besides, what would I have said anyway.

Much to my parents' distress, I left for California the summer after my sophomore year in college. I was nineteen. Before taking off, I stood for a while in front of the long mirror in the hallway of our apartment and saw myself for the first time with some clarity. It was time to go. Blaine helped me pack my clothes (in silence) and the books I hadn't sold back to the store, and drove me to the airport, teeth clenched. He kept assuring me he understood, that he believed I was doing this for "us." He told me he wanted to hear all about California, and promised to call every now and then to see how I was doing. We were even cheerful and joked on the way. When I kissed him good-bye, his voice broke and he said, "Please don't go," and then before I could answer, he added, "I didn't have the right to ask you that." And I thought to myself, damn straight you don't.

The moment I was airborne I felt relief. The farther away I got the better I felt, as if suddenly a terrible weight had been lifted from me. I tried not to look back, because each time I did I remembered something I wanted to forget. Like the fact that Betsy never really went away, but gave birth to a baby that everyone back in Bluefield said looked just like Blaine. Or the fact that Dina once told me with utter sweetness, as we shared a double scoop of toasted almond in a cup, how she loved me and

211

I was like a sister to her, and we would always be friends. Or the fact that Lonnie called up on the phone one day when I was living in Oakland to say she missed me, when was I coming back? At the end of the conversation she asked if I could lend her some money so she could buy Alex a pair of school shoes (she was banking on my affection), and I turned her down because I suspected she'd spend it all on coke.

And then it gets vaguer at the point that Blaine followed me out to the West Coast because we weren't quite done with each other yet. I didn't exactly tell him to come and he didn't exactly say he wanted to. He said something like *I'm ready for a change,* and I said, *Yeah, well, California changes you.* I picked him up at the San Francisco airport in a rental car. For the next four years we lived there together like married people, I wore the ring he'd given me, and we both worked hard and finished school, and everyone thought we were a terrific couple. Blaine started a job with Alameda County, and I worked over in the City for a lawyer. On weekends we'd go to movies and art openings. Sometimes we'd ride our bicycles up into the hills to the very top near Tilden Park where, pleasantly exhausted, we'd stop to look out over the Bay and imagine all the possibilities the future might bring. We talked about marriage and kids. We talked about traveling. Blaine started hanging around with a group of South African musicians and learning to play engoma drums. Our life together seemed to be shaping up and making sense. We were happy, I think, in certain ways, and sorrowful in others. But for me, something was always missing.

One day I realized I still hadn't gone far enough. I kept looking out at the wrong ocean and still waking up to the wrong man. One restless night, having awakened from bad dreams in the dark, I rolled over and said, "Blaine, Blaine, wake up, I have to leave," and he murmured through his fog of sleep that he always knew it was just a matter of time. He didn't protest when I went out and bought a one-way ticket to Paris, France, to be exact. In fact, he paid for half and bought me a French dictionary. Inside the cover he wrote, *For growth.*

But that was just the start.

And I—well, I left and wandered for some time, here and there, to other countries and other continents, learning a little of one new language and then a little less of another. There were times I felt almost invisible. Occasionally it occurred to me Blaine might pick up and come after me, and sometimes I wanted him to—to show that kind of determination— and other times I didn't. I traveled to places I'd read about in books. For a while I sent Blaine postcards because at my loneliest I missed the tenderness we once had of being so young and open. It was hard to break the habit of sharing, but I could feel the gulf widening between us.

Years later, when I heard from him again, he mentioned he'd hung up a world map on his wall during that time, and kept track of where I was with colored pushpins. We talked maybe two or three times by phone that year I was gone, which was always sad and disappointing, in part, because his voice grew fainter and more tentative, as if this time I'd gotten too far away. When he finally realized I wasn't coming back, he told me he was leaving California and returning to Bluefield. "It's just temporary," he tried to assure me, "my mom needs some help. Then I'll be leaving again—get a fresh start—maybe travel, too." But I knew that wasn't true. Blaine had gone as far as he was going to go, and now he was, in my book, heading backward. I told him this, and he grew silent on the other end. I never did get up the nerve to ask about the child. To this day, fear prevents me from knowing certain truths.

But for that odd, sweet time that Blaine and I were together again, after we'd both learned what hurt can do, we grew closer than I've ever been to another human being. I suppose I was waiting for him to undo what had been done, and he tried in his own clumsy way to do just that,

213

but such a thing isn't possible. I finally consoled myself with the fact that there's not enough sorrow in the world you can put together that will add up to love. This knowledge, like all other things we learn by living, brought us together for that briefly tranquil time. Perched as we were on the edge of the world, so far from our families, there were no more secrets, only adjustments to what we'd lost. Sometimes we went to the beach and held hands and watched the waves. Times like that I loved him so much I thought I couldn't bear it. We'd stay all day until the sun fell below the horizon, and he'd talk about the future, and his voice, like the water lapping on the shore, would soak through me, and I'd start to believe in all that he promised. But other times, hearing the hollowness of his words, I just drifted away by myself over the rocks, while he waited, hunched against the wind, on a big piece of driftwood, hands jammed in the pockets of his leather jacket. I liked to imagine what it could feel like if the tide surged in unexpectedly and washed me out to sea, leaving behind a smooth sweep of sand.

The Author

Alyce Miller has authored a collection of stories, *The Nature of Longing* (W.W. Norton), winner of the Flannery O'Connor Award, and a novel, *Stopping for Green Lights* (Anchor Doubleday), as well as more than 120 stories, poems, and essays that have appeared in literary magazines and anthologies. Other awards include the Lawrence Prize from *Michigan Quarterly Review*, *The Kenyon Review* Award for Literary Excellence in Fiction, and distinguished citations in *Best American Short Stories, Best American Essays, The O. Henry Prize*, and *The Pushcart Prizes*. She leads a double life as an attorney specializing in animal law, and a professor in the graduate writing program at Indiana University in Bloomington.